THE MASTER OF SINANJU STOPPED DEAD

The hems of his red silk kimono fluttered to angry stillness. Like a peal of furious thunder, his booming voice rang out across the empty street.

"Hold, deceiver of the Void!" Chiun commanded.

Chiun's tone was enough to freeze the black-clad figure in its tracks. Slender fingers clutched the handle of the driver's side door.

With a few quick strides Chiun shed the shadowed mouth of the dark alley. He stopped behind the immobile figure.

"Why have you returned from the dead?" he demanded.

"I was never dead." Though the voice was soft, it was not apologetic. The shoulders remained proudly erect.

"My son thought you so, and so you were," Chiun said.

The figure turned slowly to him. The black hood hung low over eyes as cold as steel.

"Did you not think I was dead as well?"

Created by Murphy & Sapir

THE

Destroyer™

DISLOYAL OPPOSITION

A GOLD EAGLE BOOK FROM

WORLDWIDE®

TORONTO • NEW YORK • LONDON
AMSTERDAM • PARIS • SYDNEY • HAMBURG
STOCKHOLM • ATHENS • TOKYO • MILAN
MADRID • WARSAW • BUDAPEST • AUCKLAND

For John F., who wasn't even a zygote last time around.
For John and Mary Howard, who were.
And for the Glorious House of Sinanju,
e-mail: housinan@aol.com
Assassins to and of the stars.

First edition April 2001

ISBN 0-373-63238-X

Special thanks and acknowledgment to James Mullaney
for his contribution to this work.

DISLOYAL OPPOSITION

A shadow has fallen upon the scenes...from Stettin in the Baltic to Trieste in the Adriatic, an iron curtain has descended across the Continent.

—Winston Churchill

All I know is, if there'd been a real Iron Curtain, I'm the one who would've had to schlepp it to the Laundromat.

—Remo Williams

The Cold War is over, and we have won.

—Former U.S. State Department Official, 1992.

War? What war? Why was I not told? How like you whites to have a war that doesn't even have the decency to be a proper war and then not tell anyone important about it.

—Chiun, Reigning Master of the House of Sinanju

P.S. And don't listen to a word Remo says. I'm the one that does all the heavy lifting around here.

To the Glorious House of Sinanju,
e-mail: housinan@aol.com

PROLOGUE

The explosion heard round the world came a full fifteen years before Boris Feyodov would become a whore. On that great day in January 1986, he gave no thought to betraying his country or the great socialist cause, nor to spreading his legs to the capitalist dogs of the hated West.

Indeed, when the Russian general saw the beautiful white cloud from the explosion on his small monitor, he was one of the few people on the face of the planet who realized the triumph it represented for the Soviet Union over the mewling, complacent Americans.

The grainy image of the blast was transmitted live via satellite to the many Japanese television screens that ringed the cramped control room buried beneath the frozen ground of the Sary Shagan Missile Test Center in Kazakhstan.

As the big white cloud expanded, shooting milky streamers into the blue sky, a cheer went up in the small room.

"Perfect!" exulted a white-coated scientist. The thick glasses Viktor Churlinski wore were at least twenty years out of date by Western standards. He eagerly adjusted the glasses on his blunt nose as he spun in his seat to face the standing general. "It went exactly as expected, comrade General," he boasted proudly.

Pieces of the test craft streaked toward the ocean.

"Impressive." General Boris Feyodov nodded. Though it was warm in the small room, Feyodov still wore his heavy greatcoat. His huge peaked Red Army hat brushed the low ceiling as he leaned back from the console.

"It is more than impressive, comrade General," Dr. Churlinski insisted. "The curvature of the earth would make this impossible for most. Even the Americans cannot do this at the moment."

So excited was he, the scientist failed to notice the flicker of disdain on General Feyodov's harsh face.

"We have bounced the stream off the atmosphere itself," Viktor continued. "And to hit a moving target seven thousand miles away? It is—" he shrugged "—well, it is more than just impressive."

Viktor spun from the general to his team of scientists.

Men were slapping one another on the back. One had smuggled in two vodka bottles. Drinks were poured and congratulations filled the cramped room.

As the scientists celebrated their achievement, the ringing of the wall telephone went unnoticed to all but General Feyodov.

It was the hotline. There was no doubt that someone from Moscow was calling with congratulations.

When the general answered the phone, he was surprised to recognize the voice on the other end. He began to offer a rare smile of satisfaction. But his face froze abruptly.

As he listened to the speaker, the color drained from the general's face.

"But, comrade—" he questioned.

The argument he was about to offer was cut off. With a final order, the line went dead.

When he hung up the phone, General Boris Feyodov seemed suddenly drained of life. The excitement in the bunker was such that no one noticed. Picking up the receiver once more, Feyodov dialed a number on the base. After a few hushed commands, he hung up the phone again.

No one in the bunker noticed the hard scowl that had settled on the fleshy face of the Red Army general.

The party went on for several minutes before the knock came from the hall. Slipping silently from the celebrants, Feyodov stepped over to the sealed metal door of the chamber. Pulling it open, he gave a sharp, angry hand gesture.

Only at the sound of marching boots did Viktor Churlinski and the rest look up. Their exultant faces fell.

Six Red Army soldiers had filed into the room, forming a line on the far side of the consoles near the door. Their youthful faces were etched in stone. And, to the horror of the gathered scientists, their rifles were raised.

A single vodka glass slipped from sweating fingers, smashing on the concrete floor.

Viktor's face held a look of horrified bewilderment. He shook his head in confusion as he turned to Feyodov.

"Comrade General?" he asked fearfully.

General Feyodov did not answer the terrified scientist. He stood at attention beside his men, eyes locked on the far wall.

For an agonizing moment, no one said a word. The only sound in the tiny room was the frightened breathing of the huddled scientists. Finally, Feyodov lowered his gaze. With agonizing slowness, his eyes sought those of Viktor Churlinski. In the brown depths of his unflinching orbs, General Feyodov offered something close to an apology.

The general took a deep breath.

The scientists watched expectantly.

"Fire," ordered General Boris Feyodov.

And chaos erupted in the room.

A bullet slapped Dr. Churlinski square in the forehead, burrowing deep into his brilliant brain. Bits of hair-mottled gray matter splattered onto the console behind him.

The other men were shot in the chest and face. Those who tried to run were shot in the back. Flowers of crimson bloomed on white lab coats.

The metallic stink of blood flooded the underground bunker.

A stray bullet crackled into the face of a monitor, sending blue sparks and glass shards into the room.

"Watch the equipment!" Feyodov growled as the last body sank to the floor.

Leaving the soldiers near the door, the general strode into the room.

Viktor Churlinski was sprawled back on a console, his glassy eyes staring ceilingward. Feyodov dragged the dead man by the collar, dumping him to the cold floor. Stepping over the corpse, the general inspected the shattered monitor.

The damage was superficial. It would not have affected the primary systems. Seeing that everything else had survived intact, he ordered the soldiers from the room.

As the men marched back through the door, Feyodov crossed the room. He would shut off the power from outside.

Before closing the door on the grisly scene, Feyodov cast one last look around the bunker.

The bodies of Viktor and the others were a minor distraction. His dark eyes were drawn to the computer consoles. The image of the explosion he had helped cause was being replayed by the American news services on several of the monitors.

The world would forever after call the explosion of the space shuttle *Challenger* an accident. General Boris Vanovich Feyodov knew otherwise.

With a hard tug, Feyodov closed the heavy iron door.

He would not open it again for another decade.

1

The socialism that governed Barkley, California, was the cute Western variety where the windows of all the organic bakeries and herbal garden shops were always full and everyone kept their lawns trimmed to a city-council-mandated one and one-quarter inches year-round. If it was true that every ridiculous fad to sweep America first began in California, those same fads had first been born on the politically correct streets of the college town of Barkley.

Barkley was the undisputed Mecca for the counterculture, both old and new. On the carefully swept sidewalks of its tidy tree-lined streets, hippies could still be found in all their tie-dyed, potbellied splendor. Aging beatniks prowled the byways in black turtlenecks, bongos tucked under arms. Youths pierced and tattooed represented the new avant-garde.

Couples in bell-bottoms berated neighbors for destroying the planet with Huggies while earnestly washing the cloth diapers of their lone ''experience'' child under the spray of the front-lawn sprinklers. Men who thought the internal-combustion engine represented the single greatest threat to the world pedaled rusting ten-speed Schwinns to work. Women with filthy bare feet and furry legs lashed themselves to trees that had a date with the chain saw.

The main streets of Barkley were potholed obstacle courses. Someone had noticed a few round rocks at the bottom of one of the holes and instantly declared that they were cobblestones from the days Spain ruled California. In an act of misguided historical preservation, the holes were left to widen. After scented candles and hemp underwear, shock absorbers were one of the best-selling items in town.

The Barkley Historical Society wasn't quite sure what it would do once all the cobblestones reemerged. After all, they were a sign of Spanish imperialism, as well as the subjugation of indigenous peoples. The head of the society thought the townspeople could pry them up and throw them at Antonio Banderas's car if he ever came to town.

A reed-thin woman in her early forties, she was picturing herself hurling a rock as a stunned Melanie Griffith looked on. The woman wore a glimmer of a smirk and a muumuu that looked as if it had been dragged through every historically significant ditch in town.

No one noticed the pleased smile on her face. The rest of those gathered in the small auditorium in Barkley's city hall were too busy discussing the two most significant things to descend on their hamlet since Fritz Mondale and Geraldine Ferraro made a campaign stop there back in 1984.

"How are things going with Buffoon Aid?" asked an overweight man who sat on the dais at the front of the hall. As he spoke, he continued to eat from the container of ice cream on the table before him. The man's own image was plastered across the side of the carton.

Before a hostile takeover that had cost him his business, Gary Jenfeld had been half owner of the famous Vermont-based ice cream company Zen and Gary's. His partner, Zen Bower, sat in the chair next to Gary.

After losing the company that still bore their names and likenesses, the two men had slinked bitterly across the country, settling in the socially conscious town of Barkley.

"Everything's cool, you know," drawled a black woman who sat down the main table from Zen and Gary. She pushed a string of dirty cornrows from in front of her dark glasses.

Yippee Goldfarb was an actress, comedian, producer and middle box on the syndicated game show "Tic-Tic-Blow!" For someone with not an ounce of discernible talent, her success was incredible even by Hollywood standards.

"I got my boys Leslie and Bobby comin' in tonight," Yippee said laconically. "Home Ticket Booth will be beaming us coast to coast via satellite for the next three days."

At the mention of the cable network, Zen offered a thin, knowing glance at the rest of the council.

"Good," he said with an efficient nod. Zen began shuffling through his notes so they could move on.

"Uh…a little snag," Gary said. As he bit his lip, dollops of melting ice cream dripped down his coarse beard. "It's about Huitzilopochtli." He raised his hands to ward off the council's sudden worried looks. "The statue's fine," he said quickly. "You can see it if you lean this way."

Gary leaned far to the left.

Long windows lined one wall of the room. The dusty venetian blinds were twisted open. A dark, looming shape—taller than the city hall itself—could be glimpsed through the slats. Fat and tall and menacing, the slab of rock seemed to swallow up sunlight. A dark shadow cast from the huge statue fell like an ancient blight across the windows.

From this angle, a single black eye—as big as a small car and carved in angles of pagan fury—glared at the men and women in the crowded auditorium.

"Four stories of rock-hewn Aztec scariness towering over the main square," Gary winced, shuddering. Chunks of brownies were like brown grout between his yellowed teeth. "The statue's not a snag, per se. It's just that we got a call from Fox News about it this morning."

A ripple of concern passed across the stage.

"How did they find out about it?" Zen asked.

"Don't know," Gary replied. "They didn't say. Maybe from some blabbermouth *National Review* reader over at the university. Anyway, they wanted to know if, since it was the Aztec sun god, we planned on sacrificing any hearts to it. I think they might have been yanking me."

Zen's face fouled. "That's ridiculous," he

snarled. "We shelved the heart-sacrifice proposal months ago." His narrowed eyes found a few people in the back row who stubbornly mixed paper and plastic in their recycling bins. "For now," he added under his breath. More loudly he said, "I hope you told them the statue's just a link to the true, non-white, original gods of this hemisphere."

Gary nodded. "Then I steered them to the Buffoon Aid benefit. Oh, but I did mention how the kids of Barkley are pledging allegiance to Huitzilopochtli. But they're offering flowers, not hearts. I made that clear."

A hand shot up in the front row. It was Lorraine Wintnabber, chairperson of the Barkley Historical Society. As her dirty arm stabbed high in the air in an unintentional duplication of the Nazi salute, the woman scrambled to her feet.

"No flowers," she insisted.

Men on either side leaned away from the ripe smell rising from her exposed underarm.

Even Zen didn't seem to have patience for Chairperson Wintnabber. Thanks to her one-woman pothole crusade, he was on his tenth set of BMW shocks in as many months.

"What's wrong with flowers, Lorraine?" he asked with a sigh.

"They're living things," Lorraine snarled. Her filthy neck craned out of her muumuu. "'Pick' is just a euphemism for 'kill' when you're a flower. I for one do not think that it's good for the children for us to teach them horticide."

"I hadn't thought of that," Zen frowned. He bit his cheek. "I suppose we could use fake flowers."

Lorraine's arm Sieg Heiled once more. "Not plastic," she warned. "They have to be made from biodegradable paper."

Zen nodded reluctantly. "You're right," he sighed.

"Super," Lorraine enthused. A soiled notebook appeared like magic from the sleeve of her muumuu. "How many hundred should I put you down for?"

The next few minutes were spent haggling with the only woman in town licensed to produce handcrafted biodegradable flowers. It was finally decided that eight hundred was the perfect number that would satisfy the powerful Aztec god Huitzilopochtli without siphoning too much of the budget from the annual Kent State Reenactment and Flea Market.

"I'd better get started on this right away," Lorraine announced to the room when they were done. Notebook clutched in her grimy hand, she hurried from the auditorium.

At the back door, she bumped into a man who was just striding into the hall. Too busy at the moment to accuse him of contact rape, Lorraine scurried around him and was gone.

Far up on the stage, Zen noted the appearance of the new arrival with a flicker of approval. His lips curved to form the superior smirk common to political-science majors and devout Marxists.

The crowd failed to notice the stranger as he took up a sentry position near the door.

"Now, on to the most important item on the agenda," Zen announced from the stage. "I am pleased to finally announce that your council has been doing extensive secret work on the whole United States of America problem. I am sure that most of you had resigned yourselves to living under the oppressive boot heel of the fascists in Washington for the rest of your time on this polluted planet. I am pleased to report, however, that as far as Barkley is concerned, the American century is finally over."

There were sighs of relief around the hall, accompanied by a smattering of applause. "Thank Gaia *that's* over with," one man muttered.

Zen held up a staying hand and the noise died away.

"I can't go into all the details at the moment," he said. "But I can tell you that we have recently acquired the means by which Barkley can at last declare its independence from America. We will become the first socialist state ever to exist on this benighted continent. We will shake the pigs in Washington from their fat complacency, collapse their fragile police state and signal to the rest of the world that the Revolution has finally begun."

His voice had taken on the strains of a revival meeting preacher. Throwing his arms wide, he gestured to the back of the room.

"And though your council deserves most of the credit, a small measure of our newfound liberty must go to a true hero of the People's cause. My fellow Barkleyites, I give to you the man who will help deliver us to our utopian paradise, Barkley's supreme military commander!''

All eyes turned to the man in the back of the room.

The old soldier was clearly uncomfortable with the sudden attention. As the crowd broke into applause, his back stiffened. The buttons of his Red Army uniform strained to the bursting point from the motion.

The uniform no longer fit as it once did. In the past fifteen years, his flat stomach had given way to a middle-aged paunch. Soft streaks of silver lined the dark hair that peeked out from under his hat. But the one thing that had not changed was the eyes.

Flat brown eyes looked out across the sea of blissful, dimwitted faces. A notch formed in his brow.

As the applause grew soft with confusion, then fell to silence, General Boris Vanovich Feyodov looked from one corner of the room to the next. When he was through scanning the crowd, he turned from the room and was gone. Back out the door to the People's Hall.

A few more feeble handclaps trickled to silence.

On the stage Zen Bower hid his anger with clenched teeth. He leaned over to Gary Jenfeld.

''For what we're paying him, he'd better stop jumping at every shadow,'' he whispered.

Giving only passing thought to what might make his Russian general so twitchy all the time, the retired ice cream man quickly turned his attention back to making reality from his great socialist dream…and America's nightmare.

2

His name was Remo and he had lost faith.

It wasn't so much a religious thing, although he didn't know anymore if he towed the orthodox line like the nuns back at St. Theresa's Orphanage, where he'd spent his formative years. Experience had taught him that there was something bigger out there somewhere. He just wasn't sure if anyone—including himself—knew exactly what that something was.

It wasn't a loss of faith in himself or his abilities. Remo was a Master of Sinanju. To be Sinanju was to be at the peak of one's physical powers. To say that he was one of the two most lethal human beings to currently walk the face of the earth was neither boast nor delusion. It simply was. Like the oceans or gravity or the sky above his head.

It was certainly not a loss of faith in friends or family. For one thing, Remo didn't have any friends. And though the orphaned Remo Williams had discovered in recent years that he did indeed have some family, he didn't see them enough to lose faith in them. The only real family member he saw on a regular basis was more constant than even sea or stars. In this individual, he could never lose faith.

No, the thing that Remo had lost faith in was man. Both man as a species and men as individuals.

The sad erosion of trust that brought him to this state seemed to have taken many years. But on reflection, he realized it had been with him for a long time. So long that he didn't much think of it. And so, even though it had sat there as big as can be in the middle of his life for years, he had only just noticed his complete and utter lack of faith in all of humanity that very morning.

Truth be told, he had been nudged into this realization by a meeting with his employer earlier in the day.

Because of circumstances beyond his control, Remo was currently living at Folcroft Sanitarium in Rye, New York. Folcroft was cover for CURE, a supersecret government agency set up outside the pesky confines of the Constitution in order to protect the American republic from those who would do it harm. Remo was CURE's enforcement arm, answerable only to his employer, Harold W. Smith.

The circumstance that had put Remo in such close proximity to his boss was a fire. Specifically, a fire that had burned to the ground Remo's home of ten years.

Remo had been planning a trip to Massachusetts to collect a few items in storage that he had left behind after the fire two weeks before. Since he was heading that way already, Smith had stopped by Remo's Folcroft quarters with a small assignment in the area. It was when he learned the nature of the assignment that Remo realized he no longer had even an ounce of faith in his fellow man.

Remo was pondering just how vast was this pool of personal disillusionment as he parked his rental car on the snowy streets of Lowell, Massachusetts.

The air was cold as Remo stepped onto the sidewalk. There wasn't a hint of the elusive February thaw that was spoken of by many New Englanders but hardly ever seen. Remo suspected that the alleged thaw was a comforting myth the people of the region told one another in order to get them through the last long months of winter.

Even though he was dressed only in a white T-shirt and dark gray chinos, Remo didn't feel the cold. As soon as he left his car, his body compensated for the extreme temperature. Indeed, if passersby had looked closely enough they would have seen just a faint heat shimmer around his bare forearms. Like a desert mirage on an open highway.

Without even a hint of a chill, he walked up the street, stopping on the sidewalk before an old brick structure.

The building was two stories tall with an open cupola sitting high on its slate roof. Three big whitewashed garage doors sat almost directly on the street. Above the middle door, the legend Engine No. 6 was etched into the brick.

The garage doors were all closed. To their right was a man-size door, also closed.

When Remo tried the door, he found it locked. Frowning, he rapped a knuckle against it.

It took two whole minutes of knocking, but a four-inch-by-four-inch peephole finally opened in the door.

A pair of very tired eyes looked blearily out on the street. Below them, a giant handlebar mustache sagged out the opening like the paws of a dead ferret.

"What is it?" the fireman yawned. "It's two o'clock in the afternoon. We were all asleep."

Remo smiled. "Hi, I'm a corrupt and stupid mayor who wants to increase my fire department's budget," he said sweetly. "Is Firefighter Joe here?"

The eyes above the mustache grew skeptical. "Yeah, he's here. But he usually deals with fire chiefs, not mayors."

Remo's smile relaxed just a bit. "It's a very sad story about our chief," he confided. "He was with the department for eighteen years but, for some reason we still can't figure out, he went to see a fire last week. It was his first one. He was so scared at all the hot and the orange, he had a heart attack and dropped dead right then and there."

The man nodded. "I been with the department ten years this summer," he commiserated. "So far I been lucky enough to keep away from all that fire stuff."

And, having decided that Remo's story did indeed check out, the man opened the door.

Apparently Remo's knocking had awakened the rest of the firehouse personnel. As he entered, several men were lumbering down the wide staircase at the side of the building, wiping sleep from their eyes with pudgy fingers.

The name Bob was stitched on the T-shirt of the man at the door. He had been given the nickname "Burly Bob" by his fellow firemen. It was a sobriquet that hardly acted to distinguish him from his firefighting brethren, since most of the sleepy-faced men who were even now stumbling tiredly out into the main garage bays of the station house tipped the scales in excess of five hundred pounds.

Scanning the sea of ponderous bellies and sagging bosoms, Remo worried for the fate of any cat unfortunate enough to get caught in a Lowell tree. Come autumn, he envisioned a lot of bent ladders and crippled cherry pickers, as well as dozens upon dozens of feline skeletons clutching desperately on to naked maple branches.

"Hey, Joe!" Burly Bob yelled up the staircase. "Guy's here to see you! Says he's a mayor!" He stumbled away from the door to join his comrades at a big coffee machine.

As the men slurped coffee and devoured pastries from an aluminum-foil-lined tray near the coffee-maker, Remo crossed his arms patiently. He hummed quietly to himself.

Smith's computers had caught Joe Bondurant while tirelessly searching the Internet. Online, he went by the name "Firefighter Joe," offering via the electronic ether a service that was at once abhorrent and completely contradictory to the goals of his chosen profession.

When Joe appeared a few moments later, Remo saw that he obviously didn't share with his brother firefighters a fondness for sweets. Firefighter Joe was tall and thin. His blue T-shirt and trousers looked like collapsed sails. If it weren't for his red suspenders, he would have been tripping on his pants as he walked over to Remo. Like the others, he wore a long mustache that sagged morosely to his chin.

"What can I do for you?" Firefighter Joe asked as he shook Remo's hand. He had no sooner spoken than a bell began ringing loudly throughout the station.

The men at the coffee machine reacted angrily.

"Not *again*," one man complained through a mouthful of sticky Danish.

"It's probably just a whatchamacallit," said another, scowling as he chewed a lemon cruller. "You, know, uh…" He had to think for a second. "A fire."

"Shut it off," Burly Bob griped as he sucked the blueberry goo from the center of a bearclaw.

Someone disappeared into the radio room. A moment later, the noisy ringing stopped.

"That's better," Firefighter Joe said. He hitched up his sagging pants. "Now, Bob says you're a mayor?"

Remo nodded. "Mayor Dan Garganzola," he said. "We've got a bit of a budget crisis going on in my town right now. I've had a four-million-dollar surplus in discretionary spending every year for the past five years that I spend, no sweat. But because of some nits in the city council making noise, raising taxes is getting to be a tough sell. Trouble is, I've promised the fire department seventeen new trucks, eight new station houses, two firefighting catamarans and GPS satellite locaters stitched into their infrared union suits.''

Firefighter Joe nodded thoughtfully. ''So you're looking for, what, an event?''

''I guess,'' Remo said. ''What've you got?''

''First off, we'll handle it for you,'' Joe said, waving to the other men. ''This is our gig, exclusive.''

''But I have my own fire department,'' Remo said. ''Don't you just give me the details and I pass the info on to them?''

''No,'' Joe insisted. ''It's ours and ours alone. The deals we cut are almost exclusively with the chiefs or the unions. It's either that or no dice.''

Joe had just given him what he wanted most to know. There was only a handful of people involved in this scam.

''Fine,'' Remo agreed.

''Okay,'' Joe said. ''What we do, see, is we give you a fire. Make it big enough that you have to call for assistance from neighboring communities. That'll give us an excuse to be there. Of course, we'll have been there already, since we're the ones who'll start it for you.''

''How do I know they'll send you?''

''Trust me,'' Joe said. ''I've greased enough palms around here to make sure we're the ones who get called. Now a big fire is usually enough for most small towns looking to siphon more dough into the fire department. Warehouse, factory, mall, that sort of thing. Of course, if you want the big one—national media attention and tons of money pouring in from around the country—you're gonna have to sac-rifice. A body or two's good. More is better.''

"You've done that before?" Remo asked, a slith-ering coldness creeping into his voice.

"Oh, sure," Joe boasted. There was a smile be-neath his huge mustache. "We're all old pros at this."

Joe didn't see the hard look that settled on Remo's face. Smith's information had been accurate.

"For body duty, it's best to hire a couple of guys off the street," Firefighter Joe continued. "Guys who aren't real tight with the union yet and don't mind going out and squirting that wet stuff on fires."

"Water," Remo suggested.

"Yeah, that," Joe said. As he talked, he walked over to a nearby fire engine. "Most of the young guys are still stupid enough to be willing to do the actual fighting-fires part of firefighting. You send them into the building and then seal it off behind them with my own patented method." At the truck now, he patted the gleaming red side. "This'll be what locks the door behind them."

Remo smelled the familiar strong scent in the air.

"You filled the water tanks with gasoline," he said darkly. His eyes were flat.

Joe seemed surprised that Remo had guessed their secret ingredient. The special tanks were supposed to be tight enough to mask the smell. The fireman nodded.

"Exactly," he said. "Make it look like we're bat-tling the fire when we're actually feeding it. After-ward, invite the camera crews to watch for five weeks while you sift the ruins for teeth." His smile broadened. "Then sit back and watch the local, state and federal money pour in."

Remo seemed to be soaking it all in. As he looked from Joe to the fire truck to the men gathered around the sweets table, a somber expression took root on his face. He shook his head slowly.

"When I was a kid, Father Hannigan took a bunch of us altar boys to a fire station in Newark," he said softly. "I'll never forget it. The firemen were washing one of the engines out front. They even let us slide down the pole."

"Pete broke our pole," Burly Bob said. He jerked a greasy thumb to a particularly obese fireman. The man's blotchy red face was smeared with confectioner's sugar.

"It was a great day," Remo resumed, not listening. "It was because of that one visit that I knew I wanted a career where I could help people. I almost joined the fire department. But then I figured I could do more good as a cop."

Pastries fell from chubby fingers. All around, the firemen grew rigid, their faces drooping behind mustaches.

"You a cop?" Joe asked thinly.

Remo looked up. "Huh?" he asked. "Oh, no. Not anymore. That was a long time ago."

There was a collective exhale of sugar-scented bile.

"I'm an assassin," Remo supplied. "And officially, I was sent here to kill you guys because you're all guilty of murder and arson. On a more personal note, however, I want it to be known that I'm doing it because you have caused me to lose faith in my fellow man.''

As he spoke, Remo noted the not-so-subtle nod from Firefighter Joe. As the lanky man backed up carefully against the truck, Remo sensed movement and heard the sound of wheezing breath behind him. He felt the burst of displaced air as a fat fist was launched at the back of his head.

Remo ducked easily below the blow, turning as he stood.

Burly Bob and Fireman Pete stood behind him. The men were winded from their three-yard walk from the refreshments table. Bob was bracing palms against knees, trying to catch his breath after his unsuccessful assault against Remo. As Remo stood calmly watching the first hyperventilating man, Pete hauled back.

Another fist came forward, this one even slower than the last. Remo leaned away as the big mitt swished by.

''Damn, I gotta start on the treadmill,'' Pete wheezed.

Remo offered him no sympathy. ''Wanna see why they call those handlebar mustaches?'' he asked.

Without waiting for a reply, he took hold of one drooping fuzzy end of Pete's mustache.

As the beefy man howled in pain, Remo steered him around in a wide circle, slamming him hard against the side of the fire engine. He hit with a clang that left a big-and-tall-size dent in the truck's side. Bells ringing loud in his head, Pete fell to his back.

For an instant, the fireman clutched his face in pain. But all at once, a new idea flashed in his brain.

"Ow, my back!" Pete yelled, his eyes growing crafty. "Call the union rep. I have to go on disability."

He tried slipping his hands behind his back, but his great girth prevented him from doing so. He opted to roll histrionically in place like an upended turtle.

"Oh, hell," Remo said, his face growing sour. With the toe of one loafer, he tapped Pete's massive chest.

The fireman's eyes grew wide in shock. Sucking in a horrified gust of air, he clutched at his heaving chest. Face contorting in sheer agony, he opened and closed his big lips like a gulping fish. He went rigid, then limp. When his hands fell slack at his sides an instant later, his face was already turning blue.

And as the life drained out of Pete, the remaining firefighters suddenly seemed to grasp the urgency of the situation.

Panic erupted in the firehouse.

Men used to a completely sedentary lifestyle tried to run for the first time since high-school gym class.

They didn't get far.

Before the alarm sounded, Remo had already spun away from the dead man. As the others began their stampede for the door, Remo was already dancing down the thundering line. Flashing hands flew forward, hard fingertips tapping quickly and efficiently against bouncing chests.

One after the other, the firemen fell like obese blue dominoes. None of them had gotten even halfway to the door.

When Remo spun from the last tumbling body, he found Firefighter Joe right where he'd left him.

The thin man was rooted in place next to the fire engine, his face frozen in disbelief. Eyes wide with shock, he took in the scene of carnage. Only when Remo began walking slowly back toward him did he realize he should have fled out the back door. Like a cornered animal, he remained in place.

"You challenged my faith," Remo accused as he walked across the big bay. "I didn't even know that I had it, but I guess I did. The country's going to hell, but I still had faith in some institutions. Faith that there were people out there who were doing the right things for the right reasons. I had kept a tiny piece of my faith since the moment I slid down that fire pole when I was in fourth grade. But it's gone now. Every last bit of it. And you killed it." He stopped before Joe.

Firefighter Joe looked over at the bodies. He looked back up at Remo, trying desperately to think of the appropriate thing to say.

"Oops...?" Joe shrugged hopefully.

"And another thing that ticks me off," Remo said, annoyed. "Since when are firemen called firefighters?"

Firefighter Joe wasn't sure how to respond. Mouth

twisting, he crinkled his long mustache in silent confusion.

"Don't bother," Remo said, exhaling in disgust.

When he reached out a hand, Joe instinctively recoiled. When the hand went right past him, Joe sighed relief.

Remo grabbed something from the side of the truck. When his hand reappeared, the cringing fireman was confused to see that Remo was holding on to a long high-pressure hose. It was attached to the side of the fire engine.

"What are you doing with that?" Joe asked anxiously. For the moment he had forgotten the doohickey's name.

"Joining the volunteer fire brigade," Remo replied.

Joe didn't have a chance to ask what he meant. Before he could ask another question, Remo's hand whipped up and around. For Firefighter Joe, the world suddenly grew very dark and very, very cramped.

As he stuffed the fire hose over Joe Bondurant's head, Remo's expression was devoid of all emotion.

The hose fit down over the fireman's eyes and nose like an aggressive nightcap. Most of Joe's giant drooping handlebar mustache was still visible. When he opened his mouth to yelp in pain, Remo slipped the hose down to his neck. After that it became a tight fit.

Remo had to pop the fat steel ring off the end in order to get the hose around Joe's shoulders. Once he got past the shoulders, it was clear sailing down the length of his body.

In a matter of seconds the fireman was swallowed up by the hose. He had stopped wiggling around the time his pelvis disappeared inside. The bulge that was Firefighter Joe filled a thick spot inside the hose. He looked like the victim of some fire-engine-dwelling South American snake.

A pair of black boots stuck out into the firehouse. Remo closed the end of the hose around Bondurant's toes, then knotted it tightly. Pummeling and kneading the body, he managed to work it up the long length of the hose.

By the time he reached the tank, Firefighter Joe was no longer in one piece. With a dozen fat plopping sounds, his body hit the liquid.

When he was done, Remo folded the hose back up into the cranny on the side of the truck. He turned from the engine, looking out at the bloated bodies lying on the garage floor.

He had hoped that by getting the bad guys, some of his lost faith would be restored. It wasn't. He still felt every bit as crummy as he had that morning.

He wasn't really surprised. At this point he didn't hold out much hope for anything anymore. The world was lousy, he felt crummy and that was that. Case closed.

Still, it would have been nice to feel something.

"Crap," muttered Remo Williams, stuffing his hands deep in his pockets.

Leaving the dead firemen on the floor of Engine House Number 6, he strolled glumly from the station.

3

Edwige Soisson didn't even try to hide his anxiety as he watched the men scurrying around the concrete base near the massive metal fins of the Every4 rocket. Why should he? After all, Edwige was acutely aware of everything that could go wrong in a space launch. He knew better than anyone that little things could cause major problems.

Back in the early nineties, as a high-ranking official at the Centre National d'Études Spatiales in Paris, he had been liaison between the CNES and the space center at Kourou, French Guiana. Since Guiana was so close to the equator, it was an ideal location for launching rockets into space. Therefore the Kourou facility, northwest of the port capital of Cayenne, had always been of vital importance to the CNES.

As a rising star at the Space center with a bright future ahead of him, Edwige had been present all those years ago to oversee the ill-fated launch of the Every 44D.

At first it had been a breathtaking sight.

The launch itself was flawless. The rocket had

lifted like a timid bird from its platform, rumbling its way into the heavens.

Everything was perfect to the last detail. That was, until the rocket exploded in midair.

When the CNES was finished sifting through the debris, it was discovered that the explosion had been caused by a carelessly discarded rag left in a water circuit.

A rag.

Millions of francs in damage caused by a dirty rag.

Because of this monstrously stupid mistake, the space program of Everyspace had been subjected to endless delays. Since Everyspace was the driving force behind the entire European Space Agency, research programs across the Continent had been disrupted. All because of a single filthy rag.

Of course, a scapegoat was needed. Unfortunately, that scapegoat had been none other than Edwige Soisson. Before the accident he shuttled back and forth between CNES headquarters in Paris and the main test and research center in Toulouse. After the accident he had been put on permanent assignment at the Guianan Space Center.

He had gone to South America for a few days, only to be stranded there for the better part of a decade.

But Edwige was determined to get back to his beloved France for more than just a few vacation weeks a year. To this end his life had become a testament to perfection. Immediately upon being stationed permanently in Guiana, he had begun to inspect personally each and every rocket before launch.

As he checked feed hoses and unclipped side panels to inspect ganglionic circuitry, the technicians regularly snickered at the skinny bureaucrat in his sweaty dress shirt. Despite the jeers, Edwige would not be dissuaded. After all, it was their fault that he was down here in the first place. They were the ones who had left the rag in the 44D, not him. He was determined not to be a victim of their incompetence again.

And as the decade bled into a new century, his tenacity seemed to be paying off. There had been no major accidents since his appointment to French Guiana. His superiors at the Centre National seemed pleased with the way things had gone in the years following the accident.

In fact, Edwige had noted a certain softening toward him of late. Nothing major, but if he continued to perform his duties well, he might finally be freed from exile to return to the City of Lights, the Paris he loved so dearly.

But that would happen only if every launch continued to go flawlessly.

Edwige watched nervously as the last men took the elevator down from the bare scaffolding of the launch tower. Standing more than fifty feet tall, the tower was only slightly higher than the slender rocket itself.

The umbilical lines to the second- and first-stage dimethyl, hydrazine and nitrogen tetroxide tanks were detached. The third-stage liquid-oxygen-and-liquid-hydrogen tanks had already been separated from above.

All was ready.

In the control bunker, the dark-faced launch supervisor approached Edwige.

"The platform is clear, Monsieur Soisson," he informed the CNES representative. "We have begun the countdown."

Edwige's ratlike face puckered unhappily. "Did they recheck for rags?" he asked. Sweat beaded on his pale forehead.

The supervisor didn't flinch at the question. He had been asked the exact same thing during every prelaunch sequence since coming to work at the Guianan Space Center five years before.

"*Oui,*" the man replied politely.

Edwige nodded. "Proceed," he snapped.

He spun anxiously from the supervisor. Worried eyes looked out the angled, tinted window to the launch area.

At the bank of computer stations behind him, scientists in shirtsleeves began the last tedious steps that would put the Every rocket into orbit.

They were launching a weather satellite today, a very expensive piece of hardware developed by the Japanese to study typhoon formation in the Pacific. Millions of yen, francs and dollars were tied into this project.

Edwige bit his ragged index fingernail nervously. There was barely anything left to it. He had chewed most of it away earlier that day. As he watched tiny puffs of propellant seep from the open hoses on the launch tower, he switched over to his thumbnail.

Nearly everything here was handled by computer. Once the prelaunch sequence was begun, the machines took over. It gave Edwige some small comfort to know that he would not be relying on fallible human beings like the one who had left the rag in the Every 44D rocket years before.

"...trois...deux...un..."

He bit down harder on his nail when the rumbling ignition of the distant rocket sounded. So lost in thought was he that the countdown had hardly registered.

His eyes found focus once more, his fearful gaze directed out the blast-proof window.

As Edwige watched, the slender rocket shuddered on the launchpad, lit on its blunt end by a white-hot burst of flame. The collapsible scaffolding dropped away as the missile wobbled into the air as if pulled by some uncertain, invisible string.

The rocket cleared the launch area in seconds, screaming on its plume of belching flame into the clear sky.

Edwige watched it soar heavenward. With each passing second he allowed another short burst of suspended breath to slip from between his tensely pursed lips.

The missile passed the range where the Every 44D had exploded. As usual, Edwige had counted off the time in his head.

He was about to exhale completely to take in a

celebratory gulp of air when the unthinkable happened.

Without any warning from the scientists behind him, Edwige saw a flash of fire somewhere in the second stage. As it soared skyward, the flames enveloped the pointed nose cone, cracking the metal shell of the rocket like a cheap German sausage.

It happened in a flash. In a single, shocking, terrible instant, the entire steel body was a roiling mass of smoke and flame.

Men began shouting behind him.

Alone at the window, Edwige's heart stopped as he watched the rocket—along with its expensive cargo, his career and his hopes of returning to Paris—spread in shattered pieces across the blue South American sky.

Fragments from the rocket began their long, smoking descent to the well-tended grounds of the space center far below.

Somewhere distant an emergency siren began a plaintive wail. To the little man from France, all noise had become hissing static. Edwige Soisson failed to hear anything over the sound of his own pitiful sobbing.

4

In his Spartan administrator's office at Folcroft Sanitarium in Rye, New York, Dr. Harold W. Smith read the news digests concerning the explosion of the French Every rocket with bland disinterest.

Behind his immaculate rimless glasses, flint-gray eyes flicked across lines of scrolling text. Sitting in his cracked leather chair, his unflinching gaze directed at his computer monitor, Harold Smith affected a pose that was as fundamental to his being as the air he breathed.

Smith was nothing if not a creature of habit. Indeed, everything about him was testament to a man for whom custom was firmly rooted. For Harold W. Smith, change was an enemy that, while impossible to vanquish, was at the very least and as much as possible a thing to be kept at arm's length.

His clothing was always the same. A three-piece gray suit with a complementing striped school tie. When vests went out of fashion years ago, Smith continued to wear his. When fashion once more caught up with him, there was Harold W. Smith to greet it, sartorially unchanged.

He drove the same rusted station wagon to work

seven days a week, although in deference to the Protestant ideals of his strict New England upbringing, he tried to keep his Sunday hours shorter than his regular work days.

The office in which he toiled had remained virtually unchanged for the past forty years. The only new addition was the gleaming black desk at which Smith worked. Buried in the depths of the somber onyx slab was a computer monitor on which Smith viewed the events of the world in which he lived, but rarely ventured out into.

But although there were few things about himself or his work habits that he had changed over the years, there were some alterations he had made here and there, some out of necessity and some for the sake of convenience.

Four mainframes hidden behind a secret panel in the basement of the sanitarium had been searching the electronic ether long before the term ''Internet'' had taken its place in common parlance. Since assuming the reins of CURE as its one and only director, Smith had relied on the tireless efforts of the Folcroft Four to alert him to any criminal activity that might require his agency's attention. However, even though the mainframes were sophisticated, they weren't infallible. There were some connections that only a human mind could make. To make up for their deficiencies, during his tenure with CURE Smith had continued reading several newspapers per day. That had changed slightly in recent years.

Thanks to the increased popularity of the World Wide Web, Smith was now able to read hourly concise digests of breaking news stories that might not otherwise be of interest to the CURE mainframes. The explosion of the Every rocket was one such article.

There was nothing really new in the story. A number of similar malfunctions had occurred in recent years. An exploding Chinese rocket had destroyed an expensive Intel satellite, while another had landed in a residential area, killing many civilians. Other smaller technological firms had witnessed their share of similar setbacks.

Smith wasn't surprised. Although frugal in the extreme, he would never be so foolish as to entrust a piece of billion-dollar equipment to any nation with a spotty success record. It was a lesson his mother had taught young Harold from an early age: you get what you pay for.

Smith finished the report on the rocket's explosion, as well as the digests of the other top stories of the hour. There was some piffle about the dessert preferences of the wife of the recently inaugurated president, as well as a story about some benefit for the homeless in California featuring a large number of comedians. Smith saw nothing in any of these stories that warranted CURE's attention.

Smith was switching from the news digest to the constant data stream collected by the mainframes when his desktop intercom buzzed to life. He stabbed the button with an arthritic finger without looking up from his monitor.

"Yes, Mrs. Mikulka."

Smith's secretary was apologetic. "I'm sorry to

disturb you, Dr. Smith, but there's a problem with a patient."

His eyes flicked up to the digital time displayed in the corner of his screen. It was only 8:57 a.m.

"Dr. Paulakus is on duty," he said with a frown.

"He's the one who phoned," Eileen Mikulka replied. "He said it was one of your patients in the special wing. He thinks he might be waking up."

Head snapping up, Smith felt his heart trip.

At the moment there were only three CURE patients in the security corridor. Smith was careful to keep them separate from the rest of Folcroft's population. One was a young woman, the other was a comatose patient whom he had been told would never awaken again. He prayed that he had been given a misdiagnosis for that individual, for he dared not think what might happen if the other man ever regained consciousness.

He struggled to keep the apprehension from his lemony voice. "Which patient is it?"

"It's the one you've been giving the extra medication to. He didn't say his name. I could check," she offered.

The color drained from Smith's face. His skin went from sickly gray to ashen.

"That isn't necessary. Tell him I will be right down." He nearly choked on the words.

Rising swiftly, Smith didn't even bother to shut off his computer. His ears rang. For the first time in his forty-year stewardship of CURE, he left his office door ajar.

When he hustled out into his secretary's office,

Mrs. Mikulka glanced up, a worried look on her ma-
tronly face. A phone was pressed to her ear as she
waited for someone to pick up at the desk in the
security wing.

"Is everything all right, Dr. Smith?" she asked.

He didn't even answer. Offering a stiff nod that
could not but fuel her concern, he rushed to the door.
Smith was so hurried, he nearly plowed into the man
who was coming into the office from the hallway.

The new arrival jumped in surprise.

"Oh, excuse me," the young man apologized.

He was tall and thin, with a broad face and light
brown hair. His cheeks were flushed, his greenish
eyes anxious.

Smith didn't even acknowledge the man's presence. As the stranger spun a confused pirouette
around the sanitarium director, Smith hurried past
him and out into the hall.

Heart thudding, the CURE director rushed down
two flights of stairs. The fire door led up to a pair
of closed doors. A numeric touch pad was fixed to
the wall. Smith only realized his hands were shaking
when he tried to punch in the six-digit code.

Breathing deeply to steady his resolve, he carefully entered the number. A blinking light went from
red to green, and an unseen bolt clicked back. Smith
pushed the doors open and hustled into the hall.

An empty nurses' station was to the left. Ten
evenly spaced doors lined the right wall. Only two
of the occupied rooms were closed. Light spilled
from the third.

Bracing himself for the worst, Smith steered a certain course to the lighted open door.

When he stepped into the room, he found a Folcroft doctor leaning over an emaciated patient. Drawing open one lid, Dr. Paulakus was shining a penlight into a brilliant blue eye.

Smith cautiously noted that the room appeared to be in order. An unused television was bolted to a corner of the ceiling. Beside the bed was a bare nightstand. Nothing seemed changed in the least.

Smith allowed himself a thin slip of relief.

"How has the patient's condition changed?" he asked crisply as he crossed carefully to the bed.

The doctor turned sharply to the voice. "Oh, Dr. Smith. I didn't hear you come in." He stood up from the patient, slipping his penlight in the pocket of his white smock. "I hope I didn't worry you. It's not an emergency, but I think we need to discuss the patient's treatment."

"I have outlined his needs to you," Smith said slowly, his gaze straying to the man in the bed.

A mane of flowing, corn-silk hair spilled across the starched pillowcase. The pale, delicate face was almost feminine.

"I know," Dr. Paulakus said, shaking his head. "But the situation has changed. It's amazing given the level of potent sedatives he's been administered, but I think he's coming around. It's almost as if he's trying to will himself awake."

Smith's worried gaze returned to the doctor.

"How so?"

"Well, his pupils aren't responsive yet, but he's

giving other signs. I'd noticed over the past few weeks when I'd come in to deliver his morning injections that his hands were flexing a lot. It was a sort of repetitive clenching. At first I figured it was just a reflex motor action, but then I noticed this."

He pulled up one side of the hanging sheet. When Smith saw the patient's forearm, his jaw dropped.

For years now, the arm had been a thin, fragile thing. As delicate as the bones of a bird.

It was muscled now. Not overly so, but toned and fit. He noted with sinking dread that the wrist had grown to an unusual thickness.

As Smith watched, the hand clasped and opened, clasped and opened. The narrow chest rose and fell in rhythms that were at once hypnotic and terrifying.

"The last few days I've been asking him to squeeze my hand," Dr. Paulakus was saying, oblivious to the look of quiet dread that had settled on his employer's face. "I'm certain that my voice is reaching him on some level, because he's responded every single time."

Smith's face and voice grew stern. "That kind of contact is not advisable," he warned.

The doctor seemed surprised by the rebuke. "I don't think there's any need for concern," he said, allowing a hint of condescension to brush his tone.

Smith's expression told another story. Even his body language telegraphed his apprehension.

Of course, Dr. Paulakus couldn't know the whole story. The fact was, Jeremiah Purcell, prior to the dozen years he had spent under permanent care at Folcroft, had represented a threat like none other

CURE or its field operatives had ever faced. Remo and his teacher would not allow Smith to eliminate him. For a danger like Purcell, there was only one other real treatment option. It had worked. Until now.

"Increase the dosage," Smith ordered. "Under no circumstances is that man to regain consciousness."

The doctor hesitated. "Dr. Smith, I know you want to keep the patient's meds high," he argued, "but the circumstances are changing. He's showing signs of recovery."

"That cannot be allowed to happen," Smith replied tightly. "In this state he can do no harm. Awake, he is a danger to himself and others."

Dr. Paulakus hesitated. "Dr. Smith, I don't usually have a need to question you on matters of medical ethics," he ventured. "But these circumstances are highly unusual. I believe this man is recovering from whatever brought him into our care. Even the criminally insane have rights. Now, I don't know why such a patient would be at a private institution like Folcroft to begin with, but if he is as you say and he's regaining consciousness, rather than leave him in a perpetual medicated coma, maybe we should consider transferring him to a facility that's better suited to handle dangerously psychotic patients."

Tearing his eyes from the slumbering form of Purcell, Smith turned his full attention to the Folcroft doctor.

"Dr. Paulakus—" he began.

It was as far as he got.

There was a sudden flash of movement from the bed. Both men spun in time to see the clenching hand lash out.

It moved as if independent of the rest of the body, swinging up and around. As quick as a wink, it dropped, connecting with a pounding thump against the night table.

The thick metal surface of the heavy nightstand buckled into a V shape. As quickly as it had lashed out, the hand withdrew, settling back to the patient's side.

Purcell resumed his rhythmic breathing.

Dr. Paulakus couldn't believe his eyes. He pulled his stunned gaze from the buckled night table to the slumbering patient. The man seemed perfectly at peace.

"What was that?" the doctor gasped.

"Your patient is awakening," Smith said evenly. "I would highly suggest that you not allow that to happen."

Dr. Paulakus didn't need to be told again.

When Smith left the room a minute later, the doctor was administering a second dose of tranquilizers.

As he brought the syringe to the sleeping man's pale forearm, the doctor's hands were shaking.

5

Driving back to Quincy for what would likely be the last time, Remo took a short detour.

As he steered down the familiar street, there was a faint flicker of sadness in his deep-set eyes. Everything looked exactly as it had when he left in the dead of night two weeks before. That was, until he got to the corner.

The old converted church that had been his home for a decade lay in charred ruins. Shrunken black beams formed an angry twisted lattice on the stone foundation. Yellow hazard tape had been strung around the site. The tangled plastic streamers fluttered in the winter breeze.

The surrounding buildings looked lost and alone. The absence of Castle Sinanju was like a missing front tooth. A glaring hole in the character of the neighborhood.

On the way there, Remo had considered stopping. But now that he was here, he changed his mind. Instead, he continued on to the corner intersection and took a right.

He avoided looking in the rearview mirror.

Five minutes later, he pulled into the parking lot

of the Quincy Motor Lodge. The motel was the strip kind with two levels of doors that faced the main parking area. He left his car in a space near the swimming pool, which was closed for the season, and headed for the building. When he pushed the door to his efficiency open, he found everything pretty much as he'd left it.

Ten lacquered steamer trunks were stacked against one wall beyond two unused beds. Just where Remo had left them two weeks ago. In fact, they appeared to be completely untouched. He realized that this wasn't the case as soon as he saw the room's occupant.

Near the small stove at the back wall, a wizened figure fussed over one of the glowing orange burners. He wore a black silk robe decorated with elaborate silver-and-gold embroidery. When Remo had left a few hours before, the old man had been wearing a simple yellow kimono.

Chiun, Reigning Master of the House of Sinanju, the most lethal assassin to ever walk the face of the planet, had obviously found more than just a change of clothes in his trunks. He was steaming some rice in an old cast iron pot. Both pot and rice had apparently been stashed away somewhere in the recesses of the old Korean's luggage.

As he closed the door behind him, Remo welcomed the starched aroma.

"Inventory all done, Little Father?" he asked.

His back still to his pupil, the old man nodded. "All was as I left it," he replied, his voice a precise singsong.

Remo was relieved. He'd paid a month's rent on this room, leaving ten of Chiun's fourteen trunks here the night their house burned down. He was glad they'd been left alone, since he was in a lousy mood today. He seriously doubted that having to dispose of some nosy chambermaid's body would break him out of his current frame of mind.

"Good," Remo said. "I'll ditch the rental we brought up from New York and pick up a minivan. That should give us more than enough room to haul the rest of these back."

Chiun nodded wordlessly. The wisps of yellowing white hair that sprouted above each shell-like ear on his otherwise bald scalp danced in eddies of steam created by the boiling water. As he offered his silent agreement, a shrill whistle sounded from the stove.

Gliding into the room on silent feet, Remo saw a silver teapot on a back burner. It had been hidden by Chiun's frail body.

"No wonder those trunks are heavy as lead," Remo said. "You've been hauling half the pantry around with you for the past thirty years."

"Be grateful that one of us is prepared," Chiun replied. "For we could not fill our empty bellies with the toothbrush and spare undergarments that are your only belongings."

"So sue me for not dumping the whole K-mart housewares department in my Samsonite carryon," Remo said, hopping up to a sitting position on the narrow counter. He watched the old man work for a moment. "Can I help?" he offered.

Chiun shook his head. "Everything is done," he said, flicking off the burners with fussing hands.

A ratty old table for two sat on the worn linoleum floor of the kitchenette. Chiun had lopped off all but one foot of each of the legs, so that the table was now close to the floor. He had piled the chairs between the two beds.

Picking up the long-necked kettle in one skeletal hand, he breezed over to the table. On the cracked Formica surface sat two wooden bowls and a pair of bone china teacups—all retrieved from his trunks.

Chiun filled their cups. After tapping out a few scoops of brown rice into the bowls, the two men settled cross-legged to the floor.

Chiun used his long fingernails as chopsticks, while Remo ate with his fingers.

They sat in awkward silence for a few minutes. As they chewed their rice, each man's unspoken thoughts flitted to the same gloomy sentiment.

For years the town of Quincy had been their adopted home. The cloud that had forced them to leave in January had dissipated somewhat while they were away. But now that they were back, the gloom had settled in anew.

It was Remo who finally broke the silence.

"I drove by our house on the way back here," he said.

The old man looked up. His hazel eyes were bland. "Why?" Chiun asked, his voice flat.

"I don't know," Remo admitted. "It's Quincy. I figured I'd see if people were looting the ash piles.

I kind of wish I hadn't, 'cause it didn't make me feel any better.''

Chiun's eyes narrowed. "Better than what?" he asked.

"Than how I feel right now," Remo said. "That job Smith gave me put me in a real cruddy mood." He shook his head. "Ah, I guess I'll get over it," he muttered. Shoulders slumping, he hunched morosely over his bowl.

As his pupil chewed glumly, the Master of Sinanju silently pushed his own empty bowl away. A troubled shadow settled across the old man's parchment brow.

"Are you feeling well, my son?" the Asian asked.

"Huh?" Remo frowned, glancing up. "Yeah, I'm okay. I guess."

Chiun didn't seem convinced. "What exactly disturbed you about Emperor Smith's assignment?" he pressed.

This was the honorific the elderly Korean had applied to Smith since he first came into the service of CURE. The Masters of Sinanju had for five thousand years hired out to khans and kings. Chiun refused to work for anything less than an emperor; therefore the title had been bestowed and retained, despite Smith's early and frequent objections.

"Everything," Remo answered. "Crooked firemen aren't supposed to exist in America. But I met a bunch of them today. Worse thing is, most people probably wouldn't give a crap in a hatbox about it. They've learned not to care. America's used to a steady diet of corrupt cops and shifty politicians and people lining up to stick a shiv in their neighbor's back 'cause the dog took a whiz on the gas grill. But they don't have to live it like we do. The news to them is just another TV show. Bored with society collapsing down around your ears? Just switch over to Regis Philbin asking the dingbat du jour 'Who's buried in Grant's tomb?' But I can't switch it off. And I'll tell you something, Little Father, it sucks that I can't.''

As the younger man spoke, the Master of Sinanju's expression had only grown more troubled.

''This is not right,'' the old man intoned once Remo was through.

''Damn right it's not right,'' Remo agreed. ''I'm glad for once you see it my way.''

At this, Chiun waved a dismissive hand. ''That is not what I meant,'' he said, his face souring. ''America is as degenerate as any nation that allows its subjects to choose its king with paper ballots. If your Founding Fathers had tried this democracy foolishness in ancient Rome, Nero would have squashed their rebellion and fed them to the lions.''

''Three cheers and a tiger to Thomas Jefferson for being born at the right time,'' Remo said dryly.

''America is what it is,'' Chiun persisted. ''As assassins, we should not be troubled by this. Yet you are. It is your attitude, not this society, that is not right.''

''Yeah, you're right, Little Father,'' Remo said. ''I think I'll go out and do back flips down the street. There are firemen who do part-time work as arsonists and murderers. Hip-hip-hooray.'' His face collapsed into a scowl. "I'd think that a guy whose house just burned down would be a little more sensitive to all of this."

"My loss, while great, has nothing to do with this," Chiun said. His face sagged. "Oh, Remo, I was afraid this might happen." His tufts of hair were thunderclouds of soft despair as he sadly shook his aged head.

Remo felt a twinge of concern. "Afraid what might happen?" he asked.

"Your grave affliction," the old man intoned. "It did not expire at the proper time. Oh, why did you tempt the gods as you did?" In the deepest crevices of his wrinkled face dwelled a look of dark concern.

Remo racked his brain. He couldn't remember ticking off any deities lately. "Okay, I give up," he said finally with a shrug. "What are we talking about?"

"Your Master's disease," Chiun explained. "The Hindu curse imposed by one of their gods that makes you feel it is your responsibility and yours alone to stamp out all injustice in the world. It occurs in every fifteenth generation of Sinanju Masters. I had hoped that you would break the cycle, since you are not from the village proper, but rather from the more remote outskirts of town."

"Newark, New Jersey's about as far on the fringes of Sinanju's suburbs as you can get, Chiun," Remo pointed out. "And I thought that curse was lifted back when we were in Africa a few months ago."

"It should have been," Chiun said. "But like a

fool you could not rejoice in your recovery. In the dying days of your illness, you did open your big, foolish mouth and implore all the gods at once to leave you as you were.''

Remo bit his lip. ''Woops. I did kind of do that, didn't I?'' he said.

''Yes, you did,'' Chiun confirmed darkly. ''And I fear that your prayers have been answered.''

Remo's brow dropped as he considered the old man's words. ''I don't know about any of that fruity stuff,'' he said. ''But if it's true, it'd be just my luck. All the times I prayed for parents or a new bike when I was at the orphanage, heaven's phone was off the hook. First time I open my yap without thinking, bammo.''

Chiun raised a thin eyebrow. ''The first time you opened your mouth without thinking was the first time you opened your mouth,'' he said aridly. ''And back at the almshouse where you frittered away your youth, you were praying to the false God of the carpenter's dowagers. This time, your ill-chosen words fell on the right ears.''

''I don't know, Chiun,'' Remo said skeptically. ''I don't think my attitude's the product of any thousand-year-old curse. I think this is just the way I am.''

''It is,'' Chiun said. ''Now. And thanks to you, it is probably how you will always be.'' In a flurry of robes he rose to his feet. He gathered up their empty bowls and breezed over to the small sink.

As Chiun ran rusty water over their dishes, Remo remained seated on the floor.

"I don't think it's a bad thing," the younger man said after a few long moments of consideration. "I mean, this job rots. I shouldn't be blind to what's going on. So I get mad every once in a while. So what?"

"Mad is acceptable. Madness is not," Chiun said. "I suppose the best we can hope for, given the circumstances, is that you understand the difference some of the time."

"Maybe we can do that one better," Remo offered. He took a deep breath. "We could leave," he exhaled.

At the sink, Chiun slowly turned. His hooded eyes showed no emotion. "Leave what?" he asked.

"Leave here. America. Quit," Remo said. "Quit Smith, quit CURE. Go to work for somebody else. It's tough watching this country go to hell in a handbasket. Maybe it'd be good for me to go somewhere where I don't have to see it close up." His face turned sly. "I hear the melons are nice in Persia this time of year."

Chiun pursed his papery lips. "Persian melons grow properly only in Persia. They have been nothing but seeds and rind since the time of the Parthians."

"Okay, Mesopotamia. You like Mesopotamia, right? Didn't Master Hupka the Lesser even invent the wheel for them he liked them so much? We can go there."

"Hupka gave them the wheel to facilitate the transport of tribute back to Sinanju," Chiun said guardedly. "To this day we have not been given proper credit for its invention. However, Mesopotamia is now Iraq. And no matter what you now say, you would never be satisfied working for them."

"Yeah, Saddam Hussein is kind of a prick," Remo agreed. "Tell you what, throw a dart at a map. Wherever it lands, we pull up stakes and go there."

Chiun shook his speckled head. The gentle tufts of cotton-candy hair fluttered delicately at the motion.

"I am too old to be uprooted by your whims," he said. "America is the only nation currently able to afford both of us, and so we stay here. Someday you will leave this land. Perhaps that time will not come until the day you are forced to inter my bones with those of my ancestors. But I will not leave now because you wish to flee fate."

Remo accepted his words with a somber sigh.

"Okay," he said. "But next time you're itching to leave, don't come carping to me." He rose fluidly to his feet. "I'm gonna go rent us a van."

Turning from the kitchenette, he left the motel room.

Once he was gone, Chiun turned an eye to the closed door. On his parchment face was a look of deep concern.

Remo was making his life much more complicated than it had to be. As usual.

Eventually, the old man tore his hazel eyes from the cheap wood veneer. On silent, shuffling feet, he went to the table to collect their two empty teacups.

WHEN HAROLD SMITH returned to his secretary's office, he found someone waiting for him.

The nervous young man Smith had nearly knocked over in his haste to get down to the security corridor was seated on a drab green vinyl chair near one of Mrs. Mikulka's well-tended rubber plants.

Smith's thin lips tightened as the man rose to greet him.

"Dr. Smith," the visitor said, offering his hand as he stood. The cast on his right wrist jutted from the end of his sleeve. "I didn't realize it was you when we..." He pointed awkwardly over to the door where they'd nearly collided. "Can we talk in your office?"

Smith seemed unhappy for yet another intrusion in his normal routine. "Who are you?" the older man asked.

"He's a salesman, Dr. Smith," Mrs. Mikulka offered from her desk. "Medical supplies, wasn't it?"

The man floundered for a moment. "Well, yes," he said. He seemed unhappy with the admission.

Smith's look of displeasure become one of bland impatience. "You have no appointment," he said.

"This is kind of awkward," the man said, lowering his voice. He glanced at Smith's secretary. "I really couldn't phone ahead. If you could just give me a minute, you'll understand why."

"Perhaps," Smith said. "But I am quite satisfied with all of our current suppliers. I suggest you leave your business card with my secretary."

The man was growing frustrated. "I—I don't have one," he said. He found that he was clenching his teeth as he spoke. Forcing himself to relax, he offered a tight smile. "Just one minute, Dr. Smith. Please. I promise you, you won't be disappointed."

Smith's face soured. He glanced at his old Timex. "I will give you no more than three min—" he began.

He got no further. The jangling of an old-fashioned phone sounded from his office.

The Folcroft director looked to the door, annoyed with himself for having left it ajar. The ringing blue contact phone sat in full view on his desk.

"Please wait here," Smith said to the salesman.

Before the salesman could object, the older man marched from the room, closing the door behind him.

As the door slammed shut in his face, the young man scowled. Exhaling impatience, he took up his post in the corner waiting-room chair.

"Dr. Smith is a very busy man," Mrs. Mikulka offered thinly. The blue-haired woman didn't seem to approve of the young man's impatience.

"I can see that," the visitor muttered tightly. He did not look at the secretary as he spoke.

Rummaging on a small table near his elbow, he found a two-decade-old *Reader's Digest.* Slouching in his chair, he began reading an article about the upcoming 1980 presidential race.

SMITH PICKED UP the phone on the third ring. Through the big picture window at his back, winter wind attacked the choppy white waves of Long Island Sound.

"Smith," he said, settling into his chair. As he

spoke, he noted with a frown that he had left his computer on.

"What's with answering on the third ring?" Remo's voice said by way of greeting. "You slowing down in your old age, Smitty?"

"I was otherwise occupied," the CURE director replied. "There is a potential problem with one of our patients. I fear the Dutchman is beginning to regain consciousness."

Remo was instantly wary. "Purcell?" he asked. "Why, is he making people hallucinate there again?"

"No, nothing so extreme yet," Smith said. "It has the potential to be worse, however. He appears to be growing stronger physically, and there is some suggestion of cognitive ability. I have increased the dosage on his sedatives, but I want you and Chiun to examine him on your return."

"That's why I was calling," Remo said. "We're ready to leave now. If I run every red light, we should be back home in a couple of hours."

"I don't believe it's necessary to hurry," Smith said. "But do not dawdle."

As he spoke, habit drew his eyes to his computer. He found that the CURE mainframes had pulled an article in his absence. When he read what it was, he frowned.

"Can do, Smitty," Remo said. "See you in a few."

He broke the connection.

At his desk, Smith absently hung up the phone.

An expression like that of a curious squeezed lemon had formed on his angular gray face.

Assuming his earlier haste had caused him to err, he checked to see if he had inadvertently pulled the file from elsewhere in the system.

He found that he had not. The mainframes were functioning properly. And yet, there was the article staring up at him from the glowing depths of his black desk.

It was the same story he had read just before being called down to Jeremiah Purcell's room. The article about the Every4 rocket explosion.

Coupled with the story was another article pulled from the electronic netherworld by CURE's basement mainframes. Apparently a three-year-old NWS satellite that had been put in place to study hurricane formation over the Atlantic Ocean had malfunctioned. For reasons unknown at the present time, the satellite had abruptly gone dead.

Other than the fact that the payload of the French rocket had been a similar weather satellite, Smith saw no connection between the two stories. But he had learned long ago to trust the rigid data analysis of the Folcroft Four.

Forgetting all else, Smith turned his full attention to his computer. If there was something larger at work here, perhaps he would have uncovered whatever it was by the time Remo and Chiun returned from Massachusetts.

6

One hundred miles above the windswept New England coast, a slender object raced silently through the limitless void of space. Though night was fast approaching the easternmost shores of the continent far below, unfiltered light from the star Sol glinted starkly off the lazily spiraling object's sleek black exterior.

Though its movement appeared slow, the boomerang-shaped object rocketed with a speed surpassed only by the rotation of the planet far below.

Few nations on Earth possessed the ability to even detect, let alone track the object. Not that very many would have been interested in seeing it even if they were technologically able.

For even though the object that grabbed glimmers of white sunlight was man-made and streaked across the heavens at breathtaking speeds, it was only four inches long.

The small titanium securing bracket had been used in the repairs of the Hubble telescope. Accidentally released by one of the mission astronauts, the right-angled metal wedge had joined the thousands of other bits and pieces of junk that had been dumped into orbit around the planet in more than forty years of space exploration.

It was assumed that all of the orbiting garbage would eventually approach the Earth's atmosphere, finally burning up on reentry. And though a few voiced complaints about this sort of dumping, most experts agreed that the only real problem posed by space junk was to those who worked there. Since spacecraft and astronauts were at high risk if they were to come in contact with any debris, every piece of material abandoned in orbit was carefully logged and monitored by space-faring nations. Including the seemingly harmless metal bracket.

Named O.440B, the bracket's orbit occasionally brought it alarmingly close to an expensive CableSys commercial satellite in geosynchronous orbit above the east coast of North America.

The cable company had balked when it learned of the existence of O.440B. However, CableSys had been assured that, although their orbits sometimes made them stellar neighbors, the two objects would never, ever intersect. Since O.440B's orbit was deteriorating, it would only grow farther away. The satellite, CableSys executives had been assured, was in no danger whatsoever.

As usual, this day the wedge of metal had drawn within yards of the CableSys satellite—two cold strangers in the silent void of space. On its lower orbit, O.440B had pulled abreast and was about to draw past the bigger object when something unexpected happened.

O.440B hopped.

It happened in the wink of an eye. The bracket suddenly veered violently off course and shot sharply upward, tearing out of its decaying orbit.

Firing at an impossible velocity, the curved metal tore through the shell of the communications satellite. The satellite's delicate exterior buckled as the alien missile ripped a deep gash into the interior.

The ensuing sparking explosion was consumed by the vacuum of space.

A backup computer failed as O.440B tore an angry path of destruction through the center of the satellite. By the time it punched through the far side, circuitry was already collapsing. Wires flamed out and died.

Critically wounded, the CableSys satellite listed and grew still. A gaping hole through its middle revealed the distant white specks of billion-year-old stars.

And somewhere in that endless black sea, the melted lump of metal that had been insignificant little O.440B continued to rocket like a furious comet, trailing a tail of charge particles.

"YOU MISSED," Zen Bower complained.

"The target was acquired," General Boris Feyodov replied tersely. But in spite of the words, his fleshy face was drawn in a look of calculated displeasure.

"By *mistake*," Zen insisted, angrily noting the general's own seeming disappointment. "You hit that other—" he waggled a disapproving finger

"—doohickey thingamajig and banked it into the satellite."

They were both standing in the cramped interior of the supreme defense bunker, the secure haven built for the ruling council deep below the potholed streets of Barkley.

A few men worked around the rocky tunnel. Most were Americans from Barkley University. Only a small number of Russians had been imported for this project.

Old Soviet-era equipment lined two walls, augmented by newer American computers. One of the new Packard Bells had just finished interpreting the telemetry from space. A slow-motion simulation reenacted the collision of the piece of floating space junk with the CableSys satellite.

"I explained to you that punching through the atmosphere might warp the signal," Feyodov said as the computer-generated version of O.440B tore through the far side of the communications satellite. Represented on the screen as a simple caret shape, the small fragment of space junk raced off the edge of the monitor and was gone forever.

"I figured you were just being cautious," Zen pouted.

"I am that as much as possible," Feyodov replied. "But I am also realistic. Our tests many years ago demonstrated limitations with the device. Targets within the atmosphere can be acquired only if we are given a narrow enough window. Space launches are excellent test objects, for they originate from specific locations at predetermined times. That is how we could destroy that French rocket with such ease. There are problems, however, once we leave the atmosphere.''

"Satellites are locked in orbit," Zen argued. "They should be easy for you to lock on to."

The Russian general took a deep breath. The buttons on his old Red Army uniform strained against his protruding belly. A few moth holes were visible in the dark wool.

"'Lock on to' is an inaccurate term," Feyodov insisted. "Understand, it is like aiming a big, cumbersome gun. Rapid aiming and precise target acquisition are not possible, which is part of the reason why the research was discontinued. It was originally hoped the device could be employed to stop incoming nuclear missiles. But due to speed, randomness and unknown launch locations, at the time of its development the weapon could not be applied to hostile enemy missiles.''

"So you're saying not only can we not get the satellites like you promised, but Barkley might get nuked?" Zen complained. He put his hands on his hips. "Well, that's just perfect."

"America will not drop a bomb on California," General Feyodov muttered dismissively.

"Easy for *you* to say," Zen insisted. "You grew up in a socialist paradise. I've had to spend my entire life in this bourgeois capitalist wasteland. Genocide, imperialism, threats to cut funding to the NEA. Goddamn hostile takeovers that steal the ice cream empire you built with your own two hands right out from under you. *I* know what those Wall Street fat cats and their Washington cronies are capable of.''

The general was not convinced.

''There are forces to fear that have nothing to do with your government,'' Boris Feyodov said ominously.

Unconsciously, the Russian's dark brown eyes flickered from side to side, as if searching for ghosts in the shadows. Zen had noticed this peculiar habit of his supreme commander ever since he'd brought the general to America.

''What the hell are you doing?'' Zen demanded.

Feyodov's eyes skipped back from the darkest corner of the room. ''Hmm?'' Feyodov asked.

''That thing you always do—looking around when there's nobody there. What's with that?''

It was a habit Feyodov had developed only since the start of this enterprise. He hadn't been aware that anyone had noticed him doing it. Spine straightening, he locked his eyes on the retired ice cream man.

''There is a piece of hardware that will help us to overcome our displaced targeting problem,'' the general said, distracting Zen from his question.

Zen frowned. ''I thought you said we couldn't do it.''

''Not with the current equipment we are using here, no,'' General Feyodov agreed. ''But the technology I refer to was developed by our space program for independent reasons after the funding was pulled from this project. It could enhance our systems. However, it is in Russia and as you know, items of this kind are not easily procured.'' His eyes lowered. "With the proper *motivations* I could get it for you."

It was a pitch the ice cream man had heard far too much lately. Zen crossed his arms. "How much?" he asked.

"Three million," Feyodov replied. "American dollars, as usual."

The ice cream maker scowled at the general's favorite choice of currency.

"Why can't you ever be a good people's general and ask for rubles?" he said. "Better yet, be a purist and do it for the Revolution?"

The Russian bristled. "There is always another promised revolution on the horizon," General Feyodov said coldly. "And from revolution to revolution, we must still eat." The hint of anger that pinched his sagging face was lost on Zen.

"Yeah, yeah," Zen said.

He was thinking about how to get the money. His source wasn't tapped out; that was certain. But given his distaste of all things capitalist, Zen tried as much as possible to limit contact with his backer. Plus, there was his own stock portfolio to think of. At this point in the game he didn't want to upset the applecart.

"I'll see what I can scrape up," Zen said.

Turning from the general, he marched down the long corridor of hollowed-out rock. His sneakers squeaked once on the raised metal catwalk, then he was gone.

Feyodov shook his head at the ease with which he had just upped his payment. Of course the

CableSys satellite in its lazy orbit had been a fat, easy target. The old Soviet equipment hadn't been capable of such a feat, but thanks to the computer advances of the intervening decade, a single PC with the right programming made such precision effortless. He had just made a deal to purchase yet another shiny, worthless bauble for these fool Americans.

More money for Boris Feyodov. More wealth to corrupt his already hopelessly tainted soul.

In the hollow center of his gutted heart, he felt sick at what he had become. But that would all change soon. Soon he would have his revenge. And when the day of reckoning at last came, the very ground would boil.

Until that time, he was a prostitute.

With morose eyes Feyodov looked down at the monitor.

Although the screen was new, it was the same station at which he had watched the *Challenger* explode fifteen years ago. The digitally-enhanced contours of the CableSys satellite continued to roll in dead orbit around the planet.

The general shook his head. "The whore will have his day," he vowed softly. Dropping into a chair, Feyodov unfastened some of the more uncomfortable buttons on his uniform jacket.

7

With troubled eyes of flinty gray, Harold Smith scanned the data that slipped across his computer screen.

The explosion of the Every4 rocket had been followed too quickly by the malfunctioning weather satellite. Linking those two events, the Folcroft mainframes had identified something as a potential problem. But it remained only a possibility. Given an absence of further information, the basement computers could not make a positive connection between those two separate incidents.

At first. That had changed a few hours ago.

Two had now become three.

Smith had learned that a satellite for the company CableSys had gone black for no apparent reason.

Harold W. Smith was not a man who ordinarily trusted instinct, far preferring to truck in cold, hard facts. But he had to admit there were times in his life when his gut was a far better barometer than even his trusted computers. And at the moment he could not help but feel there was something larger going on here than three coincidental malfunctions.

Still, there was not enough yet to commit CURE's

resources. In the privacy of his tomb-silent office, Smith was looking for the link that would connect these three events.

So engrossed was he with the scrolling information on his monitor that he failed to hear the sound of a vehicle slowing to a stop behind the sanitarium. Only when the horn honked was he shaken from his worried thoughts.

Smith leaned back in his chair, the better to see the loading dock that extended from the back of the sanitarium.

Twilight had begun to crawl up from the Sound, settling like a velvet cape among the barren winter trees. In the wan gray light, Smith saw a minivan parked near the main delivery entrance. Remo hung out the window, waving him down.

The CURE director twisted from the window.

Smith quickly backed out of his system, shutting off his computer with a hidden stud. When he hustled out of the office a moment later, his secretary exhaled great relief.

"Oh, Dr. Smith," Mrs. Mikulka said. Her full face was flushed with mild tension. "You just missed him." Her troubled eyes glanced to the hallway door.

Smith frowned. "Who?" he asked.

"That supplies salesman," Mrs. Mikulka explained. "The one you said you'd meet with? He's been waiting out here for hours. I know how you don't like to be disturbed, so I didn't buzz you all afternoon. I figured you'd let me know when you wanted to see him. Should I have interrupted?"

Face troubled, she bit her lip.

Smith had completely forgotten about the salesman.

"No," he said. "I was otherwise occupied."

"That's what I assumed," Eileen Mikulka said. "Well, he'll be very happy that you're finally available. He just stepped out for a moment to use the rest room. I must admit, he's a very patient young man."

"He will have to be more patient," Smith said, edging for the door. "I don't have time for him now."

"Oh…" Mrs. Mikulka said hesitantly. "Very well." She seemed unsure what to do.

"Please ask him to return tomorrow morning," Smith said. "And this time please set up a proper appointment for him."

Turning crisply, he hurried from the room.

Mrs. Mikulka seemed uncomfortable with the order. After all, in her opinion, the young man had displayed a patience that was almost unheard-of for anyone of his generation. Still, it was not her place to question Dr. Smith.

She pulled out her employer's appointment book.

Although it was early February, there were no marks yet visible in the binder. Like most of the ones she'd purchased since coming to work for Dr. Smith, she assumed the crisp white lines would remain virtually blank for the bulk of the coming year. Dr. Smith rarely had appointments.

With a blue Bic disposable, she dutifully began to

log the Folcroft director's first meeting of the new year.

SMITH QUICKLY UNLOCKED the big garage door and rolled the sheet of corrugated steel upward.

Remo and Chiun stood on the rust-smeared concrete delivery platform on the other side. Remo's rented van was backed up to the dock. The younger Sinanju Master's face was troubled, while the older's was grave.

"Emperor Smith." Chiun bowed tightly.

"Hey, Smitty," Remo echoed, ducking under the door even before it had rolled all the way up. "Any problems while we were on the road?" Chiun padded in after him.

Smith shook his head, slipping his key ring back into his pocket. "None," he replied. "I instructed the attending doctor to call me directly every half hour if there was any change. The sedatives appear to be working."

"I must see him," the Master of Sinanju pronounced.

"Of course," Smith nodded.

The CURE director pulled the garage door back down, locking it securely. Taking the lead, he brought the two men back through the cellar. A short hallway led to another locked door, which, in turn, fed into the basement corridor where Remo and Chiun shared quarters. Passing through a pair of fire doors, the three men climbed one flight of stairs to the secure wing. Smith's security code gained them access.

When they entered Purcell's room, the Folcroft doctor looked up sharply. At Smith's order, he had been sitting at the patient's bedside the entire afternoon.

To Remo, Purcell looked as he had the last time Remo had seen him. His pale face was at peace. Soft blond hair spread like a nimbus around his head.

"Dismiss your quacksalver, Emperor," Chiun commanded as he swept to the bedside. "I would examine the Dutchman without the intrusion of prying Western eyes."

Dr. Paulakus seemed more confused than insulted. More interested now in the strange little Asian in the kimono than in his patient, the doctor allowed himself to be led outside.

Once he had escorted the Folcroft physician from the security wing, Smith returned. The CURE director closed the door to the room tightly.

Only when it was just the three of them in the hospital room did the Master of Sinanju pull back the sheet on the sleeping patient. His face darkened when he noted the Dutchman's toned arms.

Wordlessly, he went about his examination. Slender fingers tapped joints from foot to shoulder. His skeletal touch lingered lightly on the thin neck, feeling the coursing blood. When he was through, he pulled the sheet back up.

At the foot of the bed, Smith and Remo waited expectantly for an answer. The old man turned to them.

"He heals," Chiun said. His eyes were flat.

Remo shot a glance at the Dutchman. Purcell's

placid expression was the antithesis of his own worried look.

"How long we got?"

"I cannot say for certain," the old man replied seriously. He tucked his hands inside the voluminous sleeves of his black kimono, clasping bony wrists. "The Emperor's soporifics continue to keep him in this state. If not for them, he would likely be awake now. I can only say that the time is not imminent, but that it is coming."

Smith exhaled stale bile. "That is some comfort, I suppose," he said. He pulled off his glasses, massaging the bridge of his nose with tired fingers.

"Says you," Remo said.

"Master Chiun," the CURE director said, "are there any means by which you can prolong this state? You are able to paralyze others with a touch, why not the Dutchman?"

"Because he is Sinanju," Chiun said simply.

"Other means then," Smith said, replacing his glasses. "Perhaps your Sinanju amnesia technique. If you could supply the proper suggestions under hypnosis, maybe—"

"No dice, Smitty," Remo interrupted. "Rip van Winkle's on his way back to the land of the living, and there's not a damn thing we can do about it right now."

Hazel eyes directed on the sleeping form of Purcell, the old Korean took a deep breath.

"That is correct, Emperor," Chiun said. "However, that time will be later rather than sooner, so there is no great urgency. In any event, since we are bound by tradition not to harm another of the village, this is a Sinanju problem and one for which you need not trouble your regal head. When he awakens, Remo and I will deal with the Dutchman.''

''Yeah,'' Remo said dryly. ''We've done a whiz-bang job taking care of him so far. Say, maybe we should get him a balloon bouquet and a card that reads 'Welcome back to the land of the living. Sure hope you don't kill a bunch of people this time.'''

The Master of Sinanju's face was bland.

''When he finally does awaken, I certainly hope you have come up with a better plan than that,'' Chiun sniffed.

''*Me?*'' Remo asked. ''What do you mean me, white man?''

But Chiun didn't answer. His prognosis on Purcell delivered, the old man breezed past Remo and their employer. Without a backward glance, he left the room.

''What did he mean, me?'' Remo demanded of Smith.

Smith only shrugged. He clearly wasn't comfortable with any aspect of the situation.

''Very well,'' the CURE director said, sighing. ''We will cross this bridge when we come to it.''

''It ain't very damn well from where I'm standing,'' Remo said, shaking his head. ''Everything's just piling on for me lately. My house, my curse, now this.'' He sighed loudly. ''I better get Chiun's trunks before the parking brake goes and the freaking minivan rolls into Long Island Sound.''

Sullen, he turned and left, as well.

Alone, Smith cast a last troubled eye over the sleeping form of Jeremiah Purcell. Gaunt face a well of deep concern, he backed from the room. Shutting the door tightly, he snapped off the lights from the switch out in the hallway.

The clicking of his cordovan dress shoes faded to silence down the hall.

Long after Smith left, the faint rustling of sheets sounded from the darkened room as Jeremiah Purcell continued to relentlessly open and close his pale hands.

BY THE TIME SMITH returned to his small office suite, his secretary was gone for the evening.

The outer office was empty.

Relieved that he no longer had to deal with the persistent young medical-supplies salesman, Smith stepped into his inner sanctum. He found a yellow Post-it note stuck to the edge of his desk. On it, Mrs. Mikulka's neat handwriting reminded Smith of his 9:00 a.m. appointment with the salesman the following day.

As Smith read the name, something sparked his distant memory. It seemed familiar somehow.

After a moment's hesitation, he decided that it was a common enough sounding name. Smith committed the young man's name and the time to memory. Satisfied this time that he would not forget, he folded the note and dropped it into the wastebasket that was tucked in the footwell of his desk.

With practiced fingers, he located the concealed stud that turned on his computer. The glowing square of the angled monitor winked on beneath the desk's surface.

When the screen came up, a fresh report awaited him. His face grew grave when he saw that it was connected to the three earlier satellite mishaps.

Smith took but a few scant moments to read the digest. Concern grew to puzzlement.

"Odd," he said to the empty room.

Getting up, he retrieved an old black-and-white portable television set from a wooden file cabinet in the corner.

As a sop to the times, he had finally given up on his tinfoil-wrapped rabbit ears. A thick black cable wire trailed in his wake as he brought the small portable set to his desk. He had turned it on and was tuning to the proper channel when his office door popped open.

Remo and Chiun slipped into the room on silent feet.

The CURE director barely noted their arrival, so engrossed was he in his labors.

"Now the truth comes out," Remo said. He nodded to the small television as the two men crossed the room. "If you're hiding out at work watching *Judge Judy* just to dodge your wife's meat loaf, Smitty, I'm telling."

Smith was watching the TV, gray face registering confusion. "This is most peculiar," he frowned as the two Masters of Sinanju rounded his desk.

On the screen a sweating man bounced and jumped across a wide stage. His wild physical contortions were matched in energy only by his frantically flapping lips.

"You got that right," Remo said. His thin lips formed a scowl. "That's Leslie Walters."

Smith arched an eyebrow. "You know him?" he asked.

Remo shot him a glance. "Climb out of your crypt once in a while, Smitty," he said dryly. "Everybody knows him. I think he even won an Academy Award a few years back. He's been in a bunch of movies. *What's Up, Saigon, Lady Doubledees.* Oh, and he did the big-screen version of *Hagar the Horrible.* He was a stand-up comic who got his first break on some crappy TV show years ago. 'Puke and Cindy,' or something like that." He tipped his head, considering. "On the one-through-ten unfunny hyperactive dickwad meter, I'd have to rate him somewhere in the eighteen- to twenty-five range."

At Smith's side, the Master of Sinanju observed the prancing figure on the TV through slivered eyes.

"This cavorting lunatic must be of Mongol descent," Chiun determined.

"What makes you say that?" asked Remo.

The Master of Sinanju gave a matter-of-fact shrug. "He is tall and his eyes are round, but what other reason would he have to drape himself with animal pelts if not to pay homage to his Turki yurt-dwelling ancestors?"

"I got news for you, Little Father," Remo said. "That ain't a fur coat."

Chiun cast a skeptical eye at his pupil. He examined the screen carefully for a moment. All at once, his wrinkled mouth formed a shocked O.

"What manner of monkey-man is this?" he hissed.

"Told you," Remo said. "I think Walters was voted the hairiest man alive by *People* magazine. I heard a rumor that some PETA protesters even threw red paint on him backstage after a big dance number at last year's Oscars. He took off his shirt, and they thought he was wearing a mink tuxedo."

On the screen the comic wore a T-shirt and slacks. His exposed arms were covered with a thick brown thatch. Even more hair jutted from collar, ears and neck. Some said Walters had to shave his eyelids and the tip of his nose twice daily just to keep five-o'clock shadow at bay.

"Why are we watching one of the biggest A-list A-holes in Hollywood?" Remo questioned Smith.

"My computers have linked him to a chain of events that I have been investigating," Smith said. He could not hide the uncertainty in his voice.

He quickly sketched in the details of the three satellites that had been destroyed over the past twenty-four hours, including the fact that no one had linked the three events as anything more than just unfortunate coincidence.

"So what does Walters have to do with it?" Remo asked once the CURE director was through. "Was someone forcing them to beam one of his movies to cable? Because if that's the case, you can't blame any self-respecting satellite for committing hara-kiri."

"I long ago installed a program in the mainframes that allows for real-time filtering of closed-captioned programs," Smith explained. "At first it was intended as a tool to read political speeches that might not otherwise receive print coverage. I expanded the original parameters after the upgrades I made to the CURE systems a few years ago. This show is being broadcast live and is closed-captioned. Apparently, Mr. Walters has made numerous references to the destruction of the three satellites during the course of a bizarre, incoherent monologue." As he watched the comic bounce desperately around the stage, he shook his head. "Is this man on drugs?" he asked, amazed.

"He lives west of the Rockies," Remo said, as if this explained everything. "You want us to check him out?"

Taking one last look at the wildly gyrating comedian, Smith snapped off the TV.

"I think not," the CURE director said. "While the connection seems troubling, he is obviously demented. I would not put much weight in his nonsensical ramblings."

Leaving the TV on the edge of his desk, he settled into his worn leather chair.

"Suit yourself," Remo said. "The way things are going for me lately, bumping off a twit like Leslie Walters would have been a ray of sunshine. No surprise to me that I don't get to have any fun." He sank cross-legged to the floor.

Smith began typing. As he worked, he felt eyes watched his every move. After a minute of trying to ignore the two men, he finally looked up over the tops of his glasses.

Chiun still stood beside the desk, his face an imperious wax mask. Before Smith, Remo was seated on the threadbare rug wearing a bored expression. Both men stared at Smith.

"Don't the two of you have something better to do?" the CURE director asked thinly.

"Us?" Remo said. "Naw. Chiun checked to make sure all the stale mints and oyster crackers were still in his trunks back in Taxachusetts. They're all unloaded and stored in his room downstairs. Until you give us something to do, we're free as birds."

"We are not free, but we are competitively priced," the Master of Sinanju quickly inserted.

"Yes," Smith said carefully. "Perhaps you are hungry. The cafeteria is closed by now, but per your request there is an ample supply of fish and duck in cold storage. You may feel free to help yourselves."

"We ate back in Quincy," Remo explained. He patted his stomach. "Brown rice, a little dab'll do ya."

Smith pursed his lips. With a hint of perturbed frustration he returned to his work. The sound of his fingers drumming on his desktop was interrupted a few scant seconds later.

"You been dyeing your hair, Smitty?"

Drawing on deep reserves of patience, Smith raised his white head. "Perhaps I was in error," the CURE director said levelly. "It might be a good idea for you to check into Walters after all. I'm not sure if there is a connection, but it would do no harm to make certain. The event he is performing at is called Buffoon Aid.''

Remo nodded. "I've heard of that. A bunch of comics get together for charity."

"Precisely," Smith said. "The telethon is held to raise money for the homeless."

At Smith's side, the Master of Sinanju's supremely uninterested expression disappeared in a flash. "The money raised goes to those without homes?" he asked.

"Yes," Smith said, nodding.

"Remo and I are currently without a home," the old man pointed out, one eye narrowing with cunning.

"I don't think they'd be too worried about us, Little Father," Remo said. "Besides, if you need a second house, it's only because you've got so much loot stuffed in the one back in Korea it's starting to dump out the chimney."

There was a whirl of angry silk at the side of Smith's desk, followed by a rush of displaced air. Remo felt a bony toe kick him soundly in the leg.

The black blur that had flown around the desk resolved back into the shape of the Master of Sinanju.

"On fluttering wings of doves do Remo and I happily hasten to do your will," Chiun sang to Smith. He kicked Remo again. "Get up, lout," he snapped in Korean. "We are going house hunting."

"Okay, okay," Remo grumbled in the same language as he rose to his feet. "But I for one am not buying any of this. We're just getting the bum's rush because Smitty doesn't want us around.''

"And you were looking forward to listening to his wheezing and creaking? Now let us hurry, before all the best palaces are taken.'' He spun back to his employer. "Where are these generous souls located, Emperor?'' he asked in English.

"The Buffoon Aid telethon is being held in Barkley, California,'' Smith replied. "I will book you a flight.''

With a look of great relief he began typing once more, this time with earnest purpose.

"They're not gonna give you any money, Chiun,'' Remo warned the Master of Sinanju as Smith worked. "And they're sure as hell not giving you a house.''

"They will when they hear my tale of woe,'' the old man said. A frail hand brushed his thin chest. "A poor old man in the twilight of his life, far from the land of his birth, forced out into the cold streets by a cruel quirk of fate.'' He pitched his voice low. "I will be certain not to tell them that the quirk of fate was you and your firebug friends.''

"I did *not* burn down our house,'' Remo said, scowling.

Chiun waved his words away. "Be sure to play up the orphan angle.'' He tipped his head as he examined his pupil. "Your shabby clothes are perfect for the part.''

"No one cares about full-grown orphans, Little Father,'' Remo warned him.

"Try to walk with a limp,'' Chiun suggested slyly.

8

It was known only as the Institute.

The massive concrete building was a bully that menaced a block of Kitai Gorod in Moscow, east of the Kremlin. The ground-floor windows had been bricked over years before. On the upper floors, shadows played over recessed brick and mortar where there had once been panes of translucent glass.

At street level, a locked metal gate led up a short drive to the sealed entrance of an underground garage. Although this appeared to be the only way in, no one in the surrounding neighborhood had ever seen it open. The fat chain that wrapped the gate was rusted from age.

Those who came and went from that building did so by means unknown.

In the waning days of the old Soviet empire, some protesters unlucky enough to have found their way onto the streets around the Institute had vanished. Disappeared without a trace, presumably swallowed up by that menacing colorless building. They were the lucky ones.

Others who passed by with placards and makeshift weapons had died in the streets. Not from poisons or bullets. They had simply toppled over where they stood. Some said an invisible wave of fear generated by the Institute itself had caused otherwise healthy men to drop dead.

Even after the Cold War ended, the Institute remained. The Soviet Union had long collapsed beneath the relentless marching heels of history, yet when the new age dawned, that huge building was as it had always been. Unchanged from the days when the last premier walked the halls of the Kremlin.

No one was quite sure what went on inside, which was good enough for the people who lived nearby. Most did their best to keep from even looking at the building as they passed by it, let alone pry into its secrets. Many avoided the Institute altogether, taking torturous routes through the narrow, winding streets of Kitai Gorod that brought them no closer than two blocks from the sinister building that was a throwback to another era.

There was one person, however, who could not avoid the big building or the secrets it held.

The office of the Institute's director was buried deep below street level. If there was automobile traffic, it went unheard so far beneath the ground. An explosion big enough to level the building far above could go off without this area of the complex even knowing it.

The director's office was small, without ornamentation.

A television played on a pressboard stand in the corner. The used table had been picked up for twenty

U.S. dollars at a bazaar in Zagorsk. On the TV screen was a grainy image of two men walking down a crowded boulevard.

The director watched the television with a vacant stare.

On the metal desk sat a plain black phone, out of date by at least thirty years by Western standards.

Next to the phone was an open bottle of French wine and a lone glass. The wine was being given a chance to breathe. There was irony in that, which was not lost on the director.

As the silent television played to blankly staring eyes, the old-fashioned phone suddenly jangled to life.

It came as no surprise.

The weary figure pulled up the heavy receiver.

"Yes, sir."

"I have studied the information you have sent to me," the voice of Russia's president said without preamble.

The former KGB official who now ruled Russia had no time for pleasantries. It was a most worrisome attribute. The director of the Institute understood all too well that a man with power who was always in a hurry was a man to fear.

"That data is already old," the director said. "There has been another incident since the first two. A commercial communications satellite."

The president swore softly. "Do the Americans know about this yet?" he asked.

"Not that I have been able to ascertain. I have no

doubt, however, that elements of their government will eventually make the connection.''

The president hissed angrily. "Feyodov," he growled. "Who knew the coward would grow claws?"

"It is my belief that he is driven by fear, revenge and greed. All are motivations that can make the most timid man seem brave. Had I been given his dossier as I requested after the events in Chechnya more than a year ago, I would likely have seen this coming."

"Forgive me," said the president with parched sarcasm, "but when I assumed this post, my predecessor failed to tell me of your clairvoyance." His voice grew firm. "You must stop him," he ordered.

For the first time there came a flicker of emotion on the director's face. The head of the Institute leaned forward. The rusted metal springs of the desk's matching chair creaked in protest. A soft sound in the small room.

"You are aware, Mr. President, that the Institute exists only to advise. We have no field agents."

"You have an entire *building* of field agents," the Russian president insisted. "Use them."

This was the one command the director feared.

"Those men are not traditional field agents," the Institute head explained. "They were not trained for such a task. Unleashing them on American soil would surely bring unwanted attention directly to this organization. I would advise you to use SVR agents."

The SVR was the agency that had succeeded the KGB.

"No," the president declared, his voice steely. "This cannot be allowed to spread any further. If you will not use the men at the Institute, you will go yourself."

"That would be an unwise use of materials," the director said. "In addition, it would create an unacceptable risk."

"That was not a request," the president growled hotly. "You were a field agent once. Arrogant enough to think that you were better than any man, as I recall."

In another life, the two had met briefly. It was back before the director had gone into a decade of deep cover. When the president assumed his leadership of Russia, he had been dismayed to learn that this testament to conceit was still alive. Worse, that the former agent had been made head of something as important as the Institute.

"You will go to America," the president commanded. "You will kill General Feyodov, and you will suppress this information at all costs. Am I clear on this matter?"

There was no room for argument. The head of the Institute nodded to the empty office.

"Yes, sir."

"And be warned," the Russian leader said. "If you fail, there will be an open grave waiting for you on your return." With that, he severed the connection.

Coming as it did from a former KGB man, the

words were no idle threat. The black office phone fell heavily back into its cradle. So that was that. America awaited.

And in that small basement office there was an old fear in the director's blue eyes that had absolutely nothing to do with the Russian president's threat.

9

Remo and Chiun took a late flight from JFK, arriving at San Francisco International Airport at dawn.

Although the temperature was only in the high fifties this early in the day, the sun and lack of snow was a welcome change for Remo.

"This sure beats the hell out of freezing in the New England icebox," he commented as they made their way to the rental-car agency.

"I like New England," the Master of Sinanju sniffed. "It was near enough to Smith without being too near. And despite the unpleasant name, there were no Old Englanders anywhere to be seen."

"Both pluses, I suppose." Remo nodded. "Still, if we do get a new house, my vote's for someplace hot."

"And the moment your vote counts more than mine, you may live in the inferno of your choosing. Until such time, the sacred scrolls dictate that it is for the Reigning Master to decide where he and his apprentice will live."

"Where do the scrolls ever give a rat's ass about where we're supposed to live?" Remo asked, smelling a scam.

Chiun waved a hand. "Somewhere in the back, I believe. Now, please, Remo, hurry and rent us a carriage. I do not want some street-reeking lazybones to claim squatter's rights over our new residence."

Still dubious, Remo rented them a car. They took the Bayshore Freeway across the Oakland Bay Bridge. It was a short trip up the eastern shore of San Paolo Bay to Barkley.

Remo sensed trouble as soon as they hit town.

A battered Volkswagen Beetle came puttering toward them, a faded McGovern For President sticker plastered to its bungee-corded front bumper.

The Master of Sinanju's face grew displeased the instant he saw the ancient yellow car.

"Were not those ghastly contraptions banned by your government?" Chiun asked.

"No," Remo said as the car passed by. "Worse, they started making them again, even uglier than before. We won the war, but the Germans get the last laugh."

Chiun didn't hear him. A bony hand suddenly clasped Remo's forearm.

"There!" the old man screeched, stabbing a quivering nail at the windshield. "Yet another approaches." His breath abruptly caught and he squeezed Remo's arm even tighter. "Can it be?" he exhaled.

"Hey, trying to drive here," Remo said, wincing at the pressure being exerted on his forearm.

"It is," Chiun said, with a trace of unaccustomed fear in his voice. "Remo, turn this vehicle around at once!"

"What the—? Chiun, will you let go of my god-damn arm, for crying out loud?"

"A pippie!" the Master of Sinanju cried. In a flurry of frightened fingers he ducked below the dashboard as the second Volkswagen chugged by.

The car was covered with rubber daisies and peace symbols. The driver looked as if he shopped at the dump for his clothes and bathed once every two decades whether he needed to or not.

"What's gotten into you, Meryl Streep?" Remo asked.

"Turn this vehicle around at once!" Chiun shrieked in horror from the footwell.

"Huh? Why the hell should I do that?"

"Some wicked magic has obviously cast us back in time to the most odious era in your nation's history," the Master of Sinanju insisted. He tried grabbing for the steering wheel, but Remo held on tight.

"We haven't time traveled," Remo insisted. "This is just Barkley. As long as you keep your hands inside the car at all times, the locals won't bite."

A gasp from far below.

"Horror upon horrors!" Chiun wailed. "This is *your* fault for taunting the gods. I have become victim of their excess wrath. If we reverse our direction, perhaps we can escape this nightmare."

Chiun blindly tried to shift into reverse. Remo held tightly to both the steering wheel and gearshift lever.

"Will you knock it off?" he snapped. "I told you, we haven't gone through a time warp."

Hazel eyes appeared above the dash.

"I do not know what those words mean, but that was the most warped time since time began. I would gouge my eyes from my head and flee into the wilderness before reliving that dismal era."

"Okay, first order of business—no gouging," Remo insisted. "We're still in the present, those cars were really old and if you grab the wheel one more time I'm buying a banana plantation on Maui for both of us and having the natives hoist the Sinanju flag."

Sensing his pupil's certainty, the old man eased cautiously up to the edge of his seat.

"Purchase what you want where you want, but you will be swinging from your ancestral trees alone," the Master of Sinanju said. "Now explain this place quickly." Wary eyes watched the road ahead.

"Barkley *is* lost in time, but not in any supernatural way," Remo said. "I blame the college. There isn't a bigger factory for PC Jim Morrison hashhuffers than higher education. And the freaks they've got running Barkley U are the worst ponchowearing gladiolis this side of the touring company of *Hair*. Dopey professors plus dopier kids equals LSD trips on daddy's credit card and vintage Volkswagens still tooling around the streets."

Chiun was caught between skepticism and his long-held belief that any lunacy was possible in America.

"Why would your nation allow a place filled with mental defectives to exist?"

"Don't know about you, but I'd rather keep all the assorted nuts in one can," Remo said.

And because it was the first time he could remember his pupil or America ever making sense, Chiun settled cautiously back in his seat. Nevertheless, he kept a careful eye on their surroundings as they drove deeper into the city.

Remo was surprised by the large number of potholes on the main streets. Their rental car bumped and bounced its way to the center of town. As they drove, he had noted a shape looming up over some of the low buildings.

At first he ignored it, but when they came to a set of traffic lights, he saw through a break in the buildings two massive black eyes staring down at them.

"What the hell is that?" Remo remarked, looking up at the huge statue at Barkley's center.

"It appears to be the image of some god," Chiun observed.

"Some god is right," Remo said sarcastically. "Looks like a big black turd with the top lopped off."

"That's right, Remo," Chiun said blandly. "Perhaps this is the one god left that you have not yet insulted. I will bring you back to Sinanju after this latest angry deity has transformed you into a pillar of salt. The fish salter can chip bits off of you to cure the catch for the long winter months." He watched the statue with quiet reverence.

"That'd almost be worth it just to get someone in that dump of a village to do an honest day's work," Remo said.

The eyes of Huitzilopochtli followed them as they headed for the main square.

The driving soon became impossible. Remo ditched his car on a rutted side street. The two men continued on foot.

Like a full moon at midnight, the Huitzilopochtli statue seemed to always be in the sky at their shoulder as they walked along the sidewalk.

"Let's hope the Buffoon Aid benefit's inside somewhere," Remo said. "That statue's giving me the creeps."

They found a reed-thin woman on a street corner near the town square. Dressed in a big, filthy muumuu, she looked like a dirty stick draped with a circus tent.

The woman sat on the sidewalk cutting colored scraps of paper into clumsy flower shapes. As she worked her scissors, the white tip of her tongue jutted from between her pale lips. A cobblestone pried up from a hole in the street kept her paper flowers from blowing away.

As they stopped before the squatting woman, Chiun's face took on a glint of quiet fascination.

"Excuse me, ma'am," Remo said.

The scissors paused in midsnip.

"'Ma'am?'" Lorraine Wintnabber sneered up at him. "What kind of patriarchal cave did you crawl out of?"

"The kind with liquid Tide and bars of Dial that aren't dehydrated from nonuse," Remo replied.

"Soap pollutes our precious waterways," Lorraine said. She resumed clipping away.

"Since you're the first noncartoon person I've seen with actual stink lines floating off them, my vote's for sudsing up the mighty Mississip," Remo said. "Now, while my nose is still attached, you mind telling me where that big stand-up comic show is being held?"

The woman was still deeply involved in her work. She hadn't even looked up while Remo spoke.

"That way," she snarled.

Lorraine waved to a big auditorium across the street from Barkley's city hall. Remo saw HTB vans parked out front, their rooftop satellite dishes aimed skyward. The legend "An AIC News-Wallenberg Company" was stenciled in small print on the side panels of each of the vans.

"Now, beat it," she said. "I've got eight hundred of these things to do by the day after tomorrow and I've only got twelve done so far."

She finished clipping another ragged flower. With great care she delivered it to the pile of finished ones, clapping the muddy cobblestone back in place.

"This may be none of my business, Dirty Harriet, but wouldn't it be easier if you did that inside?" Remo asked.

"It's too dark," Lorraine said, her eyes on her scissors.

"Turn on the lights."

"Electricity is an invention of the military-industrial complex designed to keep the masses weak and pliable by making them stay up late watching Johnny Carson."

This time when Chiun squeezed Remo's arm,

there was a look of questioning joy on the old man's face. He was watching Lorraine intently.

"Can it be?" the Master of Sinanju whispered under his breath to his pupil.

Something else down the block caught the old man's eye. With sudden glee he bounded a few yards away.

Brow furrowed, Remo tracked his teacher. The wizened Korean stopped near a college-age man. The Barkley University student was passing out colored fliers to pedestrians. Remo noted that they were printed in the same colors as those the woman at his feet was cutting.

"In case you didn't hear out on Neptune, Johnny Carson retired years ago," Remo said to the seated woman. "Thanks for the directions."

He started to leave, but Chiun was hurrying back toward him, dragging the pamphlet-hawking student in his wake. The old man's face was rhapsodic.

"I have found another one!" Chiun squealed.

"Another what?" Remo scowled. "And stop pointing that thing at me."

He leaned back from the kid the Master of Sinanju held before him. The young man had a black sweatshirt, scraggly goatee and a shaved head.

"You wanna know the truth behind all those cattle mutilations?" the college student confided to Remo. "Think genetically engineered supercows. It's the secret Ronald McDonald doesn't want you to find out about."

He stuffed a photocopied flier into Remo's hand.

On the bright pink paper several stick-figure dead cows formed a bovine border around illegible text.

"Next time you might want to write your manifesto *after* they let you out of the straitjacket," Remo suggested. He crumpled the paper and tossed it over his shoulder.

"Litterbug!" snarled the woman snipping out the papers. She snatched up the flier and began carving it up.

"Thought I had an easy target," Remo said. "I was aiming for your mouth. What's up?" he asked Chiun.

"Do you not see?" the old man asked, delighted. He held out his hands in proud presentation. "This, Remo, is a village idiot. It is a wonderful old English tradition."

"There's nothing wonderful about the English, Grampa," Lorraine insisted as she worked. "Just a bunch of dead white males spreading syphilis and the language of conquerors."

"Lady, I got news for you," Remo said. "I've been almost everywhere there is to go on this benighted rock, and the most civilized places by far are the ones where they speak English. Furthermore, even a dead guy would jump out the window before spreading syphilis to you."

The sidewalk-squatting woman didn't even hear the last of what he said. At his use of the demeaning and sexist term *lady,* she immediately tried to stick the blunt end of her childproof scissors into Remo's leg.

"See?" Chiun said, ecstatic. "She is another village idiot. And there!'' He pointed out to the road. ''There are two more!''

Two flabby middle-aged men in short shorts and too-tight tanktops were just pedaling past on a bicycle built for two.

Chiun clasped his hands together with giddy glee.

''Why did you not tell me this was a training ground for village idiots, Remo?'' Chiun asked. ''Or perhaps it is a national secret. When the time is right, wave after wave of idiots will be dispatched from this province to amuse and delight the citizenry of this land. Look!'' he squealed.

Wrinkled face rapturous, he flounced down the street.

''Yeah,'' Remo agreed as the Master of Sinanju began joyfully stalking a placard-wearing vegan. ''And that time comes every spring at Barkley U graduation. Will you knock it off?'' he snapped down at the sidewalk.

Lorraine was still trying to jab him with her scissors. When he walked off, she gave up and instead stuck the nearby college kid in the calf. Yelping in pain, the young man promptly dropped all his fliers. As he rubbed the bruise the blunt scissors had made, Lorraine swept all of the colored papers between her folded knees.

''Go litter on someone else's planet,'' she accused.

Ever on the lookout to do her part to save Mother Earth, she began recycling the college student's discarded trash into more respectable, environmentally conscious daisies.

10

Boris Feyodov was trotting down the broad front steps of Barkley's city hall when the voice called out to him.

"General. I mean, Supreme Military— Hey, you!"

Feyodov considered ignoring the man altogether. With great reluctance, he paused in midstride. He turned.

Gary Jenfeld was huffing down the staircase, a container of Jane Funday Sundae Ice Cream in his hand.

"I am already late," the Russian said impatiently.

Feyodov was not wearing his Red Army uniform. He had agreed to that ridiculous term only on the condition that he not have to march around the street in it.

"Yeah, I know," Gary said. "You gotta get that special part. I didn't want to keep you, but—" he cast a glance back up the steps "—it's about Zen."

The look on Feyodov's face made clear his opinion of Gary's partner in the ice cream business.

"I'm not allowed to tell you some of what's really going on here," Gary whispered conspiratorially.

"It's all very hush-hush. But me and the rest of the council are getting kind of worried. Zen seems to be losing focus."

Feyodov raised a bland eyebrow. "That is of no concern to me," he said. "I am aware that you receive your money from some secret source. You pay me, and I supply that which you need. That is as far as I care."

"But I'm not sure you should leave," Gary hissed. "He's been coming unglued ever since that takeover of our ice cream company a couple years ago. With everything that's going on now, he's getting this Oliver North glint in his eye."

Feyodov scowled. "That is your problem, not mine. He leads your council until someone else takes over. If you are bothered by him, do what has been done to political opponents in Communist nations for a hundred years."

Gary's brow dropped in confusion. "Prison?" he asked.

Feyodov's eyes were flat. "Kill him."

This was obviously not the solution Gary had been hoping for. "No one ever built a socialist utopia by murdering people in cold blood," the ice cream man scolded.

"No," Feyodov agreed. "But it was not for lack of trying. Excuse me."

He turned on his heel and began marching back down the steps. Behind him, Gary hesitated for a moment before waddling unhappily back up the staircase.

Feyodov reached the main walk in front of the

building and was hurrying across the grassy town square when something across the park caught his eye.

Two men were walking toward Barkley's civic center.

His eye had first been drawn to the robe the older one wore. It was red and shimmered like wet blood. Swirling patterns of embroidered gold danced across the material.

The crowd in the square was focused mostly around the building where the American cable network's charity event was being held. Even though the mob was thick before the hall, the two men moved through it like a pair of unwavering phantoms. In the great shadow cast by the huge stone statue Huitzilopochtli, they glided through the gleaming glass front doors of the distant hall and were gone.

As they vanished through the doors, Feyodov frowned.

His glasses were in the car, so he had not seen the two men well. Yet something about their comfortable gliding movements was familiar.

For an instant his brain almost allowed him to think the unthinkable. Almost at once he remembered Zen's earlier observation. He hated to admit it, but the idiot was right. Feyodov was always watching shadows. This was just another instance of his mind creating ghosts from his own fears.

Pulling in a deep breath that filled his ample belly, Feyodov forced the two men and all they represented from his mind. Ghosts. That was all. He put them behind him.

That was in the past. A place that he did not like to visit. The present was all that mattered to him now.

As he hurried to his waiting luxury car, the flat black eyes of Huitzilopochtli continued to stare dully out over the bustling activity of Barkley's main square.

11

Smith logged off his computer at precisely 12:30 a.m.

After hours of searching, he had found nothing to indicate that the destruction of the three satellites was anything more than an unfortunate coincidence. Still, the nagging hunch that there was something more to this dogged him even as he climbed wearily to his feet.

His bones creaked as he leaned to collect his battered briefcase from beside his desk.

Remo and Chiun had left for the airport an hour ago. The CURE director feared that theirs would be a wasted trip.

At the door, Smith tugged on his heavy overcoat. On the wooden rack where it had hung, a new gray woolen scarf was draped over a dull brass peg.

The scarf had been a Christmas gift from his wife. Maude Smith had been so happy to give him something she knew he could use. Her Harold was so difficult to shop for.

She had been thrilled when he told her that it was almost exactly like a scarf he'd had as a child. He recalled many a cold Vermont night being wrapped in that scarf as he hiked to the small local library to study. That old scarf had captured all the winter aromas of his youth. It smelled of countless boiled dinners, smoke from the basement potbellied stove and his mother's pungent lye soap.

Alone in the postmidnight shadows of his office, away from prying eyes, Smith surrendered to a sudden twinge of nostalgia. Holding the scarf to his nose, he tried to get a scent of home from the wool.

There was nothing. Just the faint smell of mothballs and the even more faint indifferent aroma of a dusty old office. There was not even a hint of the neat little home he and his wife had shared for forty years.

Of course, there wouldn't be. His name might be on the mail, but his Rye residence was home only to Maude. To Harold Smith it was just a house. A place to sleep, shower and occasionally eat. His real home was here.

The sharper lines of his gaunt face softened into something resembling regret as Harold Smith drew the scarf around his narrow neck. Putting on his gray porkpie hat, he turned off the lights and left his drab office.

When he stepped through the side door to the sanitarium's administrative wing a few moments later, the cold wind that blew off Long Island Sound cut like an icy knife to his very marrow. Smith drew his scarf and collar more tightly to his neck and struck off for his car.

At this time of night the employee parking lot was practically empty.

Smith recognized all but one of the cars. It was parked in the shadows a few empty spaces down from his own. Smith assumed that a member of the skeleton crew that worked at night had gotten a new vehicle. He reached into his pocket to remove his keys.

He was clicking his key into the lock when he heard the sound of a door opening. Looking over the roof of his station wagon, he saw a figure emerge from the strange parked car.

"Dr. Smith?"

Smith was instantly alarmed. His concern intensified when he saw who it was coming toward him.

It was the young medical-supplies salesman who had spent the bulk of the day sitting outside the Folcroft director's closed office door.

The man's face was flushed, his breath nervous puffs of white steam in the cold air.

"I'm probably handling this badly, but you didn't really leave me with much of a choice," he said as he approached.

Frozen and motionless, alone and unprotected in the lonely windswept parking lot, Smith was overwhelmed by a thousand thoughts flooding his mind all at once, none of them good.

"This is highly irregular," Smith said tersely. He kept his movements subdued even as he continued to stealthily unlock his door. "I do not know what you hoped to accomplish by lurking out here in the middle of the night, but you may consider our appointment canceled."

"It's a little more complicated than that," the salesman replied.

At first, Smith was worried that he would not be able to protect himself against this stranger. After all, the young man looked to be some fifty years Smith's junior. And the CURE director's automatic pistol was in a cigar box hidden deep in the back of his bottom desk drawer upstairs. But the salesman didn't seem threatening in his manner. In fact, once he got as far as Smith's station wagon, he stopped. The two men faced each other over the roof of the rusted car.

"I'm Mark Howard," the salesman said. "Your new assistant." He glanced nervously over his shoulder.

Black trees clawed up from the snow-streaked landscape around the parking area. Weak yellow overhead lights bathed the frozen asphalt.

"I know your name," Smith said. "As does my secretary." This was said as a warning. "And if you think that this is an acceptable way to seek employment, young man, you are—"

"You don't understand," Howard insisted. "I've already *got* the job. I'm not here to work for the sanitarium."

He glanced around once more. He gave the look of a man peering for enemies in the distant shadows. It was a habit the CURE director knew all too well.

When he turned back around, Howard pitched his voice low, as if shadow or snow might overhear his words.

"I was sent by the President to help you, Dr.

Smith,'' he whispered. ''I'm the new assistant director of CURE.''

The shocking words were like a fist to the thin chest of Harold W. Smith.

Mark Howard offered a weak, apologetic smile. Smith didn't even acknowledge it.

The older man blinked behind the cold lenses of his glasses. And when they slipped from his stunned arthritic fingers, the sound of Smith's keys striking the pavement was swallowed up by the howling, desolate wind.

12

Despite the wishes of the Russian president, the head of the Institute had not come to America alone.

A team of six SVR men with foreign experience had been drafted into service directly from the Moscow offices. When Pavel Zatsyrko, the head of the SVR, found out one of his squads had been activated by someone with security clearance greater than his own, he would not be pleased.

It had been a calculated risk. The Institute director's reasoning was simple. The mission would either be a success and this minor defiance would be overlooked, or the mission would end in failure and no amount of disobedience would alter the director's fate.

The six agents had worked as a unit years before, assigned to the Soviet embassy in Washington. Time had been as kind to them as it had to the nation they once served. The men were mostly twitchy and balding, with growing bellies and the relentlessly scanning eyes of former KGB agents.

One was a hulking brute whose youthful muscle had long ago started the middle-aged slide into flab. At the other end of the evolutionary scale was Vadim Zhdanov, their leader in the SVR. A short man with deep, intelligent eyes, he scrutinized every move the Institute director made.

Zhdanov had not wanted to come back to America, especially after all these years. His men were no longer the field agents they had once been. Nor was he. Even though he had done his best to stay fit over the years, time had slipped past all of them. Yet the activation orders came from so high up they could not be refused. And so he and his five men had reluctantly returned to America.

Guns bulged beneath six armpits.

All seven Russians were crowded into a balcony box above the hall where the Buffoon Aid fundraiser was being held. The six SVR men were stuffed in behind a thick red curtain. The Institute head alone sat in a seat. A pair of infrared binoculars bathed the crowd in spectral green.

"There," the director announced, aiming a certain finger at the main floor of the auditorium.

Vadim crept forward, accepting the binoculars. Sitting next to the director, he trained them to the front of the vast crowd.

In the fourth row from the back on the left-hand side of the stage sat a stone-faced man. While others around him laughed uproariously, his expression never changed.

"That man is Yuri Koskolov. He is a known associate of General Feyodov," the director said, quietly. "You and your men will *capture* Koskolov. Repeat that order, for I do not want you to claim a misunderstanding if you blunder and kill him."

At this, Vadim frowned. "I am not a child," he said.

"No," the director agreed. "You are worse. You are a man. Now repeat the order, or I will put one of these others in charge."

Vadim had heard of this brusqueness. It was somewhat legendary in certain intelligence circles. He had always found the hushed tales amusing. Now that he was on the receiving end, however, his own attitude had changed.

As his five snickering men looked on, he repeated the command.

"We will capture Koskolov," the old agent said. "We will not kill him."

The director nodded curtly. "There is one other thing, this more important than anything else. There might be two men here in town looking for General Feyodov. One is a thin Caucasian with very thick wrists, the other an Oriental who is very, very old. If you see either of them, run. Do not approach them, do not speak to them and under no circumstances attempt to engage them either with weapons or physically. If you happen upon General Feyodov and they are in the vicinity, shoot the general and then run for all you are worth."

Vadim wasn't sure if this was some attempt at humor. The look on the director's face was deadly serious.

"You are joking, yes?" the SVR man asked.

"If you are stupid enough to involve yourself in a contest with these two men, you will be dead before the breath of shock reaches your throat," the

Institute head continued icily. "With any luck you will not even encounter them. If you successfully apprehend Koskolov, he will lead us to our renegade general. Perhaps we can clean up this mess before anyone here finds out the truth. Now, go."

Vadim Zhdanov nodded. Getting up from his seat, he herded the cluster of hiding SVR agents out from behind the curtain and through the balcony door.

After they were gone, the director raised the special binoculars once more. A green glow descended on the crowd.

With precise movements, the director scanned the mob, looking once more for the face of General Feyodov.

It was worse than looking for a needle in a haystack. Intelligence had put the general in San Francisco. Sketchier were the reports that had placed him in Barkley. It was only after seeing Yuri Koskolov, a former Red Army major and associate of Feyodov's, enter this building that the director knew they were on the right track. But the prize was the general himself, and every moment he remained at large increased the chance that the director would be—

The spyglasses abruptly froze in place.

Two new figures had just entered the hall. When the Institute head saw who they were, a wave of cold fear slipped across the director's body like a ghostly fog.

One was a thin man with exceptionally thick wrists. Beside him stood an ancient Korean.

It had happened. After all these years.

And to the shaking director, the terrible dream that

had haunted many a sleepless night for more than a decade had finally become a waking nightmare.

"PEE-YEW. I smell Russians."

Remo's face was puckered in displeasure as they entered the hall where the Buffoon Aid event was being held.

At shoulder level beside him, the Master of Sinanju turned his unhappy button nose into the air.

"There are at least eight," the old man replied. Hazel eyes scanned the balconies to the left of the hall where the bulk of the odor seemed to be concentrated.

"Dammit, they've had democracy for—cheez, gotta be ten years by now," Remo griped, fanning the air with his hand. "Why can't those Volga-paddlers smell like something other than turnips boiled in Stolichnaya?"

"Were I American born, I would not be so quick to find fault with the cultural odors of others," the Master of Sinanju droned in reply. "Until my delicate senses adapted, my first five years in this heathen land I could smell nothing but frying cow flesh. Although in defense of America, most of that issued from your smelly pores."

The old man's eyes narrowed when he noted the last balcony box far down near the stage.

"Yeah, well, I'm here 'cause Smith wanted us outta his hair, not to stamp out any beet-eating Russians," Remo said, "so they can watch us till their mutant Chernobyl cows come slithering home. I don't care. I'm not looking back."

On some level that Remo never quite understood, he could sense when he was being given more than just casual attention. Such was the case now.

Instead of looking at the person observing them, Remo turned his determined gaze on the distant stage.

For his part, Chiun was staring at a pair of very big lenses. They obscured the face behind. A pair of small, pale hands held them in place. Beyond was shadowy blond hair.

"Yes," the Master of Sinanju said, "by all means, Remo, do not look." The old man's tone betrayed just a hint of some buried emotion.

Remo failed to notice the catch in his teacher's voice.

"I'm not," Remo said firmly. "Just said so."

Chiun's slivered gaze never wavered.

"Binoculars, right?" Remo said absently. "If you ask me, binoculars are just a big fat cheat. Oh, they're gone. Good riddance to Bolshevik rubbish."

Whoever had been watching them had abruptly stopped. Remo felt the cessation of pressure waves on his body. He didn't seem interested in the least in their silent observer.

The auditorium was large, the seats filled nearly to capacity. Given the three-day nature of the marathon event, people didn't feel as obligated to stay put as they otherwise might. Streams of concertgoers were coming and going up and down the six long aisles that ran the length of the big hall.

The houselights were dimmed, the stage lights up full.

Remo was busy watching the man onstage. To his surprise, he had found upon entering that he actually liked the comedian who was performing.

The portly old man wore a black suit and red tie. He had once starred in a movie about a successful businessman who enrolled in college to be closer to his estranged son. Even though it was now more than ten years old, whenever he passed by that movie on TV Remo still stopped to watch it.

"Let's find some seats," Remo said.

Chiun's somber weathered face did not reflect his pupil's uncharacteristically bright tone.

When the binoculars had lowered, their owner had already been darting back into the balcony box. The old man had seen just a flash of a face. But it was enough.

Chiun looked as if he had seen a ghost.

Far down the hall a set of doors opened. In the general commotion of the hall, they went unnoticed. Six men hurried through them and began marching up the aisle.

"The Russians are coming," Chiun observed. He cast a wary eye at his pupil. He seemed relieved to find that Remo had not so much as glanced at the balcony. The younger Master of Sinanju had not seen the specter in the box.

The Russians were coming full steam ahead, elbowing people aside in their haste to reach the back of the room. Although they had not yet unholstered their side arms, the hands of all but the leader strayed under their jackets.

"Russians, schmussians," Remo griped. "I'm

sick of Russians. Don't they know they're not even topical anymore? They should have the decency to be Chinese. C'mon, there's two empty seats down there.''

He had no sooner spoken than the man onstage completed his act. There was a round of thunderous applause during which the comedian departed and a slight, balding man with a curly fringe of black hair stepped up to the microphone.

''Oh, balls,'' Remo griped when he saw who it was.

Bobby Stone was a film actor, occasional Oscar host and one of the three regular emcees of Buffoon Aid. He had been in one hit film about a group of middle-aged men who signed aboard a ship as merchant mariners for a two-week adventure vacation. Aside from *Land Lubbers,* Stone's movies were generally bombs so large the studio should have fired their PR team and replaced it with a demolition squad.

As Stone lapsed into a painfully unfunny improvisational routine, Remo spun to the Master of Sinanju.

''Let's get out of here,'' he griped.

Chiun remained motionless. ''Smith would want us to see why those Russians are here,'' he said.

''Since when do you give a turd in a tailpipe what Smith wants?'' Remo said. ''And besides, they're coming up to nab that other Russian who's stinking up the fourth row.'' He shot a thumb over his shoulder, roughly to where Yuri Koskolov sat. ''You coming with me or what?''

The old man shook his head. "You cannot leave."

"Course I can," Remo disagreed. "I can ignore whatever they're going to do and go outside and sit in the grass in the shadow of that chunka-chunka scary rock. Bye."

He hadn't taken a single step for the exit when he heard the first shout in Russian behind him. It was quickly followed by a single gunshot. After that, pandemonium.

"Well, crap," Remo observed, slamming on the brakes. Placing firm hands to his hips, he spun.

The seated Russian was now trying to claw his way across the panicking row toward the center aisle. In his wake came the gaggle of men who had raced up the aisle. A hulking member of the hit squad carried a smoking gun in his paw.

The single, ill-advised warning shot had sent a flood of concertgoers to the exits. The first wave was racing toward Remo and Chiun. The crowd broke around the unmoving men, crashing through the gleaming exit doors behind them.

Remo shook his head in disbelief. "They don't leave for Bobby Stone's Ricardo Montalban impersonation, but they stampede over one single gunshot?" he complained.

"Quickly," the Master of Sinanju pressed.

The center seats were empty by now. Chiun bounded from the floor. Toes barely brushing the top of one of the back seats, the old man launched himself forward.

With a resigned sigh, Remo followed, toe to chair

to air. The two men propelled themselves to the fourth row down, spinning in midair. In a heartbeat they landed on either side of the pack of armed Russians.

The huge Russian with the gun was running along in front of the other five. Lumbering toward his fleeing countryman, he was startled to suddenly find himself staring down into a pair of hard, deep-set eyes. Halting, the SVR agent quickly twisted his gun, aiming it into Remo's face.

"Here's where I've got a problem," Remo said. "My country's falling apart, sure. No argument there."

As a pudgy finger squeezed the trigger, something went wrong. Instead of aiming toward the little American's face, the gun was now pointed in the opposite direction. The hulking SVR agent didn't have time to ponder the significance of this strange turn of events before the bullet fired by his own hand blew off the top of his Soviet-era head.

"But *your* country," Remo continued as he bounded over the falling mountain of flesh and into the next man in line.

The next Russian came up short, stunned by both his collapsing comrade and the stranger leaping over him.

"Now if we want to talk a *real* mess, *that's* the shithole to end all shitholes," Remo said as he planted a finger deep into the second man's occipital lobe. "I mean, rather than pester me, why don't you use this energy where it might do some good? Take a mop and a pail to the Urals and don't stop until you reach Iran.''

When he crushed the third man's chest to jelly and found a fourth one beyond the toppling agent, Remo frowned. There were only six in all, and he was up to four.

"What, you sitting this one out, Little Father?" he complained loudly as he planted a gun deep into the next man's pumping heart.

Chiun didn't respond. The row was too narrow. Remo couldn't see the Master of Sinanju beyond the next two men.

With a punishing overhand blow, Remo sent the penultimate agent's head down deep into his thoracic cavity. Collapsing vertebrae clicked together like fastening Legos. His chin now nestled onto his sternum, the suddenly short SVR agent tipped forward onto the floor.

All that was left behind the man was one very shocked Vadim Zhdanov.

The Master of Sinanju was nowhere to be seen.

When he realized he alone was left standing among his SVR agents and that a man who fit the description given by the director of the Institute was wading through the bodies of his team toward him, Vadim Zhdanov did the only thing he could do under the circumstances.

Gulping audibly, the Russian agent placed his own gun to his own temple and pulled the trigger.

As the last body fell, Remo scowled. "Typical," he said to the man with the smoking hole in his head.

"He gets me all rah-rah worked up and then takes a powder."

Still frowning, he turned.

The crowd had all but dispersed. A few stragglers were pushing through the doors near the stage. Remo was grateful that there weren't any cameras aimed his way. Most were directed at the stage, but some were positioned to get audience-reaction shots. But the crew from the cable network airing the Buffoon Aid special had fled, as well.

At the end of Remo's row, beyond the line of fallen SVR agents, a man was sprawled across two seats.

Hopping from head to chest to head, Remo skipped across the bodies and approached Yuri Koskolov.

The single shot intended to warn had accidentally found a target. Lying back uncomfortably across the seats, the Russian was clasping a hand to his heart. His fingers were stained bright red. His skin was already growing waxy.

"What's your story?" Remo asked.

Yuri Koskolov shook his head in weak incomprehension. "I just vanted to see funnyman Jackoff Smirniv," he gasped.

Then he died.

Remo straightened. His brow had only sunk lower over his eyes.

"Russia," he mumbled in disgust. "What a country."

Expression still dark, he went off in search of the missing Master of Sinanju.

13

The clandestine rendezvous was held in the broad daylight of San Francisco's Golden Gate Park. Boris Feyodov leaned back on a bench, his heels digging comfortably into the pebbled path. Hands folded and resting on his paunch, he watched the joggers as they ran by.

The retired general was glad he had worn a jacket. Though the sun was warm, the occasional gusts of cool, salty wind from off the Pacific chilled the air.

His tired eyes watched a young jogger approach. The girl was all of twenty-five, with a bobbing knot of natural blond hair, red shorts and a scandalously revealing tank top.

The sweating girl smiled at him as she ran past. Feyodov returned the smile, tracking her with his eyes.

Her smile was one of politeness. She wasn't interested in him. Couldn't possibly be. She had seen him looking at her and decided to give a dirty old man a cheap thrill.

As he thought of his age, his physical condition, his current career and the life that had somehow claimed all he had once been, the remnants of the smile he had offered the pretty young American girl slowly faded into the broad lines of Boris Feyodov's sad, sagging face.

A sudden stiff breeze made him shiver.

Feyodov was scowling at the cold when a dark shadow fell across him, blotting the sun. Eyes hooded, he looked up.

He saw little more than a bushy black mustache surrounded by a nimbus of brilliant sunlight.

"This is the last of it," the man grunted by way of greeting. He pulled a thick manila envelope from under his black raincoat, handing it over to the seated general.

Feyodov silently accepted the envelope. As the man took a seat beside him on the bench, Feyodov opened the envelope, thumbing through the thick stacks of hundred-dollar bills.

He didn't count the money. He just wanted to make sure there weren't any old *Pravda* clippings padding out the payment. This customer had tried that once early on.

With a satisfied nod, the general turned his full attention to his seatmate.

Without the blinding sun as a backdrop, he was now able to make out the features of the man.

He had brown hair that was streaked with gray and a matching mustache that drooped over his thick lips. Bushy black eyebrows hung heavily over eyes that burned with the passion of an unapologetic Communist.

In his day several years before, Vladimir Zhirinsky had been nearly a legendary figure in Russia. At that time the ultranationalist was feared by the West. As time wore on, Zhirinsky's star had faded. Now— like the Soviet Union he loved—he was relegated to the back pages of history books. But thanks to his dealings with Boris Feyodov and others in Russia's black market, he was poised to rewrite both his personal history and that of his nation.

"Everything has nearly been delivered," Feyodov said as he tucked the envelope in his breast pocket. "This will cover the rest. The most—" he paused "—*exotic* item is already on the ground in Alaska."

Zhirinsky nodded. His gray eyes seemed to be transfixed by Feyodov's nose. Often in meetings, Feyodov found that the nationalist looked people in the nose rather than the eyes.

"You will have to contact my office in Russia with the details," Zhirinsky said, getting quickly back to his feet. "You have the number. I have already told my spineless assistant, Ivan Kerbabaev, to await your call."

Feyodov seemed puzzled. "Why can I not just tell you?"

"No time. I must return to Moscow," Zhirinsky said mysteriously. "I learned only this morning that an opportunity that I have awaited for months has finally presented itself."

The nationalist whirled. He took two steps across the grass before spinning back to Feyodov. A sudden impulse grabbed the wild-eyed man.

"Join me," Zhirinsky said. "You were a general once, as well as the son of a great hero to the people's cause. Be a hero like your father, the field marshal. For the people, for the *cause*. The tide will turn soon. You have helped lay the groundwork for the new glorious revolution, share in the benefits that history will afford the strong.''

Still sitting on the bench, Feyodov shook his head.

''I was a general,'' he agreed softly. ''Once. But that rank proved to be a hollow mockery.'' Slapping hands to knees, he pushed himself wearily to his feet. His eyes were level as he addressed Zhirinsky. ''Now I am a businessman.''

The look of disgust on the face of Vladimir Zhirinsky was enough to show Boris Feyodov what his fellow countryman thought of businessmen.

Zhirinsky hadn't the time to argue. With the urgency of a man propelled by great events, he strode off across the park. Feyodov watched him go.

''Protect the world from revolutionaries,'' the former general muttered. The soft words were not so much a prayer as a cheerless desire. Thinking dark thoughts, Feyodov wandered across the park.

His car was in the lot where he'd left it.

Had this been a Moscow park, the vehicle would have been stolen two minutes after he'd left it and would be halfway to Sevastopol by now. Not that he would have any right to complain about the criminals. The fact that he was one of the greatest contributors to the current lawlessness that gripped his land was not lost on Boris Feyodov.

Feyodov was climbing in behind the wheel when his cell phone chirped to life.

When he answered, he recognized the worried,

whispered voice of Oleg Shevtrinko, one of the men he had brought with him to California from Russia.

"General, something is happening here," Oleg said.

Feyodov accepted the use of his former military title. While he had lost the title of general years ago, his black market associates were mostly former Red Army subordinates. They were the men from the Sary Shagan Missile Test Center. The men who knew him as nothing less than a god. Out of respect for what he had been, they would not dare call him anything other than general. If they only knew the truth of his career after that time...

The fact that it was Oleg calling sent up a warning flare for Feyodov. Obviously, there was some kind of problem. Yuri Koskolov was the only man authorized to contact Feyodov.

"What is wrong?" Feyodov asked. "Where is Koskolov?"

"Dead," Oleg answered. "At least that's what they are saying. There was nearly a riot at that insane charity event here. In addition to Yuri, several others are dead." His voice dropped lower. "Those we work for are *panicking,* General. They say this is a preemptive attack by their government. They have ordered the scientists to—"

The phone abruptly went dead.

"Oleg?" Feyodov demanded. "Oleg?"

He shook the phone. Nothing.

He tried calling back. Dead air greeted him.

The batteries were new. Feyodov had just changed them the previous morning. This was a very expensive phone. It filtered out background noise, so that there was not even a hiss. According to the carrier service, the phone worked in all but the most remote parts of the country. Golden Gate Park certainly shouldn't qualify as inaccessible.

Not a single sound issued from the lump of plastic in his hand. As far as he knew, the only thing that should have caused such a thing to happen would be—

Feyodov's face blanched. Slapping the phone shut, he stuffed it back in his pocket.

"*Sukin syn,*" he swore.

Throwing the car in gear, he stomped down on the gas.

Joggers jumped out of the way as the big American car steered by the renegade Russian general lurched desperately into the street.

"WHAT'S THAT ONE?" Zen Bower demanded.

On the screen where the ice cream maker was pointing, a computer-generated object whirled through the void of space. It looked like a stick-figure box with a funnel at the top. A glowing blue line extended just below the funnel.

"It's another communications satellite," answered the nervous man at the targeting console. He was an engineering professor from Barkley University.

"Is it on the chart?" Zen asked hotly.

The engineer looked at the reference book on his lap, comparing the numbers from the screen. "No," he said.

"Then blast it," Zen commanded.

The man shook his head. "The weapon's not fully charged," he replied apologetically. He cringed when Zen pounded a fist on the console.

"Dammit!" Zen growled. "Just shoot already!"

Another voice broke in from behind Zen.

"It is not possible yet."

Zen wheeled.

Oleg Shevtrinko had just come up the rock-hewed tunnel. In his hand he still clutched the cell phone he had used to contact Boris Feyodov. It had gone dead the moment Zen—in a wild selection of random targets—had ordered the destruction of the satellite through which the signal was being carried.

"Don't you dare tell me anything's not possible," Zen snapped. "It's your boss who told us we couldn't hit anything without some three-million-dollar gewgaw. We've taken out three more satellites with no problem at all."

"It is *possible* to target and hit an object in space, but it is not foolproof," Oleg lied. "The device that General Feyodov is getting will make luck unnecessary."

"Yeah, well, *maybe*," Zen said. "And he's not *General* Feyodov—he's being paid to be Barkley's supreme military commander. Although we're gonna pull back on the SMC title until we know what happened. After this I might bust him down to private and give you a battlefield promotion."

Oleg Shevtrinko's back stiffened. He had known General Feyodov for seventeen years. Back when the general was in charge of Sary Shagan, Oleg had participated in the murder of Viktor Churlinski and the other scientists that fateful January day. With ties forged in blood, Oleg's loyalty was to his general and his general alone.

"I would not accept," Oleg said coldly.

Zen's eyes widened. "You'll do what I say," he ordered. "Feyodov abandoned his post just when the U.S. government decided to attack. If that coward doesn't hurry up an—"

"We do not yet know who attacked," Oleg interrupted icily. "And were I you, I would refrain from using the word *coward* in the presence of the general."

To Zen, it was as if the air in the underground chamber had suddenly gotten ten degrees colder. He wasn't sure what unwritten line he'd just crossed, but it was obvious he had trodden on something he should stay away from.

Oleg's eyes were flinty and unblinking. "As for the incident at your silly concert that has gotten you so panicked, it is probably nothing more than random violence."

Some of the anger drained from Zen. "Violence doesn't happen in Barkley," he said dismissively, his voice growing subdued. "We've registered every man in town as a potential sex offender and forced every adult white hetero male to undergo mandatory sensitivity training. For God's sake, if the men here were any more whipped they'd all be lesbians. Which," he added quickly, lest Oleg get the wrong impression, "as a lifestyle choice is perfectly natural and beautiful and should actually be encouraged

since men are such horrible, sexist-pig rapists anyway. So if there *is* violence in town, it *has* to be
imported. America *must* be on to us.''

Conclusion made, he gave quick orders to the
seated engineer to continue firing at targets on the
approved list. Turning from the frowning Oleg Shevtrinko, Zen hurried up the tunnel. He paused to kick
a chair at an empty console.

''Get out of there,'' Zen snapped.

With a timid squeak, Gary Jenfeld came crawling
out from under the table. He clutched a cardboard
container of Zen and Gary's Chewy Newton Crunch
in his shaking hand. Runny ice cream streaked his
thick beard.

''Is it safe?'' Gary asked worriedly.

''The plan's been bumped up,'' Zen said. ''Since
they're obviously on to us, it's time we told the oppressive regime in Washington what's expected of
it.''

''Um...Zen,'' Gary said hesitantly. ''Isn't that
jumping the gun? Shouldn't you tell *him* about the
dead people at Buffoon Aid? I mean, this is all his
idea. Not to mention his money. Maybe he'd think
different about this than you.''

Zen dropped his voice low. ''He *knows,* you idiot,'' he hissed. ''HTB was airing Buffoon Aid, remember? Besides, this is going exactly according to
plan.''

With that, Zen spun away from his former partner.
Without another word, he marched up the tunnel
with the brisk stride of a revolutionary.

"His plan or yours?" Gary Jenfeld wondered softly.

Melting container of ice cream in hand, Gary huffed nervously up the dark tunnel after Zen.

14

The frightened crowd from the civic center had fled
screaming into the streets, only to stop at the town
square. They stood in the shadow of Huitzilopochtli.
Faces fearful, they clogged roads and sidewalks.

The Master of Sinanju had encouraged Remo to
engage the Russians in the hall merely as a distraction. Blocked by their bodies, the old man had
slipped out a side door. He emerged into the tightly
packed crowd.

His hazel eyes scanned hundreds of faces for one
in particular. He had nearly given up, thinking that
his advanced years had somehow given way to hal-
lucinations, when he caught a glimmer of movement
across the square.

While most everyone's interest was focused on
the hall, one figure skulked off in the opposite direction. The peaked black hood of an obscuring cape
could be seen bobbing across the distant road that
bordered the grassy square.

The hood slipped beyond the gleaming window of
an apothecary shop. It turned up an alley and was
gone.

Before the figure had disappeared, Chiun was off.

Pipe-stem legs pumped furiously as he bounded across the road in front of the hall.

The crowd seemed possessed by some reflexive instinct of preservation, for it parted as if connected to a single mind. The split formed across the park, beneath the giant statue's shadow and over to the distant street. And through the new-formed passage—a wall of human flesh on either side—flew the Master of Sinanju.

Sandals barely brushed sidewalk as he raced past the apothecary shop with its hanging crystals and jars of herbs. His path free of people and now at a full sprint, Chiun raced up the alley.

Hazel eyes searched for a face that mocked the grave.

The long alley was deserted.

Chiun was a blur.

Past bundled trash bags and broken asphalt he ran.

The Main Street alley fed into a narrower gap between a pair of two-story buildings. And on the street beyond, Chiun caught up with the fleeing figure.

The black hood was racing to a parked car.

Upon exiting the alley, the Master of Sinanju stopped dead. The hems of his red silk kimono fluttered to angry stillness. Like a peal of furious thunder, his booming voice rang out across the empty street.

"Hold, deceiver of the Void!" Chiun commanded.

Chiun's tone was enough to freeze the black-clad

figure in its tracks. Slender fingers clutched the handle of the driver's door.

With a few quick strides Chiun shed the shadowed mouth of the dark alley. He stopped behind the immobile figure.

"Why have you returned from the dead?" he demanded.

The hand finally slipped from the door handle.

"I was never dead." Though the voice was soft, it was not apologetic. The shoulders remained proudly erect.

"My son thought you so, and so you were," Chiun said.

The figure turned slowly to him. The black hood hung low over eyes as cold as steel.

"Did you not think I was dead, as well?"

Chiun stomped his foot. "That does not matter," he insisted. "You were dishonest to make him believe you no longer lived. And now—at the most precarious time of his Masterhood—you return. Remo cannot afford you as a distraction. You will go. Now and forever. Leave this land and never return."

"You stop me only to order me to go?"

"Pah!" Chiun waved. "You were not going anywhere. You are on some fool errand for your Kremlin lords. Now that Remo has dispatched your men, you would be forced to lurch and blunder around yourself. I will not allow your path to cross my son's. I tell you now, leave not only this province, but this nation, lest you bear the wrath of the Master of Sinanju."

Two small hands reached up and the hood finally came down, revealing a short crop of honey-blond hair and a familiar high-cheekboned face.

"I *cannot* go. Not yet."

Chiun's expression began to harden when his sensitive ears suddenly detected swift footfalls behind him. With flashing hands, he grabbed for the door.

One bony hand clutched the handle, the other held firm to the cloaked figure's bicep when Remo came exploding from the alley mouth an instant later. The younger Master of Sinanju's eyes darkened when he spied his teacher.

"I've been looking all over for you," Remo groused. "Next time you badger me into snuffing out a Russian hit squad, I'd appreciate it if you did at least two seconds of actual work before punching off the clock for your afternoon rice break." Face still a scowl, he glanced at the figure Chiun was manhandling into the car. "Hiya," he added.

He looked momentarily back to Chiun. Then his face fell.

For an instant the world stood still.

Remo's head snapped back around.

When his eyes alighted once more on the stranger's face, anything Remo might have wanted to say froze in his throat.

Eyes growing wide in shock, his jaw dropped open. He seemed desperate to speak, but could not. He looked the figure up, then down.

Remo wheeled on Chiun. The Master of Sinanju's wrinkled countenance was pinched into an unhappy knot.

"Chiun?" Remo asked, bewildered.

"Go back to the center of town and wait for me," the old man advised darkly. "No good can come of this, my son."

Remo spun back to the Institute director.

"This *can't* be," he insisted.

With a frustrated hiss, the old Korean released his grip on the head of Russia's secret Institute. "Your eyes do not deceive," the Master of Sinanju insisted angrily.

The Russian agent nodded gentle agreement. There seemed a hint of shame in the movement.

It was almost too much for Remo to take. A swirl of emotion, confusion, amazement, spiraled around him in a crazed, impossible kaleidoscope. For what seemed an infinite moment, he lost all voice, all reason. When he finally caught up with his swirling thoughts, it was as if the one word he spoke echoed up a ten-year-old tunnel that led to the depths of his very soul.

"Anna?" Remo Williams asked. His voice was small and faraway.

And with equal emotion, buried under a practiced veneer of cold rationality, Anna Chutesov nodded sharply.

15

They stared at each other for what seemed like an eternity. It was Remo who finally broke the silence.

"You're dead," he insisted.

"Obviously not," Anna replied. She shot an uncomfortable glance at the Master of Sinanju.

"Oh, no," Remo snapped. *"No.* You're not gonna worm out of this one. I *saw* you dead."

"Impossible," Anna said. "What you should ask yourself is, did you see me die?"

Remo opened his mouth to speak, his finger raised authoritatively. Sudden memory made him hesitate.

"You see?" Anna said, nodding. "You remember. You did not see me die, nor could you have, because it is apparent that I did not."

"A situation easily remedied," offered the Master of Sinanju thinly.

"Back off, Chiun," Remo snapped. He was regaining his senses. The shock of seeing Anna Chutesov after so many years was worse than any physical blow. "But Mr. Gordons killed you," he said to Anna, some of the fight draining from him. "He was wearing your face when I kicked his mechanical ass years ago."

"Gordons," Anna nodded. "The android that was programmed by your space agency to take any form that would aid in its survival. He looked like me, you say?"

"He was you by way of Xerox and Lockheed-Martin," Remo said. "But, yeah, he looked like you when we zapped him."

"I suspected as much," Anna said, pleased with her deduction. "It determined that mine was a form that would aid its survival. It hoped to confuse you, a plan that I gather failed, given the fact that you both still live."

"Maybe it didn't fail," Remo said, suddenly cautious. "I took out its central processor." He took a step back.

"You did not," Chiun sniffed. "It was I who slew the mandroid that time."

"No, it was the amusement park that time, Little Father," Remo said. With narrowed eyes he studied Anna.

"I know where it was," Chiun said haughtily. "And we were not amused."

"No matter which one of us whacked the robot that time, we still met up with him twice since then," Remo pointed out. "He's like the wind-up version of Freddy Krueger. He keeps coming back with a new Roman numeral tacked to his caboose. Who's to say this isn't him again?"

Chiun shook his head. "The machine man is dead," he said firmly.

"Yes, Remo," Anna begged. "Do not complicate this any further. I *tried* to shoot Gordons. When that had no effect, I determined that there was only one prudent course of action available to me.''

''Which was?''

Anna shrugged. ''I ran.''

''And Gordons didn't follow?'' Remo said skeptically.

''You were its enemy, not me,'' Anna said logically. ''After I fled, it must have decided that since we were allies, it would muddy the waters by transforming itself into my likeness.'' She nodded appreciatively. ''A strategy that I would probably take under the same circumstances.''

''My point exactly,'' Remo said. ''How do I know you're not wearing a set of tin-plated long johns under that Captain Marvel cape?''

Anna considered but a moment. When she lunged at Remo an instant later, he braced for an attack. He arrested the forward lethal movement of his own hand when—instead of striking him—Anna grabbed him by the shoulders and planted her lips firmly on his.

Remo tensed. After a few seconds he relaxed. A moment later his arms fell limp at his sides.

Beside them the Master of Sinanju's wrinkled face tightened into a tangle of disgust.

''Stop that this instant,'' he snapped. ''I endured my fill of this vulgar exhibitionism back when I did not have a heart condition.'' Though they were harsh, there was a worried undertone to his words.

Anna and Remo unlocked lips. Despite her best efforts, the Russian agent's pale cheeks were flushed.

"Okay, no android busses like that," Remo admitted.

Embarrassed by her lack of physical control, Anna looked down, brushing wrinkles from her long, dark cloak.

"I am sorry to hear about your heart problem," she muttered to Chiun.

"He doesn't have anything wrong with his heart," Remo said. He was still staring at Anna in disbelief.

"Yes, I do, O heartless one," Chiun disagreed. "And it is aggravated by proximity to aging Russian harlots. Go this instant," he instructed Anna, "lest your presence alone causes me to drop dead on this very street corner."

He pulled open Anna's car door. Remo slapped it shut.

"A clone," Remo announced. "Maybe the Russians grew another you in a test tube."

"Now you are being ridiculous." Anna scowled.

"Yes," Chiun agreed. "Russia has always produced more than sufficient numbers of prostitutes without having to resort to unholy means."

Anna pointedly ignored the old man.

"If I tell you something only I would know, would that satisfy you?" she asked Remo.

"I guess," he replied reluctantly.

Anna leaned in close to him. Her breath was warm on his ear as she spoke in a barely audible whisper.

"Stop shouting," Chiun groused.

When Anna finished, this time it was Remo's face that was flushed. His ears burned red.

"Anna," he said, his voice soft with incredulity. Until that moment he hadn't permitted himself to fully believe. He looked at her now with new eyes.

The Russian nodded sharply. She tugged off the big black poncho she'd been wearing since arriving in Barkley that morning, tossing it through the open window of her car.

"It is a wonder the two of you got any work done at all, with all of your groping and grunting," Chiun huffed. He turned a stern eye on his pupil. "Remo, I have always kept to myself my opinions about the way you fritter your life away. Though presented with opportunities to criticize that were more numerous than the stars in the sky, always have I held my tongue. I have allowed you to stumble and bumble and rut like a mad donkey with every debauched hussy who invited you to share her bed. Never did I scold or complain or offer even a single sharp opinion."

Remo gave the old man a heavy-lidded stare. "Don't make me start doubting you're you," he said flatly.

Chiun pointed a long-nailed finger at Anna Chutesov.

"I never liked this woman," the old man insisted. He folded his arms angrily. "There. I have said it. And to speak this truth, I have been forced to break my steadfast and ironclad rule against meddling. *Her* fault, *again.*"

The Master of Sinanju's words were like white noise. Numbly, Remo turned back to Anna.

"It's really you," he said. "I don't get it. Why didn't you tell me?"

His voice was small. In his eyes was the lost-little-boy gleam that had always stirred some long-repressed maternal instinct deep within Anna Chutesov's ice-princess heart. But she well knew her feelings for Remo had never been truly maternal.

"You know the answer," Anna said. "It was too dangerous for me. I was an outsider who knew of your organization. Dr. Smith had already expressed his desire to see me terminated. That loomed over my head for the year we worked together. Long before our encounter with Gordons, I had been working on a way to get away alive. Our last meeting presented an opportunity I could not resist."

"Never would have happened," Remo insisted, shaking his head firmly. "You were never in danger."

"Yes, Remo, I was. And if you already thought me dead, you would not have come to kill me. With so many deaths, I assumed I would be counted among the missing at the amusement park. When it was demolished afterward, so, too, was my existence as far as you and Dr. Smith were concerned. Because of my deception, I have lived the last thirteen years of my life in peace."

"Anna," Remo said. It still seemed so strange to speak her name. "I *never* would have killed you. Ever."

Her expression remained unchanged. "If not you, him," she said, nodding to Chiun.

"The day is young," the old man offered thinly.

"I wouldn't have let him," Remo said.

"You could not have stopped me," Chiun volunteered.

"Stay out of this, Chiun," Remo snapped. His flashing fury melted instantly. "Don't," he begged. "Okay? Just don't."

He turned back to Anna. "I loved you," he said softly.

Her expression hardened.

"That is not what you told me in Smith's office thirteen years ago," she said. "Or do you not remember?"

Remo thought back to the last time he'd seen Anna Chutesov. There had been a long gap between encounters. So long that in the intervening months Remo had gotten engaged to someone else.

At the time Remo—the perpetual outsider, the orphan with no real roots—had been determined to get married. He wanted to force happiness on his life if it killed him. In the end it was not Remo who was the victim. His single-minded quest for the elusive normal existence enjoyed by the rest of the world had claimed but one life. Mah-Li, Remo's Korean bride-to-be, had paid the ultimate price for the life he led. Killed by the Dutchman, Jeremiah Purcell.

Before Mah-Li died, Remo had met Anna for one last joint mission. It was then that he had told her of his intention to marry someone else. Always cool, always in control, Anna believed that it was she who had the upper hand in their relationship. But the news of Remo's plans to wed another had been worse than any physical blow.

At the time she pretended it didn't matter. But it was a lie. The truth was, in the end, she had been shocked to learn that she loved Remo more than he loved her.

Anna had used the first opportunity that presented itself to flee. Her claim that her disappearance was motivated by concern for her personal safety was only partly true. Yes, she wanted to live. But the act had as much to do with emotional self-interest as physical. Given all that had happened between them, she needed to stay away from Remo.

Remo had accepted the lie, assuming Anna dead. Not long after, Mah-Li had died, as well. After that loss, Remo had thrown himself into his work, allowing little room for emotional contact. In the past decade he had come to realize that his marriage to Mah-Li had been more for his sake than for hers. A selfish desire for a life that could not be. But Anna...

Anna had always been another story. Remo wasn't really sure what it was he felt for her. Was it emotional? He didn't know. It was certainly physical. He didn't know if he could possibly still love her. At the moment all else had been short-circuited by the shock of discovery and his anger at her deception.

"Remo?"

The voice sounded far away. Remo was numbly aware of a pair of slender fingers snapping in front of his face, like a hypnotist trying to bring a subject out of a deep trance.

He blinked hard once, looking down into the beautiful upturned face of Anna Chutesov.

"As much as I would like to stand out on this

sidewalk for the rest of the day, we should go,'' Anna said.

The Master of Sinanju was already scurrying into the back of Anna's car. Sitting in the center of the seat, he folded his billowing kimono neatly around his bony knees.

''Why can't anything ever be easy?'' Remo exhaled quietly.

''There is a saying in my country,'' Anna said as she slid efficiently behind the wheel. ''Simplicity is for children, fools and the dead. Did you kill all my men?''

''An even half dozen,'' Remo confirmed as he got into the passenger's seat.

''What about Koskolov, the man they were after?''

''Dopey-looking guy? Partial to Russian stand-up comics?'' Remo said. ''The big guy who looked like one of the dancing bears from the Moscow circus shot him.''

''Idiots,'' she muttered, jamming the key angrily into the ignition. ''They killed our only lead to the lunacy that is going on here.''

Yet another surprise for Remo. ''So this isn't just Smith getting us out of the house?'' he asked. ''You wanna fill me in on what's really going on here?''

When she looked at him, her blue eyes were charged with sparks of dark concern.

''The end of the world,'' Anna Chutesov replied ominously.

Twisting the wheel of her rental car, she pulled carefully away from the curb and into the potholed street.

16

For Harold W. Smith, the end of the world had begun after midnight the previous evening. His impending personal Apocalypse loomed large and full in the gloomy gray hours before dawn. With the rising of the cold winter sun, the threat did not fade, but grew greater still.

As the tired sun swelled from bleary red to bright yellow, the light spilled through the one-way picture window at Smith's back. The shafts of widening sunlight stabbed across the room, illuminating the figure that slept on the sofa of his Folcroft office.

Mark Howard was using his coat as a blanket. It was tucked up under his chin as he slept. Howard was oblivious to the old man who was staring at him from across the room.

Smith had remained awake the entire night. Though exhausted, his eagle's gaze had not once shifted.

Smith's lower desk drawer was ajar. The lid of the cigar box that was ordinarily tucked far in the back was open. Inside the box Smith's old service automatic sat atop his cracked leather shoulder holster.

His first concern after his shocking encounter in the parking lot was that this was some sort of trap. Some individual, agency or government had learned of CURE.

But upon rapid consideration he realized that the means by which such an enemy would announce himself would almost certainly have been different.

To send no one but a shivering young man to stand alone in the nearly empty Folcroft parking lot didn't make sense.

After frisking Howard for weapons and recording devices and finding neither, Smith had reluctantly brought his guest back up to his office.

By then it was one o'clock in the morning and far too late to call the President.

At other times Smith would not have hesitated to call the White House, even at so ungodly an hour. But it was barely two weeks into the new President's first term, and the chief executive had yet to contact the head of CURE.

At first, most presidents were reluctant to communicate with the agency. When they did finally call, some merely did so just to see if there would be an answer on the other end of the line. Others waited until there was a crisis. In either case, the introduction was always an awkward moment, and so Smith made a habit out of not being the first to make contact.

This was the worst scenario he could think of to break that custom. If the new President had not sent Howard here, then the young man had found out about CURE by other means. Were this the case, then security had been compromised.

Smith's relationship with the last President had been strained. After the past eight years, this was not the kind of introduction he wanted to make to a new chief executive. It could only be worse to call in the middle of the night. And so, to dull the edge of what might be a disaster for CURE, Smith waited for a more respectable hour to call.

Through the night, he had not even been able to use work as a distraction. He dared not turn on his computer. Dared not expose any more of what was going on here to the snoring stranger across the room.

And so he sat. Staring.

Smith was still watching the man on his couch when he was startled by the abrupt opening of his office door.

Smith instinctively darted for his gun. When he saw who it was entering his inner sanctum, he quickly slid his desk drawer shut, concealing the automatic.

"Good morning, Dr. Smith," Eileen Mikulka said pleasantly as she walked into the room. She balanced a small serving tray on her forearm. On the tray was a steaming cup of coffee and two slices of dry toast.

This was one of Mrs. Mikulka's daily duties, and one that she made it a point not to miss.

In days long gone, Dr. Smith had sometimes found time to golf in the mornings. Once in a while when he was gone there were important sanitarium documents that needed his attention. The papers were couriered to his home. On these occasions, according to sanitarium lore, Mrs. Smith had always been delighted to greet company and insisted that they have something to eat. Afterward, when next there came a time that something needed to be delivered to the Folcroft director's home, whoever went last invariably refused to go.

Everyone around Folcroft knew that Mrs. Smith was a very nice, very lonely woman, as well as a notoriously bad cook.

And so Mrs. Mikulka had taken it upon herself to see to it that her employer at least ate something decent during the day. At 7:00 a.m. every morning, come rain or shine, she delivered a plate of toast and a cup of coffee to the Folcroft director's office.

Mrs. Mikulka was stepping across the threadbare carpet when a noise behind her nearly caused her to drop her tray. Startled, she looked over her shoulder.

Someone on the couch was just stirring awake.

"Oh," she said, surprised that her employer was not alone. She grew even more surprised when she saw who it was pushing himself to a sitting position on Smith's sofa.

When she glanced at her employer, she saw that his tired gray eyes were rimmed with dark bags.

"Is everything all right, Dr. Smith?" Mrs. Mikulka asked. When she looked back, the patient young medical-supplies salesman from the previous day was rubbing sleep from his eyes. Standing in front of Smith's desk, she seemed unsure whether she should say hello or call security.

"It's quite all right, Mrs. Mikulka," Smith said.

"Oh. Very well." Hesitantly, she set plate and mug to Smith's desk. She still was not sure what to make of this. "Would you like something, sir?" she asked Howard.

"No, thanks," Mark said, stretching. "How late's the cafeteria serve breakfast?"

"Oh, um, eleven o'clock."

"I'll grab something later," he said, smiling.

Mrs. Mikulka nodded. Clutching the plastic tray like a shield to her ample bosom, she left the room.

As she was closing the door, Mark climbed to his feet. Stifling a yawn, he checked his watch. Because of the cast on his wrist, he wore it on his left arm.

"It's probably okay to call now," he ventured.

Smith nodded crisply. Before opening the right-hand drawer where the special White House line was secreted, he pulled open the lower left drawer, once more exposing his automatic pistol. Smith took out an old-fashioned cherry-red phone, placing it on the desk next to his toast and coffee.

As Howard stood patiently before him, tie loosened and suit rumpled, the CURE director lifted the receiver.

THE PRESIDENT of the United States was getting dressed when the pager on his belt buzzed.

His wife was sound asleep beneath a mound of blankets. Although she had been a political wife for some time, she had not been prepared for the attention she was getting as First Lady. The past few weeks had worn her out.

Leaving his jacket at the foot of the bed, the President tiptoed from the room. Walking briskly, he headed down the main hallway of the family quarters, past the private elevator. He ducked into the Lincoln Bedroom.

Like many other rooms in the White House, the Lincoln Bedroom had recently been hastily refurnished with antiques from the Smithsonian Institution. The remodeling became necessary after it was discovered that the previous occupants of the White House had left under cover of darkness with a wagonload of priceless antiques. Over the past week some of the missing national treasures had begun quietly showing up at an online auction house. The highest bid for the framed original copy of the Emancipation Proclamation was currently $2,350.50, not including shipping.

Sitting on the edge of the bed, the new President opened the bottom drawer of the nightstand and removed the dial-less red phone that sat alone inside.

Hand on the receiver, he steeled himself for a moment before lifting it to his ear.

"Yes?" he said. His faint Southern twang was noticeable even on the single syllable.

"Good morning, Mr. President," a sharp voice replied.

The President was surprised at how tart it sounded. His predecessor had been right about the voice. It was like lemons mixed with grapefruit.

"This is Smith, I presume?" the President said.

"Yes, sir," Smith answered crisply. "Mr. President, do you know a man by the name of Mark Howard? He claims to have been sent here by you."

That was it. Straight on to business. No apologies for the early hour, no further pleasantries, no nothing. After the endless parade of smoke blowers he had dealt with over the past year, this Smith was like a breath of fresh air.

"Yes, I sent Mark there," the President replied.

"May I ask why?" Smith said.

Phone pressed tight to his ear, the President sat forward on the bed, resting his elbow on the opposite wrist.

"I know what goes on there, Smith," the President said. "What's more, I understand that it's necessary. I mean, I've gotta assume that four decades' worth of presidents from *both* parties wouldn't have left you in business if you weren't important to the nation. But the guy who held this office before me said there were only three of you there who know what's really going on. Is that true?"

Up the East Coast, in the privacy of his Folcroft office, Harold Smith's gray face clouded.

"Yes, Mr. President," Smith admitted. With Howard still in the room, he was careful to keep his answers short.

The young man stood before Smith's desk. He seemed determined to mask any nervousness he was feeling.

"Has anyone else ever learned of your group?" the President asked.

Smith already knew where this was heading. With an eye trained on the man before him, he nodded. "From time to time that has happened," he admitted.

"I figured. So what happened to them?"

The CURE director pursed his lips. "I believe you have already deduced the answer to that question, sir," he said.

"Yes, Smith, I have. When I assumed this office two weeks ago, I was briefed by the outgoing President about you. He's the one who chose Mark, not me. The screening process was done months before I even won the election. So in the middle of my inauguration and hundred-day honeymoon period, I had this mess dropped into my lap. I had only two options, since Mark already knew about you by this time. I could either send him to you and have you take care of him like you have the others who've found out about you over the years, or I could send him there as your assistant. I was understandably reluctant to spill an innocent man's blood—as I imagine you would be—and so I went with the second option."

Smith did not deem it the proper time to inform the president that some of those who had learned of CURE and subsequently died at his order had been innocents, as well.

The CURE director pushed up his glasses, pinching the bridge of his nose.

"And in so doing you have installed him here as my assistant," Smith said.

"That's right," the president said. "And let's be reasonable here. I don't want to be insulting, but the last President said you weren't a young man."

"That is true, sir," Smith sighed. He refrained

from mentioning that this call was making him feel older by the minute.

"And it's true, as well, that there are no contingency plans in case you, um..." His voice trailed off.

"Yes, sir, that is true," Smith offered.

"Well, there you go," the President said. "Problem solved. You teach Mark the ropes there, and so if there ever comes a day we need someone else to take over your group, we don't have to send someone in blind. It's a necessary thing, Smith. In spite of what the last President thought of you, I have to assume that you perform a vital national function. This measure will keep CURE going for years to come."

Smith stopped massaging his nose. When he pulled his hand away, his glasses dropped back into place.

This was new territory for CURE. From the outset there had been only a few rules governing the agency. Though under the auspices of the executive branch, Smith was actually autonomous. He alone decided what crises merited CURE's attention. The President could only suggest assignments. Beyond that, the chief executive had only one other explicit power over the agency. If he so deemed it, the President could order CURE to disband. That was it. And since it was not expressly stated that a given chief executive could not install a second in command at CURE, such an action fell beyond the stated original boundaries of CURE.

Smith looked up at the very young face of the

man hovering before his desk. The CURE director suddenly felt very old, very tired.

"Perhaps you are right," Smith sighed.

"It makes perfect sense," the President reasoned. "You've served your country well. With Mark there, this'll give you a chance to pull back a little. Who knows? Maybe you can even retire someday."

Smith's eyes were dull. There was only one way he would ever retire. A coffin-shaped pill in his vest pocket awaited his last day as director of CURE.

"Is that all?" Smith asked.

"No, there is one more thing," the President said. "This phone of yours. Is there any way to move it into my bedroom? It seems odd that you'd have it here in the Lincoln Bedroom. After all, this is really just a guest room. Anyone could find it here."

"I will see what can be done," Smith promised. Without another word, he broke the connection.

Smith replaced the red phone in his desk drawer, sliding it shut with a click. He closed the cigar box lid on his gun before easing that drawer shut, as well.

Once he was done, he sat up straight, placing hands to his desk, his fingers intertwined.

His eyes were flat as he looked up at Mark Howard.

Given the circumstances, there was only one thing he could say to the eager man with the wide, innocent face.

"Welcome to CURE," Smith said tartly. "I will have Mrs. Mikulka see to finding you an office."

He did not offer Howard his hand.

17

The girl always asked a lot of questions, especially for a Barkley U graduate student.

As was the norm for most colleges, the bulk of the student population enrolled at the famous California university was just there to kill time before heading out into the real world. Parties, protests and pills dominated life on campus. But Brandy Brand had been the inquisitive type ever since she showed up in Professor Melvin Horowitz's office at the end of the previous semester. She had stayed during the break, when life at the school generally quieted down.

The Barkley physics professor had been worried she might take off to become a cog in the capitalist machine when the new semester began. After all, she never seemed to go to any classes. Then again, that was hardly unusual for the lifer students at Barkley U. To the delight of Dr. Horowitz, however, she'd stuck around when the other students returned.

Behind her horn-rimmed glasses her intelligent eyes seemed to absorb everything. That was another odd thing about her. She actually seemed smart. Not just in the bookish sense, which some of the Barkley professors still had, in spite of years of academic dumbing down. She had the kind of vigorous mind that used to inspire educators to teach back when school was all about books and facts and learning.

Melvin himself felt inspired to teach her a thing or two. Most of the time it was when she was standing on a ladder getting a book from his office shelf and he stole a good glimpse of creamy white inner thigh.

He never quite figured out what she was doing there. But that was no big deal. People came and went as they pleased at Barkley University. He was just glad she had picked his office to roost in, settling in beneath the academic radar as a sort of uncredited teaching assistant.

Many days Melvin Horowitz found himself daydreaming about the girl. In class, at lunch, bouncing through the pitted streets of Barkley in his VW van.

She inspired in him the sort of longing he hadn't felt in thirty years. And the way she smiled and seemed to be fascinated by everything he had to say made him actually think he might have a shot with the beautiful young thing. In spite of being fifty-seven, with a substantial potbelly, bad comb-over, perpetual worn brown cardigan sweater and a weary, foot-dragging walk that he called the academic's shuffle, Melvin had started to convince himself that he might not be as pathetic as he'd always thought he was.

When Melvin bustled into his office this busy day, Brandy Brand was wearing her most distracting outfit yet.

Thin white spaghetti strings held her see-through halter top in place. Beneath it, Melvin could clearly make out the shadow of her black bra. Her black skirt was conservative for her, running down to just below her knee. A slit far up the side revealed a slice of heaven that Melvin had spent many a tortured night dreaming about.

Despite the breathtaking view, Melvin Horowitz couldn't enjoy it. As he held the door open for the man who was entering the office with him, the professor's troubled thoughts were elsewhere. He barely offered the girl a nod.

"Oh, hi, Dr. Horowitz," Brandy said, smiling. She was sitting in a chair beneath the high windows.

If Melvin had looked hard enough, he would have seen that the young woman's smile was devoid of any real feeling. She turned her attention to the man who was stepping into the small office behind the lumpy physics professor.

He was tall and pale with black-rimmed eyes and a mouth that looked as if it would shatter his lower face if it attempted anything other than the frown he now wore.

As Melvin's companion turned his suspicious gaze on the young woman, Brandy's flat smile never wavered.

"Who's your friend, Professor?" Brandy asked.

"Him?" Melvin said, distracted. "He's with the, um, city. Where did I leave that notebook?"

Even after years in academia, Dr. Horowitz hadn't succumbed to the slovenly stereotype perpetuated by many of his colleagues. His numerous books and papers were all neatly bound and filed. But for some reason the notebook in question wasn't where he thought he'd left it.

"Notebook?" Brandy asked. Still sitting, she glanced around. She found one sitting on the edge of the photocopier. "Is it a blue one?" she asked, grabbing it.

"Yes," Melvin nodded. "Oh, there it is." He hustled over, taking the book from her outstretched hand. "I could have sworn I left it on my desk."

He waved it to his companion. "This is all I need," he said.

With a passing frown, he hurried back to the door. Melvin was rushing into the hallway when the other man called to him.

"Wait," the stranger ordered.

Professor Horowitz stopped dead in his tracks. When he spun impatiently, his mouth dropped open.

The man in his office now held a gun in his hand. To Melvin's shock the barrel was aimed at the lovely young graduate student. The man's face was dead.

"Your bag," he ordered Brandy. "Kick it over here." His Russian accent was thick.

Brandy's hands were raised. "Professor?" she asked fearfully. There was confused pleading in her eyes.

"What do you think you're doing?" Horowitz demanded, hustling up to the man.

"Quiet!" the Russian barked. With his free hand he shoved the professor back. The cold barrel of the weapon never wavered. "Do it now," he commanded, "or I will fire."

His back pressed against the wall, Melvin Horowitz watched the drama with utter incomprehension.

To make things even more bizarre, Brandy Brand's attitude suddenly seemed to change. It was a strange, subtle metamorphosis. The flirtatious young graduate student seemed to visibly steel. The normal terror and confusion that Brandy had been displaying at the sight of the gun abruptly melted into a look of cold anger.

There was a blue knapsack at her feet. Hands still above her head, she kicked the bag across the floor. It slid to a stop at the man's shoes.

With the gun still trained squarely at her chest, the Russian stooped and unzipped the bag.

Inside, he found exactly what he'd expected. He pulled out a thick sheaf of photocopied papers. Standing, he stuffed the sheets into Melvin's hands.

"Do you recognize these?" he asked.

The physics professor glanced at the papers. When he saw his own handwriting, alarm turned to bafflement.

"Yes, they're—" He looked at a few more.

They were all in his writing. Many had been copied from the notebook he now clutched in his sweating hand. The notebook he *swore* he'd left on his desk and that Brandy Brand had conveniently found on the photocopier.

"Oh, my," Melvin said softly.

His flabby face was bewildered when he looked up at the woman sitting in his office. Melvin couldn't believe it. It was as if he were seeing her for the first time.

His fear returned when the man pulled a nickled revolver from the depths of Brandy's bag. The Russian stuck Brandy's gun into his belt.

"Who are you?" Professor Horowitz asked her, shocked.

The young woman screwed her mouth shut. With angry defiance she stared at the office wall.

"I don't have time for this now," the Russian snapped at Horowitz. "You are wanted at the site immediately. Call your campus police. Have them hold this woman until she can be transferred to local authorities."

He turned back to Brandy. For the first time something resembling a smile cracked his frozen features. "Once I have delivered the professor, I will enjoy questioning you personally."

Melvin Horowitz didn't like the sound of any of this.

With fading hope that he would ever succeed with the only romantic prospect to cross his path since his brief dalliance with a nearsighted Chinese exchange student his junior year at MIT, the physics professor hurried obediently to the office phone.

REMO WILLIAMS HAD SEEN a great many things during his time as America's official assassin. So much so that he had long assumed that he was immune to those things that might shock the faint of heart. But as this depressing day rolled on, he found the walls of casual certainty he had constructed for himself rapidly crumbling.

Remo had barely begun to come to terms with

Anna's amazing return from the dead before having to cope with the reason she had come back into his life after all these years.

"Are you people nuts?" he demanded of Anna as they drove onto the campus of Barkley University.

"Russians have always been insane," Chiun observed from the back seat. "Ivan the Good was the only sane Russian, and look what it got him. Maligned by white historians with half-truths and baseless innuendos."

"Ivan the Terrible was mad," Anna said, peeved. She was trying to talk to Remo and didn't appreciate the old man's distraction.

"He had a right to be angry," Chiun sniffed. "Perhaps he knew what was in store for his nation. Tzar-hating fomenters running hither and thither, sticking their pointy beards into everyone else's bank accounts. Leave it to the Russians to find the only form of government more foolish than representative democracy. And need I remind you, Remo, that every moment we squander here, someone less deserving is acquiring the deed to the next Castle Sinanju? We should be back in the village of idiots, not this training ground."

"The party's over back there, Chiun," Remo said. "No stand-up comic wants to follow seven dead Russians and a riot. No Buffoon Aid benefit means no houses getting passed out. Not that there were any to begin with."

"This is *your* fault, woman," the old man accused Anna Chutesov. "You are not returned five minutes and you have already cost me my second beloved home in less than a month. I say we bind her by hand and foot and throw her on the next freighter bound for Istanbul. During Tzar Ivan's time they paid a high price for blond-haired blue-eyed slaves.''

''No white slavery,'' Remo said firmly. ''At least not until she's finished laying out this mess.''

He turned to Anna, steering her back to the topic at hand. ''What the hell is a particle-beam weapon?''

''It follows the same principle as a laser,'' Anna explained. ''The beam produced is a stream of sub-atomic particles, which, when accelerated, is able to nearly reach the speed of light. It is like an invisible cannon with a destructive force unmatched on Earth.''

''Sounds like science fiction to me,'' Remo grumbled.

''It is science fact,'' Anna said darkly. ''In spite of problems early on in the development. At first the beam was bent and dissipated by Earth's magnetic field or disrupted by air molecules. But this was all eventually overcome. For our current dilemma, the worst breakthrough was miniaturization. The original design had a device two miles long, four miles wide and weighing more than five hundred tons. Thanks to the diligence of the scientific team that developed it, it was shrunk considerably. It could now be hidden in any building, wooded area or even on this campus.''

''That's just swell,'' Remo said sourly. ''Just because you people lose one dinky little cold war is no reason to let your whole country go to hell.

How'd you let something like that fall into the hands of some whacked-out general?''

The corners of her mouth twisted, as if Feyodov's corruption were somehow a personal affront.

"Boris Feyodov is no longer a general," Anna said thinly. "He was disgraced more than a year ago. It was after his dishonorable discharge that he further sullied his uniform by joining the black market."

"Big whoop there," Remo said. "Isn't a Russian in the black market like a Kennedy in a cocktail lounge? The world's in shock when they're *not* shaking down Shoeshine Boy for booze and quarters."

Anna's tone grew frosty. "I am not in the black market," she said, insulted.

"No, but you *are* hiding something," Remo replied absently. He drummed his fingers on the door handle.

As she drove, Anna shot him a glance. "What do you mean?" she asked innocently.

Anna did her best to conceal it. In fact, she did a lot better than most. But as Remo had suspected, when she spoke her body stiffened slightly and her voice rose just a hair.

"Definitely hiding something," Remo nodded. "Wouldn't you say so, Little Father?"

"She is a Russian, she is a female and she lied to us for the last ten years by pretending to be dead," Chiun said, his tone flat. "Forgive me, Remo, if I do not express grave disappointment that she would continue to deceive."

Anna's fingers had tensed on the wheel.

"Relax," Remo said. "You're a good liar, Anna, but we're better—" He paused, tipping his head to consider. "We're just better, and let's leave it at that."

In the back Chiun harrumphed quiet approval at his pupil's description. He continued to stare out the window.

Anna was relieved when Remo didn't probe further.

"So what are we doing here?" Remo asked. He looked out at the college students who were walking along the sidewalk.

They were passing by the dorms at the edge of the campus. Vines clung to the big brick buildings. Although nothing in California ever seemed old to him, this place appeared to have some sense of history to it.

"If Feyodov smuggled the device to Barkley, as I suspect he has, he still would not have the technical skills to reassemble and fire it," Anna explained. "He would need individuals possessed with knowledge in physics, engineering and computer sciences."

Remo snorted. "Good luck finding anyone here who can do any of that stuff," he said.

"Why do you say that?" she asked. "This is one of the most famous universities in your country."

"Fame doesn't equal good, Anna," Remo said. "Anyone who's ever seen a Jim Carrey movie knows that. Community colleges laugh at Barkley's curriculum. They're the folks who pioneered challenging courses like Touching Yourself 101, Crapping on Canvas and Why It's Art, and Introduction to Why White People Suck.''

Chiun quickly chimed in from the back seat. ''If I did not know you were trying to be clever with that last one, I would have the female stop at the office of admissions,'' the Master of Sinanju said. ''It would do you both good to expand your minds.''

As she drove, Anna punched an angry fist against the steering wheel. ''If those SVR idiots had been able to collect Koskolov quietly instead of shooting him dead, we would already have Feyodov by now instead of having to waste our time searching for him,'' she muttered.

''Yeah, Russian hit teams just aren't as trustworthy as they used to be,'' Remo droned. ''And maybe this General Fabio doesn't need any outside help. He could have brought the original team over here with him.''

Anna shook her head angrily. ''Feyodov had the team scientists executed fifteen years ago.''

Remo's brow sank. ''Why?''

This time Anna felt the tension clutch her body. She shook her head, annoyed at her own lack of total control.

''That is a state secret,'' she said. ''But I can tell you that the weapon was constructed at the Sary Shagan base, which was under Feyodov's command at the time. It was test fired once, and it did work. What's more, a recent audit of equipment found that much has been looted from the base, including the weapon in question. And Feyodov was seen a great deal in the area, as well as near here. Given the fact

that there have been three satellites destroyed in the
past two days, I have concluded he is using the
weapon. Most likely, for a client. As far as the client's purpose, I do not know. Feyodov's motivation
is an easier thing to determine. He is largely inspired
by greed.''

Remo crossed his arms, exhaling angrily. ''Anyone else here miss the days when Russian generals
were in it for the boots and the chicks and that whole
world-domination thing?'' he grumbled. ''Now
they're all having sword fights over who's got the
bigger IRA.''

Anna's face was grave. ''That is not his only motivation, Remo,'' she said. ''But it is the simplest.
The rest goes to his psychological makeup, which is
too lengthy to get into right now. Suffice to say that
Feyodov is a deeply disturbed man. And he has stolen the means to throw mankind back into the technological dark ages.''

''Don't you think you're overstating it?'' Remo
sighed. ''Even if you're right, what's a couple of
satellites? Just have NASA launch a few more.''

''They cost millions, some *billions* of your dollars,'' Anna said. ''No one could afford to put any
more in orbit if they are just going to be destroyed
once they get there.''

''Still don't see how my life'll change one jot,''
Remo muttered.

Anna shook her head, amazed. ''Do you have any
idea how much the human race relies on space-based
technology today?''

"Gonna take a wild stab and say too much," Remo said.

"Hear, hear," Chiun echoed.

Anna nodded seriously. "You are correct. Telecommunications, computer networks, national defense, entertainment, scientific research. Even something as simple as weather forecasting could be affected."

"Don't like to talk on the phone, TV sucks since they took *Gunsmoke* off and since when can the weathermen do anything more than make the sports guy look bright by comparison?"

Anna simply couldn't believe his attitude. She gave up trying to convince him of the seriousness of the situation. "You have changed since last I knew you," she said quietly.

Remo nodded. "Unlike you, I haven't been dead." As soon as he spoke, he reconsidered. "Well, maybe once or twice. But never for ten years at a stretch. Guess I've just learned not to sweat the small stuff so much."

At this Chiun snorted. "Please, Remo," the old man chided. "Unlike your other conquests, this one was never a fool. He *has* changed," he told Anna. "He has accepted who and what he is. He knows his place in the universe and no longer feels the need to be something that he is not. But in spite of all this, he will always feel the need to redress the wrongs of the world. It is a curse that I fear he will carry to the grave." His voice dropped low and he focused all attention on Remo, concluding darkly, "And he owes it all to his own big, blubbery, careless mouth.'' Brow dropping low over accusing hazel orbs, he sank back in his seat.

''What is he talking about?'' Anna asked.

''Long story,'' Remo said. ''Short version, I pissed off some gods in Africa.''

''Ah,'' Anna said, nodding. She had heard such fanciful tales from the two men before.

As they wended their way through the campus, Remo looked back out the window at the passing students. All at once he sat up straighter in his seat.

There was a young boy standing alone on the sidewalk. He couldn't have been more than six. A knot of coarse black hair capped his head. As they approached, his flat Korean face was barely visible in profile.

Remo seemed about to speak when the boy turned. As soon as he saw the boy's full face, the tension drained from Remo's body. Almost at the same time the boy ran over to a young woman. Hand in hand the two walked off across the grass.

Behind the wheel Anna noted Remo's interest in the boy. ''What is it?'' she asked.

Remo frowned. ''Nothing,'' he grunted, tearing his eyes away from the mother and child. ''Lot of Asians at this school.'' He stared glumly out at the road ahead.

There was an awkward moment of silence during which the Russian agent fidgeted uncomfortably.

''I do not see a wedding band,'' Anna announced all at once, regretting the words as soon as she spoke them. For an instant she turned a bland eye from the road.

"Yeah, and you don't see a feathered boa, either," Remo said. "There's a parking space."

Swallowing the embarrassment she felt for her blurted observation, Anna kept her mouth screwed tightly shut as she pulled into the space in the student parking lot.

They left the rental car and followed a winding, tree-lined path into the main quad of Barkley University. Since the first building they came upon was the mathematics center, Anna decided they should start there.

The three of them were climbing the broad front stairs when the main door burst open. A young woman who looked a little too old to be a student was being carted out into the sunlight, flanked on either side by campus police officers. The two men began dragging the girl down the stairs.

"Let me go!" she yelled.

The woman was struggling desperately to pull free. The group was halfway down the stairs when her frantic, darting eyes fell on the three individuals coming up the steps. Shocked hope sprang full on her panicked face.

"Remo!" the girl cried.

Surprised to hear his name, Remo glanced at the student as she passed by. When he got a good look at her face, he blinked. His eyes darted to the Master of Sinanju. Chiun's own brow had knotted in recognition.

"Don't just stand there, get me loose!" Brandy Brand shot back over her shoulder as the campus security guards hauled her down the stairs.

Remo shook his head. "It never rains..." he muttered.

Spinning from Anna and Chiun, he bounded back down to the foot of the stairs.

"Who is she?" Anna asked the Master of Sinanju. She tried to hide her look of thin displeasure as she studied the very, very young woman Remo was running after.

Chiun shrugged indifferently. "Remo has met so many comely, *youthful* females since he discarded you like a worn-out sandal that it has been difficult for me to keep track," he offered. A single careful eye looked Anna's way.

With an impatient hiss, Anna glanced down the stairs.

When the guards hit the sidewalk, they found Remo barring their path.

"Okay, Barney and Andy," he said. "Your choice. You wanna let her go the easy way or the hard way?"

The campus security guards didn't have guns. One of them drew his billy club. When he tried to hit Remo with it, Remo split the nightstick up the middle and jammed both halves up the man's nostrils.

"They always pick the hard way," Remo said as the two men staggered away.

He turned his full attention to Brandy Brand. "Okay, what are you doing here?" he asked.

But she had already spun away from him. Without so much as a thank-you, she raced back up the stairs.

Remo followed her, shrugging confusion to Anna and Chiun as they ascended. With Brandy in the lead, the four of them hurried through the big glass-and-chrome door and into the cool interior of the building.

Inside they raced down the hallway.

"Who is she?" Anna demanded of Remo as they ran.

As soon as Anna spoke, Brandy stopped dead. Her head snapped around, her eyes shocked.

"You're Russian," she accused.

"Yes," Anna admitted. She quickly held up a hand. "I suspect, however, that we are on the same side here. You are a government agent of some sort?"

Brandy shook her head. Before she could issue any denials, Remo jumped in.

"Her name's Buffy something-or-other," he supplied. "She's with the FBI. Or maybe it was the CIA. Anyway, it's one of those dipwaddle agencies that's always poncing around making messes I've got to clean up. She helped me out a couple years back." To Brandy he said, "And, yes, Anna's Russian, but it's like a mole or a wooden leg. For the sake of politeness we try not to mention it. And apparently we're all here to stop what's going on. Whatever the hell that is."

Brandy clenched her jaw tightly as she considered his words. Finally, she shook her head violently.

"I don't have time for this," she barked. "I'm FBI, not CIA and it's not Buffy anymore, it's Brandy."

She turned and ran. The others followed.

The door to Professor Horowitz's office was

locked. At Brandy's urging, Remo popped it open with the flat of his palm. The four of them slipped inside.

Her knapsack sat on the professor's desk. Brandy went straight for it, tearing it open. As she expected, all of the papers were gone. She dug around at the bottom, tearing up a Velcro strap that looked like part of the seam. Wrapped tightly in a small hand towel was a second revolver. Brandy pulled the weapon out, glancing at Anna.

"Since the Cold War ended, you people have gotten sloppy," she said to Anna.

Brandy pulled out a hip holster. Hooking it on to the belt of her skirt, she slipped the revolver inside.

Anna didn't hear her. The Russian agent had stepped over to a cork message board that was fastened to the wall. Thumbtacked in the center was a crude drawing.

"My God, I was right," she whispered.

Frowning, Remo looked at the doodle. What appeared to be a long tunnel led to something that looked like an upright mechanical claw gripping a large cylinder. Pencil rays shot into the sky. On the side of an exploding satellite, Dr. Melvin Horowitz had drawn a smiley face.

"Yep," Remo nodded. "Looks like the peaceniks have got themselves a death ray. If I cared, I'd probably be wondering right about now what they plan to do with it."

Anna shot him a baleful glance.

"Tell me again how apathetic you are, Remo,

when you have to communicate with two tin cans on a string,'' she said, turning full attention back to the drawing.

Her voice was hollow.

18

The first great technological war in the history of the human race began fourteen months into the twenty-first century. Even though war had been officially declared and embarked upon by one side, the contest had raged for more than two hours without any nationally elected official in the Western world even knowing they were under formal attack. It might have gone unnoticed for days, with America unwittingly bearing the brunt of the punishing and costly first salvo, if not for a lowly White House intern.

Charlie Worrel was sifting through e-mails in the communications office of the old Executive Office Building that fateful morning when war was declared. It was his job to sort the mail into three distinct categories: those requiring form-letter responses, those that might merit personal responses and those notes written by kooks.

There were two ways of submitting e-mail to the White House. The first involved a form that could be filled out online. However, it required the sender to give a name and a street address. The second e-mail address required neither, allowing the sender more anonymity. However, if need be, letters could still be traced.

The note in question came through on the regular president@whitehouse.gov address.

When he clicked on it, Charlie assumed that this was one of those notes that was going to require further attention. The subject line read simply "Declaration of War." The sender was barkleycouncil@barkley.org.

When Charlie began reading the note, he wasn't sure what to make of it. It seemed to be very carefully worded gibberish. There were all sorts of whereases and wherefores and many references to the "pig United States." The mention of satellites was what caught Charlie's eye.

He had seen a small blurb in the paper that very morning about three coincidental satellite accidents. Whoever these particular kooks were, they were claiming credit for the destruction of all three satellites.

Unsure what to do, Charlie turned the note over to the manager of the White House mail section, who in turn passed it along to the woman who ran the President's mail affairs. From there it found its way directly into the hands of the chief of staff, who carried it in to the Oval Office.

The President sat behind his broad desk. Sunlight streamed through the high windows onto the dark carpet.

The rug that had been there when the President assumed office two weeks ago had been removed. The team of restorers who were attempting to clean it were doubtful that the many splotches and stains in the fabric would ever come out.

The President was on the phone.

"You want a good laugh, sir?" the chief of staff whispered. He placed a printout of the note on the desk.

As he talked, the President glanced down at the letter. After reading just a few lines, his face darkened.

"I'll have to get back to you later," the President said quickly. Hanging up the phone, he picked up the note. "When did this come in?" he asked worriedly.

"The time's at the top, sir," the chief of staff said, confused. "It's just a joke. I mean, it has to be."

When the President looked up, his face was serious.

"I have to make a call," he said.

Leaving his puzzled chief of staff, America's chief executive hurried up to the family residence. For the second time that morning, the President of the United States picked up the red phone in the Lincoln Bedroom. It was answered on the first ring.

"Yes, sir," the lemony voice of Harold Smith said.

"Smith, I was just given a very strange e-mail," the chief executive said. "Trust me that I ordinarily wouldn't bother you with something so silly, but I just got off with the Senate majority leader, and he said he and the speaker of the house got one, too. They figured it was a joke."

He was going to explain further when Smith interrupted.

"You are talking, Mr. President, about the intention of Barkley, California, to secede from the Union," the CURE director said. There was not a hint of mirth in his voice.

"Oh, you heard," the President frowned. "I guess it's one of those joke e-mails that's making the rounds. It's just that they're saying they're the ones who blew up that French rocket and those two satellites."

Smith's reply and assuredness of tone made the President grip more tightly on the red receiver.

"They are claiming credit, Mr. President, because as far as I can determine, they *are* responsible," the CURE director said somberly. "Not only that, but over the past hour and fifty minutes, they have rendered inoperative an additional nine satellites. They are disabling them at a rate of roughly one every ten minutes."

The President felt his hand tighten on the computer printout. "How?" he demanded. "Who are they?"

"At the moment I am not certain who is responsible," Smith said. "However, according to my operatives, they are using a weapon that is able to concentrate particle streams that they have smuggled into the United States."

"Are you saying that these attacks are originating within our own borders?" the President gasped.

"That is correct," Smith said brusquely. "We can only assume that the first three—spaced apart as they were—constituted a fine-tuning process with the device. However, they appear to have worked out any problems they might have had, for they have stepped up their attacks considerably.''

''And declared war on the United States,'' the President said. He looked at the crumpled printout in his hand. The paper was wet with sweat. ''So this nonsense here about Barkley seceding from the Union—that's true?''

''I have accessed the White House e-mail system and read the note in question,'' Smith said. ''Stripping away the extreme language, their desires are clear. As well as what they are willing to do to achieve their ends.''

The bed the President was sitting on suddenly seemed as remote and vast as the deepest ocean. He felt as though he were sinking into it, with nothing to grab on to.

''My God,'' the commander in chief said. ''How can this be? A civil war in this day and age. It's absurd.''

''It is also happening,'' Smith said, with infuriating calm. ''Someone in Barkley, California, has the means and the desire to carry out their goals. In our favor is the fact that, unlike the Civil War of two centuries ago, this is small and localized. Barkley is seen as a fringe community, well outside the American mainstream. But given the power they wield, they cannot be dismissed. Hopefully, Mr. President, we can avert catastrophe before the situation reaches critical mass. My men are on the ground there and are working on the situation even as we speak, so I would advise you to keep any combat forces out of the area for the time being. An armed invasion might only exacerbate the situation. However, in the event that CURE fails, I advise you to seriously consider what you are willing to do to prevent them from achieving their desired objective."

The President balked. "You mean the United States should declare war on an American city?"

"I remind you, sir, that they have shown no qualms about preemptively attacking us," Smith said seriously. "While unpleasant, this is an alternative you need to consider. And now you know as much as I do. I have only learned some of these details within the last few minutes. Please excuse me, but my enforcement arm is on the other line at the moment."

"Wait," the President called anxiously. He was feeling queasy. The fate of his fledgling administration—of perhaps the entire nation—rested squarely on his shoulders. It was something he thought he had been prepared for. Now he wasn't quite so certain. "If they're knocking out satellites, how will I talk to you if this line goes out?"

"This is a dedicated line," Smith explained. "It relies on ground, not satellite technology. We will be able to communicate throughout this crisis."

And with that, Smith severed the connection.

Thoughts spiraling, the President hung up the phone.

He sat for a long moment on the edge of the bed.

He was afraid if he stood, he might keel over onto the floor.

The job he had fought so hard to get now seemed like the most terrible victory he had ever won.

Suddenly feeling much older than his years, the President pulled himself leadenly to his feet. With the shuffle of a man twice his age, the leader of the free world headed wearily for the door.

"IT'S ABOUT DAMN TIME," Remo complained when Smith rejoined him on the line. "Did you have to explain to little Timmy exactly where California is on a map?"

Remo was sitting on a windowsill in Professor Horowitz's Barkley University office, the desk phone resting on his knee. Chiun stood beside him, peering out at the campus. Anna and Brandy were searching the desk and file cabinets.

"The President just learned of the situation," Smith explained tersely. "Now, what else have you to report?"

"That's pretty much it," Remo said. "Some shrub-puffers here got hold of the mammy of all bang-bang machines and now they're pointing it at the sky making things go pop."

"You have no idea who's behind it?" Smith asked.

"Just a sec," Remo said. He cupped his hand loosely over the mouthpiece. "We have any clue who's pulling the strings on the magic cannon?" he called over to Anna and Brandy.

"I think it's the Barkley city council," Brandy

replied. She and the Russian agent were pawing through piles of paper. Until five minutes ago she'd thought she was working on a simple smuggling case. Thanks to Remo and Anna's quick explanation, she had undergone a rapid conversion to the true urgency of the situation in town. "It could be one or two council members, though. I don't know for sure."

"City council, Smitty," Remo said into the phone. "And if it's true you get the elected officials you deserve, they've probably got Cheech and Chong as lifetime aldermen and smelly-beard Castro moonlighting as mayor."

"The e-mail stating Barkley's intention to secede from the Union was sent from the Barkley council web address. Unless someone else has access to their system, we can assume for now they are involved, at least peripherally. I will research the council," Smith vowed. "Who was that you just spoke to?"

"Remember that FBI agent we ran into back during that whole Ranch Ragnarok mess in Wyoming a couple years back?" Remo asked. "The one we left at the hospital on the way out of town?"

"Buffy Brand," Smith said. "Yes, I remember."

"It's not Buffy anymore, for some reason," Remo said. "But she's on the case here, too. And you'll never guess who else we bumped into." He was watching Anna as she leafed through a thick file.

At Remo's words, the Russian's head snapped up. She shook her head frantically.

Remo hesitated.

"Who?" Smith asked after a moment's pause.

Beside Remo, the Master of Sinanju's face fouled.

"A cabal of Russian home wreckers, that is who, Emperor Smith," Chiun called. "They scattered the jesters before I was allotted my house. If not for the fact that you have opened the doors of your palace to Remo and myself, I fear your servants would be out in the streets with a box for a roof and a shopping cart to transport our meager belongings. Songs of gratitude we sing to you, Smith the Generous, for your continued kindheartedness and generosity."

Across the room Anna exhaled relief. With an angry look of warning for Remo, she returned to her work.

Remo nodded gratefully. "Nice save," he said to Chiun, careful to keep his voice low.

"Look before you speak," the Master of Sinanju hissed quietly in Korean. "If she did not want Smith to know she lived these many years, what makes you think she would want you to blab it to him now?"

Remo nodded. "Check," he agreed. "Chiun's right, Smitty," he said into the phone. "There was some Russian hit squad at the Buffoon Aid benefit. They had that cabbagey KGB smell all over them."

"SVR," Smith corrected. "That is the group that succeeded the KGB. I assume you eliminated them?"

"Yeah," Remo said. "They were going after another Russian who I guess helped bring that zap gun here. But thanks to that old KGB habit of murdering first and asking questions later, that's another dead end."

"That is unfortunate," Smith said. "It would

have helped to have one of them to question. Still, if the SVR was after this other man as you say, then we can eliminate the involvement of the Russian government in all this. They would not be attacking one of their own men.''

''No,'' Remo agreed. ''But they're not too keen on their ex-men. There's a guy running around here who supposedly brought that doohickey over from Russia. General Fedora, or something like that.''

Remo could hear Smith's chair creak over the phone. The CURE director obviously had found this fact intriguing enough to come to seated attention behind his desk.

''Feyodov?'' Smith asked. ''Do you mean General Boris Feyodov, formerly of the Sary Shagan Missile Test Center?''

''Yeah, that sounds right,'' Remo said. ''Rumor has it he stole the gun from that Sally Shaghole place.''

''Hmm,'' Smith mused. He began typing at his keyboard. Remo could hear the certain tapping of the older man's fingers at the edge of his high-tech desk.

''That a good hmm or a bad hmm?'' Remo asked.

''Feyodov was drummed out of the military over a year ago,'' the CURE director explained as he worked. ''If memory serves—'' The typing stopped abruptly. ''Ah, here it is. Yes, it *was* he. Feyodov was in command of the Russian forces in the break-away republic of Chechnya. There were several routs while he was in charge. The most notable was a massacre of Russian troops that garnered interna-

tional attention. It was thought that heavy bombardment had caused rebels to flee the capital of Grozny.
Feyodov led a convoy personally into the city. But
the rebels were merely setting a trap. When the Russian forces moved in, the guerrillas closed in behind
them, slaughtering the Russians to a man.''

At this Smith let out a confused hum.

''Sounds like you just did the math in your head,''
Remo said. '''To a man' means Fredo shouldn't
have gotten out.''

''Yes,'' Smith agreed, puzzled. ''But apparently
he did. There is no record of how he escaped harm
in the translation of the official report that I have
accessed. The current Russian president, who was
prime minister at the time, relieved Feyodov of his
command and stripped him of his rank. Yet it seems
as though everything was done very quietly. Still,
given the facts of the case, I would imagine the general returned to civilian life in disgrace.''

''And bitter to boot, I bet,'' Remo groused. ''Why
is it when people get pissed at the world, they always
take it out on our part of it?''

''And on poor homeless me,'' Chiun chimed in
dolefully.

''I don't think anyone factored you into the equa-
tion, Little Father,'' Remo said.

Still at the window, hands behind his back, the
Master of Sinanju turned a hard eye on his pupil.
''That is their mistake,'' he said. He turned his
weathered face back to the Barkley University quad.

''What of the weapon itself, Remo?'' Smith ventured. ''Do you have any idea where it might be?''

"Hold on," Remo instructed. Off the phone he said to Anna and Brandy, "You find anything over there about where they've got that thing stashed?"

Anna kept her mouth clamped shut, not wanting to risk even a sound that the CURE director might hear.

"It looks like whole departments of the university have been turned over to the project," Brandy supplied. "Seems everyone's jumped on the bandwagon to get it up and running. From what you told me, this thing could be run from anywhere in the world, but there are so many locals on the list I'd bet J. Edgar Hoover's bloomers it's somewhere in town."

"You get that, Smitty?" Remo asked.

"Yes, and I concur," Smith said. "It is of paramount importance that you stop that weapon. The entire future of man's technological mastery of space is at risk as long as it continues to operate. Begin with the council. Excluding General Feyodov and him alone, any Russians you meet are distractions. Eliminate them an—"

The line abruptly went dead. With a frown Remo hung up the receiver.

"What did he say?" Anna asked as he returned the phone to the physics professor's desk.

"The usual," Remo said. "Kill all Russian spies, fate of the world rests in my hands, blah-blah-blah." He raised a seductive eyebrow as he glanced at Brandy. "Am I turning you on?" he asked.

The FBI agent ignored him as she stuffed papers into her knapsack. "I don't think any of this will do us much good now," she said tightly to Anna. "I thought these numbnuts were smuggling bomb supplies, not ray guns. Should've figured Barkley U would be into the more heavy-duty stuff.''

"It is not the university staff that is the problem," Anna said. "They are merely lackeys. Although given what I have seen on this campus, I have no idea how you people won the Cold War."

"America doesn't have mental institutions—we have higher education," Remo explained. "Okay, let's go check out the council. Anna, keep your eyes peeled for that general of yours. He should know how to pull the plug on this thing."

"He might have skipped town," Brandy said evenly. "My partner was in Barkley with me. He followed Feyodov to San Francisco this morning, where your general met with someone my partner recognized. Some other Russian."

"Who?" Anna asked with a frown.

"He wasn't sure," Brandy said. "Last I heard from him, he'd left Feyodov to follow the other guy." Her voice grew deadly serious. "They found him severely injured and stuffed inside a maintenance closet at San Francisco airport an hour later. Whoever the sick bastard was, he tore my partner's nose clean off. They couldn't even find it to reattach it.''

Remo suddenly found himself trying to remember if Chiun had left his side at any time while they were at the airport that morning. When he turned a worried eye on the Master of Sinanju, Anna seemed to pick up the thread. Confused by their reactions, Brandy glanced at the frail old man.

Standing at the window, the wizened Asian was the very picture of innocence.

"What did he look like?" Chiun asked, his eyes hooded. "After all, I meet so many people."

"Wait," Remo said to Brandy. "When was that meeting?"

"About two hours ago," she said.

"We got in town way before that. You're off the hook, Little Father."

The old man's lips thinned. "Thank you, Remo, for having such confidence in me," he said acidly.

"No offense," Brandy said carefully as she eyed Chiun, "but he doesn't look very dangerous."

"I am not," Chiun sniffed. "I am but a poor homeless old man who has given everything to an adopted foundling who repays the kindness he has been shown with baseless suspicion. While you are thinking of more unsolved mysteries to blame on me, I will be waiting in the car."

As the old man breezed between them, Remo said, "It was just a passing thought. Besides, I never blamed you for the *Titanic,* the *Hindenburg* or the Lindbergh kidnapping."

"See?" the Master of Sinanju said knowingly to Brandy. "Where I actually deserve credit, he gives none."

With that he swept from the room.

"Don't listen to him," Remo assured the FBI agent. "Now he's just bragging."

As the trio headed to the door, Anna Chutesov shook her head. "Men," she muttered.

"Tell me about it," Brandy agreed.

"Maybe we better keep the top up for the ride across town," Remo said as he pulled the office door shut. "One stiff breeze and both your Bella Abzug hats could get blown into the Timothy Leary Memorial Pot Plantation."

19

General Boris Vanovich Feyodov hated his country with every fiber of his existence. It was a hatred forged from betrayal and humiliation. A personal, visceral loathing that could not help but be stronger than everyday antipathy.

This attitude was newly born. The old Boris Feyodov had loved the old Mother Russia. It was this new bastard incarnation of the nation he loved that Feyodov so reviled.

The son of a field marshal who had fought in the Great Patriotic War, Feyodov had learned early on that rank equaled privilege. For the family of Marshal Gregori Feyodov, there were no food lines, no stores with empty shelves. Their needs were small, of course, as was right for all good Communists, but those needs were always met. There were houses and cars and an old Armenian woman who helped his mother with the cleaning. Once every year there was a summer vacation at a Party dacha on the Black Sea.

By studying his father, young Boris Feyodov had come to understand exactly how the world worked.

When Boris came of age, his father had pulled

strings, getting his son an early commission in the Red Army. Clever, resourceful and possessed of an innate sense to know whom to stroke and whom to avoid in the Party leadership, Feyodov had quickly climbed the ranks. All who watched his rapid rise to general could not help but be impressed by the way Feyodov played against both the strengths and the weaknesses of the Communist system. The little boy from Smolensk, son of the great Field Marshal Gregori Feyodov, was truly a virtuoso. His instrument? Communism itself.

Feyodov achieved the rank of general in the 1970s, back during the time of SALT and détente.

Back then, it was understood that the West was in its death throes. Capitalism was bloodied and reeling, desperate to appease. The Union of Soviet Socialist Republics was respected and feared. When the great Russian bear arched its mighty back, men from Washington to Peking to all points in between quivered like frightened children. At that time to be a Russian general was to be a god among men.

It was as a god that General Feyodov assumed command of the Sary Shagan Missile Test Center. The collection of hangars and bunkers was his own personal Olympus. He strode through halls and across tarmacs, head held high, never out of full uniform. The soldiers under his command worshiped him, and the civilian workers were terrified of him.

It was at Sary Shagan that Feyodov's true reputation began to grow. Until the time of his appointment there, he had always been his father's son. Certainly he was clever enough, but Party leaders assumed that he had gotten where he had largely because he was son of a field marshal. That was only partly true. Sary Shagan was the turning point of Party sentiment toward the younger Feyodov.

There was never a challenge sent to the base that was not accepted by its commander. Projects sent there were completed on time and under budget. The ironhanded rule of General Boris Feyodov kept order and garnered results.

When in the 1980s the Americans announced their desire for a missile defense program, Boris Feyodov and Sary Shagan were given the task of producing a Soviet version.

Feyodov had driven the team of scientists like dogs. The men worked, slept and ate at the Kazakhstan facility. Only one weekend every four months were they allowed to go to visit their families off base.

The work schedule was brutal, even by Feyodov's normally harsh standards. If questioned, the general would have claimed that he was only doing his duty. But the truth was, he had another motivation. One he dared not speak aloud.

Like a religious visionary, Boris Feyodov had detected something that had gone unnoticed by his countrymen. The son of Field Marshal Gregori Feyodov had seen the end.

The West was no longer timid. Unlike the cowardly days of the sixties and seventies, America had now gone on the offensive. Challenges to Soviet authority that would not have been dared a generation before were becoming common. Afghanistan, El

Salvador, Nicaragua, Grenada. For the first time in years, Mother Russia had begun to lose ground.

Feyodov was one of the first to smell change in the air. And it terrified him.

General Feyodov understood communism. He knew how to exploit the nuances of that system to his advantage. Without it, Boris Feyodov was hollow. And it was this fear of what might be that motivated him to push his men.

For more than a year he drove the scientists to complete their task, hoping that their work would hold together the splitting seams of socialism.

When the work was done on what was supposed to be the prototype for a line of high-tech Soviet weapons, the order to test had come down from the Kremlin itself.

At the time the head of the USSR had been in office for less than a year. This new general secretary was younger than any who had preceded him. Swiping away the cobwebs of fear, he had been appointed to give a smiling face to Russian communism. This fact alone was offensive to General Feyodov. Who cared if the hated West ever saw you smile?

Still, the order had given Feyodov hope. Especially after he learned what his target would be.

The test had gone flawlessly. When the American space shuttle burst apart in the blue sky like a clod of white dirt, the general had allowed himself a moment of hope for his country. His first in several years.

The moment was short-lived.

As soon as the spacecraft was obliterated, Feyodov received the call. He was stunned when he recognized the uncultured voice of the general secretary.

"You are calling with congratulations, comrade General Secretary," Feyodov had said proudly.

"Yes," the general secretary agreed, in a way that made it sound as if the opposite were true. "I did not think you could do it," Russia's premier said.

"We are Russians," General Feyodov had said. "Proud sons of the Revolution."

"Yes, yes," the general secretary said. He actually sounded anxious. "Feyodov, I am beginning to rethink this program. It was instituted before I assumed this office. What we—what *you*—have done today…" He took a deep breath. "The Americans, Feyodov, will not understand."

Though tempted, Feyodov refrained from instructing the general secretary of the Soviet Union on the indifference he should feel toward the concerns of the Americans.

It was then that the general secretary had issued the most shocking order General Boris Feyodov had ever received. The general was commanded to obliterate every member of the team responsible for creating the particle-beam weapon.

Feyodov wanted to resist, but to refuse a direct order from the premier would be to invite the considerable wrath of a system that the general understood all too well.

In the end he had done his duty. The civilian scientists were killed on the spot. The technicians and military personnel were shot later on. When he was finished, knowledge of what had truly transpired that day was limited only to Boris Feyodov and the highest levels of the Kremlin.

The explosion that should have heralded a great new day for the struggling Soviet Union ended up sounding its death knell. The world began to unravel not long after.

The great technological advance Feyodov had helped usher in was minuscule when weighed against the achievements of the West. The Soviet Union simply could not afford the arms race with America. Funding to the military was cut. This included the Sary Shagan base.

For his obedience and silence, the general secretary eventually transferred General Feyodov to another post.

A new espionage agency was being created. If Russia could not beat its enemies with brute military force, it would do so with cunning. It was to be the most secret agency ever to exist. Formed ostensibly to battle internal problems, it would actually be an international force like none other. More clandestine than the KGB, Cheka or Shield, it would employ only three men: General Feyodov and a pair of very special field operatives.

The general secretary himself had blackmailed the Americans into turning over two of their top agents. When given his appointment to this start-up agency, Feyodov had his doubts that a pair of American agents would willingly work for the sworn enemy of their country. He was told by the premier that they were mercenaries, based in Communist North Korea, and thus were not beholden to any nation. To Feyodov's disgust he learned that the two men who would be his new stealth operatives worked purely for monetary gain.

And so General Boris Feyodov, late of the Sary Shagan Missile Test Center, had come to Kitai Gorod in Moscow to set up his clandestine agency in an ominous concrete building with bricked-up windows and no visible entrance.

And there he waited for the agents that never came.

It turned out that there was some problem with the contract of the two operatives. General Feyodov became head of an agency of which he was the sole member. Not that he had time to nurse this latest humiliation.

Almost before he had time to settle in, he was ordered to vacate his post as director. The Institute, as his agency was called, was being turned over to a special adviser to the head of Russia. A person who had been a field operative and who, because of some terrible secret, could no longer work abroad.

He had met his successor briefly. To make his disgrace complete, Feyodov had been shocked to find that it was a woman. A mere slip of a girl with cold blue eyes, an attitude of snide superiority and a fat briefcase locked with the seal of the Soviet president.

Feyodov left the Institute gladly. Let this woman have her big empty building and whatever secrets she carried with her in her government attaché case.

By now he knew that the end was near. For him and for his beloved Russia.

He had become just another general after that. With postings at crumbling bases all over the dying empire. When the Soviet Union finally collapsed, Feyodov had remained in the military, dutifully obeying the commands of his civilian superiors. Eventually, he had gone to Chechnya, accepting a battle command for the first time in his lifelong army career. For Feyodov, this would be the final nail in the coffin of a grand life grown pathetic.

Chechnya had been a trouble spot ever since the death of his beloved Soviet Union. Like many others before it, the predominantly Muslim republic craved independence. Another bleeding scrap of meat to tear off the wheezing, dying body of the shrunken Mother Russia.

Feyodov didn't see the situation as very complicated. The Muslim separatists were infected with the same disease that had plagued what had once been the great Soviet empire. The rebels embodied all the disloyal, anarchic traits that had killed the USSR.

Boris Feyodov took command in Chechnya with one thought on his mind: revenge. These miserable Muslim dogs would pay for all of his own personal defeats and humiliations.

The bombardment against the capital of Grozny was vicious. They bombed from land and air. Day after day of punishing, endless assaults against the city, ordered by Boris Feyodov with the blessing of the Kremlin leadership.

When the bombing stopped and the smoke

cleared, Feyodov declared victory. The rebels were defeated. Those left alive had fled the city.

The taste of triumph thick in the air, the general had climbed into the lead truck in the convoy that would reclaim Grozny for Russia. He and his men rode down from the hills, through the pathetic barricades and into the heart of the city. For a few brief moments—as he beheld the buildings, collapsed at his order, and passed by the burning cars and along cratered streets—Boris Feyodov was once more a god.

As apotheoses went, this one was short-lived.

The first gunshot came from the darkened doorway of a tumbledown apartment building.

In the lead truck, General Feyodov jumped. He wasn't quite sure what the noise was. After all, he had never heard a bullet fired in battle before. At first he thought it might be a firecracker.

The next shot sounded an instant later, followed by the next and the next until they became a nightmare chorus. His uncertainty sprouting wings of desperate fear, Feyodov dropped down. Bullets whizzed overhead.

Panicked, he jerked his head around.

His driver was dead, slumped over the steering wheel. The men in the back of his truck had already suffered heavy casualties. Bodies were tumbling from the trailing trucks. Terror washed over the Russian troops.

Bullets thudded into metal.

He ordered his men to attack. They were already firing.

He ordered them to protect him at all costs. No one could hear him over the raging gunfire.

He ordered retreat. They were surrounded.

Blinded by fear, Feyodov grabbed for the door handle. Twisting it, he fell to the ground. As the men above him fought for their lives, their commander crawled beneath the dark belly of the lead truck. Terrified hands covered ears; elbows and toes dragged him forward.

The truck was at the side of the road. A stairwell led into the shadowy basement of a bombed-out building.

Unnoticed by rebel or soldier, Feyodov toppled down the concrete stairs. Bloodied and dirty, he scurried beneath the collapsed archway and crumbled ceiling.

As the battle raged in the street far above his basement hideaway, General Boris Feyodov fled deeper and deeper into the shadows. He crawled until he could go no farther. As the final shots were fired and the last Russian soldier spilled his blood on the streets of Grozny, the general who had abandoned his troops was far away, cowering in a dank corner of his basement haven, his knees tucked up to his chin, rump settled into a cold, muddy puddle.

He was found eight days later.

The general was malnourished and dehydrated. He had soiled himself, drinking from the same filthy puddle.

As soon as he was pulled from the basement he was shipped back to Moscow. To have the leader of the Russian forces in Chechnya appear weak, gaunt, disheveled and cowardly, would only help to further the rebels' cause.

The war would be fought without him.

It was during the long months of his recuperation that Boris Feyodov the loyal Soviet, Boris Feyodov the *aparatchik,* Boris Feyodov the Communist Party virtuoso, finally learned the truth about himself. He had found that—no matter what his service rank was—he had never been a soldier.

Feyodov had gotten where he had by manipulating the Communist system. Early on it was his father's intervention. Later it was a flawlessly executed practice of strategically alternating between political backstabbing and bootlicking. He had compelled others to follow his orders at gunpoint so that his star might shine more brightly. At his various cozy appointments, his successes came on the strained backs of others. But *he*—Boris Vanovich Feyodov— could never claim credit for personally achieving anything in his life.

On the day he was released from the hospital, Feyodov learned that he had been dishonorably discharged from the military the day he had been discovered in the Grozny cellar.

For Boris Feyodov—with his career gone, his country lost and the only world he understood vanished into the mists of history—there was only one way out. In his service trunk he found his father's old World War II revolver, a treasured memento of the only Feyodov who had truly earned his rank.

With a bottle in one hand and the great field marshal's gun in the other, Feyodov staggered out into the cold streets of Moscow. Near a chain-link fence that overlooked the river he took a last bracing swig of vodka. Smashing the bottle to the frozen ground, he slurred a curse at the cold air and stuck the barrel of the gun into his open mouth.

And there he stood. The night wind cutting through his greatcoat. The twinkling lights of the city reflecting on the rolling waves, now a garish siren call to capitalism.

Feyodov struggled with the gun. His teeth and tongue tasted the metal. His finger almost touched the trigger.

But in the end he was too much the coward.

Drawing the cold barrel from between his chapped lips, he hurled the gun into the Moscow River.

Boots crunching on the broken glass, the general fell sobbing against the fence.

The weeks after that were a blur of hard drink and a hazy gray twilight of pitiful anguish. He barely remembered being approached at a bar by a former subordinate in the Red Army—a colonel who had been stationed at Sary Shagan. The months-long hangover hadn't even lifted before he found himself working for the black market.

So he became a criminal. So what? Wasn't everyone in Russia a pimp or a whore to the West these days? And since it seemed unlikely he would ever work up the nerve to kill himself, he would have to eat. Besides, this new Russia inspired corruption. No, it *deserved* it.

Many of his new associates were former military

men like him, betrayed by the system that had made them all gods.

No one knew of his disgrace. The war in Chechnya was too important for the Kremlin to allow news of its cowardly general to be leaked to the public.

Almost without effort, Feyodov climbed the ranks. He soon learned that capitalism and communism were not so different at their most basic levels. He applied his old tactics to his new life, killing or currying favor until in scarcely more than a year's time he became one of the new power elite in Russia. A crime lord.

Many who marveled at the way he worked the system assumed the old Communist had become a born-again capitalist. But the truth was, Boris Vanovich Feyodov was the hollowest of hollow men, loathing life but frightened of death. He did what he did only because he had no idea what else to do.

When he was approached by the fools of Barkley early on in his new career, he agreed to see them only because of their promise of money.

Zen Bower and Gary Jenfeld had met with Boris Feyodov at the Moscow McDonald's. The men had owned an ice cream shop in the city and out of necessity knew well of the Russian underworld. Their contacts had pointed them to Feyodov.

"We hear you're someone who can get things done," Zen had said craftily at that first meeting almost a year before.

Zen and Gary hunched over their trays of food.

Feeling very much like spies, they glanced at doors and windows.

"What do you want?" Feyodov demanded. He was a busy man now, with no time for nonsense.

"We come from a small community in America," Zen whispered. "But please don't hold that against us. The truth is, we've had it with being part of that whole love-it-or-leave-it, apple pie, racist, sexist, homophobic testament to dead-white-maledom. We want out, and we're willing to pay."

"You want out of what? America?" Feyodov scoffed. "I have seen your kind before. You men are fools."

He started to get up. Zen grabbed his wrist.

"You don't know what we're willing to do. Or *pay*."

There was an intensity in his eyes and voice that Feyodov hadn't seen in years. It was the earnestness of a diehard Communist. Someone willing to do anything for the great People's cause. Feyodov retook his seat.

Zen smiled. "We need nuclear weapons," he hissed.

"Although we're firmly antinuke," Gary interjected.

"That way, pig America would never dream of attacking," Zen said. "We could bury a couple ICBM silos on the Barkley U campus, target L.A. and San Diego. You give us one of the long-range suckers, and we could even threaten the East Coast. That way Washington *has* to stay off our backs. Without the jackbooted threat of Uncle Sam breathing down our necks, we can finally create Marx's dream of a socialist utopia.''

Feyodov looked hard at Zen Bower. ''I would not sell you idiots a water pistol, let alone a nuclear weapon.''

He stood once more.

Zen was growing desperate. As Feyodov started walking across the dining area of the restaurant, the ice cream man called frantically after the former general.

''Don't you want revenge against the filthy capitalists who destroyed your workers' paradise?'' the American shouted.

The words seemed to echo at him from down a long tunnel.

It was a moment like no other Boris Feyodov had ever experienced in his life. It was an epiphany. An instance of pure, crystalline realization.

These men had money and hated America. Feyodov hated both America and Russia. What's more, he had contacts, power and a decade-old secret. And the weapon that went with it.

The outline of a plan came to him in a flash.

On wooden legs, he returned to the table. He accepted their money. Seemed to do everything they asked. He gave them their weapon, the means by which they hoped to secede from the country that had given them everything in abundance. But even as he brought over the particle-beam device piece by piece and set it up in that wealthy California community, the former Red Army general kept secret a scheme of his own. One he hoped he had the nerve to execute.

Boris Feyodov would get his revenge against this Russia that had made him face the mirror and see his true self. He would have vengeance, too, against America for bringing the land of his birth to ruin. He would play both sides against each other in a final showdown. He alone would bring the Cold War roaring back to the boiling point. And in order to do all this, he would manipulate the imbeciles of Barkley just as he had the Communist leaders of old.

And when the bombs started to fall like summer rain, General Boris Vanovich Feyodov might just be sitting there to greet them. A smile of triumph on his tired, sagging face.

20

As he stormed through the network of underground tunnels beneath the city of Barkley, Boris Feyodov did not smile.

His boots clattered urgently along the metal plates. All around heavy insulated pipes channeled power to the smuggled particle-beam weapon.

The idiots had been charging and firing nonstop for more than three hours. The constant operation shocked the very ether in the fetid underground rooms. The short hairs on his neck rose and his fillings ached as he charged into the main tunnel. The air was ripe with nervous mingled body odors.

Zen and Gary were back, standing above one of the monitors. Professor Melvin Horowitz sat at the console, nervously tracking the latest targeted satellite.

Oleg Shevtrinko stood anxiously behind the trio. When he saw the general emerge into the tunnel, relief bloomed wide on Oleg's face. Feyodov didn't even acknowledge him. He brushed past his fellow Russian, marching up to Zen.

"Are you out of your mind?" Feyodov snapped.

The Russian's jowls were pulled back in a furious scowl.

Zen's head snapped around. "It's about time," the Barkley council leader barked. "We're under attack." He turned his full attention back to Professor Horowitz.

"Attack by whom?" Feyodov growled. He didn't wait for a reply. "Stand down!" he commanded the men in the tunnel.

"Belay that order!" Zen countered. He tapped an angry finger on Melvin's monitor.

A satellite spun through computer-generated space, the glowing letters ANW beneath it. A program neatly identified all registered satellites with simple codes.

"Not that one," Zen warned authoritatively. "Leave all the ANW ones alone. Any others are fair game."

Melvin Horowitz knew that ANW stood for AIC News-Wallenberg, the biggest communications conglomerate in the world. It was the company that owned HTB. For some reason unknown to the Barkley professor, Zen seemed particularly interested in preserving only that company's satellites.

Professor Horowitz nodded dull agreement. It was difficult to avoid the AIC News-Wallenberg satellites. For some reason, they had more of them floating around up there than they could ever possibly need. As sweat poured down his forehead, the professor got a lock on an NBC satellite.

"It'll be another minute before we're fully

charged," the Barkley University physics professor said.

As the device charged, Zen spun. "We had a riot while you were gone. Bodies piled everywhere. You should have been here. If I wanted a coward in charge, I'd have picked Gary to be Barkley's supreme military commander."

The instant the insulting word was spoken, the former general's eyes saucered. Raging brown pupils swam in a sea of bloodshot white.

When he saw the look that gripped Feyodov's face, Gary Jenfeld gasped. He dropped the cardboard container of Cherry Rubin ice cream he'd been eating.

Suddenly remembering Oleg Shevtrinko's earlier warning, Zen took a half step back. "We had to step up the timetable after the attack against Buffoon Aid," he said, trying to force a rough edge to his voice even as he inched back from Feyodov. "We've officially declared war on the oppressors in Washington. So far they've remained silent, so we're following through on our threat. Operation Clear Heavens has eliminated sixteen satellites."

The general's jaw was clenched so tightly his molars squeaked. His wild eyes darted to Oleg Shevtrinko's hip holster. The automatic pistol was within reach.

By sheer force of will Feyodov overcame his more murderous impulses. Tearing his eyes from Zen, he did some rapid calculations in his head.

Thanks to these imbeciles his own plan might have been put in jeopardy. He had taken too long to get back here from San Francisco. Retaliation from the United States government might already be imminent. But there was still time.

Eyelids drooping over his maniac's eyes, he refocused on the ice cream men.

"What happened?" he asked, forcing calm. *"Exactly."*

"One of your men got killed by a bunch of other guys at the benefit," Zen said. "Somehow they got killed, too."

Feyodov gave Oleg an angry questioning glance.

"Not by us, General," Oleg said seriously. "They were killed by hand, not by weapons. At least not by any weapons I know of. There was much panic, so the eyewitnesses cannot be trusted completely. They say there were two men in the area at the time. An old Asian and a young white. I cannot see how they were responsible for all six deaths. And the force exerted on some of the bodies was inhuman. One man's head was forced down into his chest." He shuddered at the memory. "I have never seen anything like it, General."

Feyodov's face grew deadly calm. Somehow the lack of any emotion was more frightening than the look of rage that had gripped his flaccid features a moment before. When he spoke, his voice was small.

"I have," Feyodov said quietly. Shoulders deflating, he fell back against the console. Melvin Horowitz had to pull his hand away before it was sat on.

"There was someone else here, too," Zen said. "At the university. Some kind of government agent or something."

Feyodov was hardly listening. "Your government or mine?" he asked absently.

"Neither," Zen said. "She was *American*. Campus police were supposed to hold her until your men could collect her for questioning, but someone helped her escape. He fits the description of the guy at the Buffoon Aid benefit. The old Asian was there, too. And an unidentified woman."

Feyodov's eyes darted to Zen. "This woman," he said, his brow furrowing. "Was she blond and attractive, perhaps with a smug, superior attitude?"

"I don't know about any of that," Zen replied. "Is she an enemy of yours? Because if she is, the council will have to reevaluate our relationship. We didn't pay you, General, to drag any of your personal problems into this."

At this Feyodov remained mute. These fools had no idea that all of this had been engineered as a direct result of Boris Feyodov's personal problems.

Before the ice cream man could question the general any further, a phone on the console table buzzed to life. Zen saw that it was the line to the council chambers. He grabbed it, assuming they'd finally heard from Washington.

Zen listened for only a few seconds. As the frightened caller spoke, the ice cream man's face visibly paled.

"I'll be right there," he snapped. Slamming down the phone, he wheeled on Feyodov. "We're under attack again! My God, they're assaulting the city hall building!"

He turned from the general and was off. The metal

plates rattled furiously as Zen and Gary ran down the tunnel.

Feyodov's reeling brain had still been trying to absorb all that was going on. But as soon as the two men were gone, he seemed to reach a sudden decision. He shoved Melvin Horowitz aside, diving for the nearby keyboard. With shaking fingers he entered a new code into the system.

The image on the screen shifted from the targeted NBC satellite that Horowitz had been tracking. A new computer-interpreted figure appeared on the monitor.

The object in orbit was far bigger than a satellite. Assembled by pulsing space telemetry and translated to the computer screen, it was a stick-figure cigar shape.

"When that comes in range, fire upon it," Feyodov ordered the Barkley University professor.

The general's worried eyes strayed to the roof of the cavern. Who knew what was going on up there at the moment? He couldn't fail. Not now.

"But I already have a target," Horowitz apologized. "Besides, I don't know if I'm supposed to shoot that." His worried eyes followed the familiar object through the void.

Above the seated man, Feyodov glanced around. Oleg still stood at attention behind him. Reaching over, the general wrenched the gun from Oleg's hip holster, jamming the barrel against Melvin Horowitz's sweaty temple.

The general leaned in so close, Horowitz could

see the fine hairs growing from the end of his venous nose.

"You have a new target," Feyodov whispered, his finger twitching over the trigger. "You will fire, or I will."

"Yes, sir!" Dr. Horowitz snapped, lunging for his keyboard. Desperate, stubby fingers mashed the keys.

As the professor frantically went about executing his new orders, Feyodov straightened, slapping the pistol back into Oleg's outstretched palm.

The former general shot a glance down the far, dead end of the tunnel. The particle-beam weapon was barely visible behind a ganglia of connecting power lines. A stab of sunlight washed down from far above.

Soon it would be over. And the hollowness of his life would have meaning.

"I will not fail," he said quietly.

The soft words were a promise to his own cowardly soul.

WHEN ZEN AND Gary burst into the Barkley council chamber, they found the small auditorium empty. Zen didn't know whether or not he should be relieved. He'd expected to find storm troopers from the U.S. government smashing windows and firing tear-gas canisters filled with Agent Orange and Philip Morris tobacco products around the room in an orgy of fascistic meanness.

"Where is everybody?" Zen whispered harshly as they stepped into the silent hall.

Gary was in midshrug when a timid voice chimed in.

"Under here."

Only then did Zen see the row of sandals sticking out from under the council table on the main stage.

One of the Barkley residents on the council insisted on wearing nothing but Indian moccasins in order to show his support for the plight of Native American master craftsmen. The hand stitching was usually unraveling before he even took them out of the box and the genuine artificial leather material imported from China reacted poorly with air, water, slight temperature changes and all the other environmental stimuli of Earth's precious ecosystem. Zen saw the council member's distinctive shoes, as well as his nervously wiggling toes, which were sticking out of the holes in the seams.

Allowing a slip of relieved breath to pass his lips, Zen hurried up to the stage.

"What's going on?" he demanded.

"Lookout on the roof said he saw those guys heading this way," a disembodied voice replied. "The youth-impaired, culturally rich Asian-heritage gentleman and the WEM."

WEM was Barkley shorthand for White European Male. Given the frequency of official condemnations against all WEMliness, it was just easier to abbreviate.

"There's nothing to worry about," Zen insisted. "We've got three sets of surplus Soviet-built superdoors, all bolted. This place is a fortress. They are not getting inside."

He had no sooner spoken than there came a distant rumble that seemed to shake the entire hall. It was followed by a terrible, muffled wrenching sound as the front door—which had been liberated from an abandoned Siberian missile silo—was ripped from its hinges.

"Last one under the table's a Republican!" Gary shrieked. He skidded across the floor in a diving leap, slipping under the tablecloth between two sets of sandals.

Gary had barely slithered from sight before a second set of hallway doors yielded with a thundering crash. Whoever the men were, they were two-thirds of the way to the chamber.

"What the hell did we pay for?" Zen breathed, shocked. "He promised me those doors would stop a tank."

Even as Zen spoke, Boris Feyodov ran into the room through the rear entrance. With him was Oleg and a handful of confused Russian black-market soldiers.

"What is happening?" Feyodov asked breathlessly.

"I'll tell you what's happening!" Zen yelled from across the room. The door to the hall suddenly began to groan in pain. Zen's head snapped around. "I want a refund, that's what's happening!"

And as he spoke, the last door to the outside world surrendered to the punishing force that had penetrated the outer defenses to the Barkley seat of power.

The door to the chamber was four-inch-thick steel

with a titanium mesh interior and a mortar-proof facade. It split up the middle like a cracked eggshell and plopped to the floor in two fat halves. Dust rose high into the air.

"Lucy, I'm home," said Remo Williams as he stepped over the remnants of the door into the main council chamber. Chiun breezed in beside him.

Behind them came Anna and Brandy. Both women clutched guns in their hands. Cool, alert eyes scanned the room. When Anna saw Feyodov and his retinue of shocked Russian expatriates in the back of the room, her mouth thinned. She was quicker with her gun than they were with theirs.

"Do not move!" Anna commanded the Russians.

Hands going for weapons, the men froze. Slowly, the Russians raised their hands into the air.

"*You,*" Feyodov growled. He didn't even seem to notice Remo and Chiun. He glared hatred at Anna Chutesov.

"Great," Remo grumbled. "This another old boyfriend who thought you were dead the last ten years? She's been yanking us all," he promised Feyodov. "So if you're looking for those Barry White albums or Bolshoi Ballet tickets she walked out with, you can just get in line."

Feyodov's anger flashed to puzzlement. He tore his eyes away from Anna.

"Are you saying you thought she was dead?" asked the former general.

"Didn't everybody?" Remo said blandly.

"But aren't you the men from Sinanju?"

"We are wasting time," Anna interrupted tensely.

"Time is never wasted that is used to discuss the glory that is Sinanju," Chiun scolded.

Anna's eyes never wavered. "That is General Feyodov," she explained. "The lunatic you are looking for."

The old man arched an eyebrow. "Do not presume to know what I am looking for, woman," he sniffed. "What I look for is respect and gratitude. Never finding either, I would settle for a roof over my head and a son who does not cavort with floozies. Thanks to you, the world continues to mock me on both of these counts, as well." And raising his chin in defiance, he stuffed his hands in his sleeves.

Anna exhaled frustration as she slid between Remo and Chiun. Her arm remained level, the gun aimed at Feyodov.

Behind the Russian agent, Brandy Brand was at first uncertain what to do. But since Anna seemed to have taken the lead from the two men who had somehow managed to bash their way through three seemingly impenetrable sets of doors, the FBI agent followed dutifully behind the Russian. Her gun was aimed at Feyodov and his men, but one eye remained alert to Zen Bower, who stood unmoving and frightened on the stage.

"Where is the weapon?" Anna demanded.

Feyodov ignored the question. A glint of cunning had appeared in his dark eyes.

"That is the Master of Sinanju, is it not?" the general asked Anna.

"That is not important!" Anna snapped.

Chiun gasped. "You see, Remo?" he said, his voice straining indignation. "You see how she continues to dismiss your poor aged father as irrelevant? It is happening all over again. Quick! Let us leave the trollop to her nefarious business, lest she convince you to cast me into the dark dungeon of a home for the unwanted elderly." He grabbed Remo's wrist.

Though Chiun pulled, Remo remained in place.

"Sorry, but I gotta go with Anna on this one, Little Father," he said. "Looks like Boris Badenov here has turned his boom-ray death device over to the Frostbite Falls granola set." He nodded to Zen.

Chiun's hands fell to his sides. "Of course," he said, his voice flat. "Why would I expect that you would ever take my side against this lying Russian hussy? As my heir and future Reigning Master of Sinanju, you could ask this one how he has come to know of us, perhaps to better help us advertise our services, but no. By all means worry about whatever it is *she* tells you to worry about. I only ask that once you are through doing her bidding, we may drive past the home she has cost me on our way out of town. I would like to take one longing look through the windows as the indigents and gypsies who are not me root through my cupboards and relieve themselves on my carpets."

Across the room, Feyodov's raised hands lowered an inch. "So you two still do not work for the Institute?"

"Institute?" Remo asked. "What the hell's the—?"

It was as far as he got before the explosion.

The bullet fired by Anna struck Oleg Shevtrinko hard in the shoulder. With a shocked expression, Feyodov's assistant spun halfway around before slamming solidly into the rear wall of the hall. As Oleg sank to the floor, a streak of blood staining the wall, Anna swung the gun back to Feyodov.

"Another word that is not about the Russian property you have stolen and you will be next," she said coldly.

Feyodov's hands shot back up high in the air. Any curiosity the general might have had about Remo and Chiun's current employment abruptly gave way to cowardice.

"It is here," the general volunteered quickly.

Anna's face held no emotion. "Take me to it."

Feyodov nodded sharply. Arms still high in the air, he began to step over his bleeding compatriot.

Anna had taken but a single step to follow when she felt a hand suddenly grip her arm, holding her firmly in place.

Remo. He was fooling around again. He had always constituted an audience of one for his own childish antics. He was still behind her. With the traitorous Russians standing before her, she did not dare turn to look at him.

"Remo, let go," Anna urged.

His hand never wavered. Worse, his thick wrist flexed.

The pain was so sharp, Anna sucked in a gasp of air. She didn't have time to question him before he spoke. When he did, his voice sounded different than she'd ever heard it. Almost…weak.

"Anna," Remo whispered.

The pain in her arm was white-hot. It was as if a vise had clamped hard, biting into flesh. His grip tightened. So strong was it, she nearly dropped her gun.

"Remo, you are hurting me," Anna said, wincing.

"Something…something's not right," Remo gasped.

Up ahead, Feyodov and the others had stopped dead. A spark of hope was growing stronger in the general's eyes.

Since Remo was holding on to her gun arm, Anna was forced to transfer the weapon to her free hand.

"Watch them," Anna ordered Brandy.

The FBI agent moved in front of Anna.

"Hands up!" Brandy snapped.

Some of the Russians had been wavering. At the command they dutifully lifted their arms higher.

Anna turned a wary eye on Remo. When she saw him, her pale skin blanched.

Remo looked as if he'd aged thirty years. His cheeks were sunken and his eyes were cavernous black hollows. It looked as though the life had been sucked out of him. Sapped of vitality, he had to hold on to Anna for support.

Behind Remo, the Master of Sinanju was in far worse shape. He seemed little more than an ambulatory skeleton.

Both men reeled in place.

"What's wrong?" Anna asked sharply.

"We have to go," Remo panted. *"Now."*

As he spoke, Anna felt a shuddering tickle, like ghostly fingers, across the downy hair at the back of her neck.

The sensation had been apparent for the last minute or so, but it had gotten worse in the past few seconds. It was as if some hidden switch had been flipped. And in the moment when the strange invisible touch reached its zenith, Anna Chutesov saw the impossible happen.

Remo and Chiun shot to attention. Arms snapped out, angled downward, fingers splayed. They stood like that for but an instant. Stiff, helpless and vulnerable.

As quickly as it came, it fled. And as Anna watched in shock, the life seeped visibly from the Master of Sinanju.

Chiun's fluttering eyes rolled back in their sockets. His frail old body went as limp as a wet rag, and he toppled over onto the hard floor.

Remo still stood. He reached a hand once more for Anna. This time he braced it on her shoulder for support.

"Remo, what is it?" Anna asked.

He shook his head. "Help me get Chiun," he gasped.

There was just a moment's hesitation before Anna did as she was told. Crouching, she helped drag the old man into Remo's arms. She had to pull Remo back to his feet.

There was not another word from him. Drawing on his last reserves of strength, Remo stumbled out the door, delicately cradling the lifeless body of his teacher.

Once he was gone, Anna dropped her voice low. "We must go," she whispered urgently to Brandy.

"What about them?" Brandy said, nodding across the room.

Feyodov and the Russians were growing emboldened. Hands were lowering cautiously. None had yet moved for a gun.

"There are too many of them," Anna answered. "We do not know how many more there might be. We can't win. Not now."

The FBI agent seemed reluctant to follow the orders of a Russian agent. Yet she had no other backup on the scene and half of her team was apparently down for the count.

Brandy nodded crisply.

Anna didn't find it necessary to say a word to Feyodov. Both of them understood her predicament. Whenever she was confronted with this sort of situation, she always left it up to the men to strut and preen and offer silly threats and warnings. She was content to escape with her life.

It disturbed the head of the Institute when Boris Feyodov found it unnecessary to say anything, as well. There was no bluster from the former general, no booming anger typical for a man. Just a superior smirk as she backed away.

And in that silent smile, Anna Chutesov felt new reason to fear. Guns raised, the two women slipped out the door.

As soon as they were gone, the Russians grabbed

for their own weapons. When they ran after the four intruders, they found that Remo and the others had already gotten past the second set of doors. Though damaged, they were still in place. Remo had sealed them from the outside. The Russian soldiers quickly returned to the hall.

Zen was climbing nervously down from the stage. The other council members were coming out from under the table.

"What was that all about?" Zen asked. "Those guys...what—what happened to those guys?"

In the rear of the hall, Boris Feyodov was glancing at his Swiss watch. As he suspected, Remo and Chiun's strange seizures had coincided precisely with the moment his precious particle-beam device would have been charged enough to fire.

The general looked up with only his eyes, a devilish smile on his fleshy face.

"Our secret weapon apparently boasts an interesting side effect," Boris Feyodov said knowingly.

And in his tired, silent heart he found delight in the fact that the end of the world was proving to be even more entertaining than he'd ever dreamed.

21

Cosmonaut Sergei Sagdeev's return to space had been a silent defeat.

Russia's space program was not what it had once been. For years it had been a testament to ingenuity, endurance and sheer stubbornness. The man was always less important than the mission. Back in the late 1980s, Sergei had been one of the cosmonauts selected to test the limits of how much time was humanly possible to spend in space.

Sergei had stayed aboard the space station Mir for just over three months. Ninety-eight agonizingly long days.

An eternity away from his native Yaroslavl on the banks of the Volga. Away from his wife, his little daughter.

Away from Earth.

At first back then, the planet had seemed enormous, stretching wide beneath the fifty-two-degree inclination of the cramped station. As his time in space grew however, the planet seemed to shrink. With each passing day it grew smaller and smaller until it was little more than an insignificant speck against the greater backdrop of eternity.

Everyone he knew, everyone he would ever know. All the great figures both present and past had lived and would die on that same insignificant speck. Thanks to his time on Mir, Sergei Sagdeev had returned to Earth with a perspective on Man's place in the cosmos few people could appreciate. Sergei was one of the few human beings on the planet to understand just how tiny and worthless he truly was.

When he finally made it back home after his long ordeal, Sergei vowed never to return to space. His future work with the space program would be done only with solid ground beneath his feet. He had no desire to remind himself just how inconsequential he was.

It was a promise he could not keep.

The Russian space program had been flailing for a number of years. There was serious talk of scrapping it altogether. With no other training in a disaster of an economy, Sergei had begun to worry about his future job prospects. Things had looked bleak for some time when a private Netherlands-based corporation stepped in to help finance some of Russia's space program. In exchange for funding, they wanted the right to use the dilapidated old Mir station for commercial ventures. And they needed experienced cosmonauts to help them get their plans off the ground.

And so, in spite of the promise he'd made to himself, Sergei Sagdeev had, at the ripe old age of forty-seven, returned reluctantly to the endless black void of space.

This time he would be on Mir for only three

weeks. Some minor work needed to be done on the dust collectors, and a few of the old data systems were getting an upgrade. A MirCorp rocket was on its way with fresh parts and supplies. It would be docking in minutes.

Alone in the crew habitat at the far end of the orbiting station as he watched the slivery needle that was the approaching rocket, Sergei pressed his hand against the cool insulated window. As he sat so far above the blue-green speck that was Earth, his heart was sick with longing.

He knew the actual distance from Mir to his small home. 360 kilometers. More than 220 miles.

The window fogged a silhouette of his hand.

Windows. The more primitive Salyut series of stations had none. Here they were supposed to be an improvement. Sergei would have preferred no windows at all.

Through the thick pane he continued to watch the approaching Dutch rocket. His heart was heavy.

In Mir's tiny dining quarters, Sergei listened to his commander's gruff voice over the station speakers.

"Dyevit. Vohsim. Syem. Shest…"

The speaker system was old and muffled.

As the small manned rocket closed to dock, the Russian voice continued to count down.

Sergei watched the rocket float to a crawl. Unfiltered sunlight sparkled off the gleaming white surface.

He hardly heard the command for the rocket to use the docking port at station control.

A single tear rolled down the cheek of the lonely, insignificant cosmonaut.

It was the sight of the rocket that did it. It came from *there*. From home.

He would be going back soon. And this time nothing would compel him to return to this cold, eternal hell.

Through a window in the nose cone of the approaching rocket he saw one of the two-man team. The cosmonaut's white gloves were moving across the control panel.

Sniffling, Sergei hardly had time to focus on the shifting gloves when the rocket vanished from sight.

It was impossible. One instant it was there; the next it was gone.

In the tiny galley the disappearance of the rocket had barely registered as an anomalous flash on the optic nerve of the seated Russian before it reappeared.

It was huge and white and blotted out the planet below. It flew sideways, faster than any propulsion system yet devised could have delivered it. And, faster than the mind of Sergei Sagdeev could reconcile what had happened, the runaway rocket collided with Mir.

Inside the fragile shell, Sergei hit the floor of the dining area in a shower of food trays and equipment. With a groan a stress-fracture cracked up the hull, splitting wide the side of the buckling station.

On his back, Sergei finally saw the face of the gloved cosmonaut who had been working the rocket's controls.

The man's eyes were wide and glassy. The rocket had been thrust forward at such a great velocity that his skull had cracked open against the headrest of his seat. Flecks of blown-out red spotted the interior of his helmet visor.

Sergei saw all this in an instant. And in the same instant he knew that the only way he could see the man so clearly was because the rocket had pierced the delicate shell of the orbiting station.

In it came, huge and heavy. Splitting the station and blasting anything that wasn't strapped down out into the cold void of space. One of those things was cosmonaut Sergei Sagdeev.

Mir creaked and vibrated and burst into two fat, jagged halves. The sections spiraled away, propelled by the same invisible force that had overwhelmed the supplies rocket.

Silent screams issued from the pressurized command module.

And through all the panic and destruction that started in space but would end on the Earth below, a lone cosmonaut floated off into peaceful, eternal repose.

An insignificant speck in an endless black sea.

22

With sirens blaring and lights flashing, the motorcade sped through the frozen streets of Moscow toward the Kremlin.

Traffic pulled quickly to the side of the street, allowing the police cars to pass. In the midst of the official automobiles was one unmarked car. In the back seat of the black bulletproof sedan, Director Pavel Zatsyrko of the SVR clutched a manila envelope tightly in one hand.

A hasty call over the radio while they were still a mile away opened the old Spassky Gate. The SVR director did not have time to wait in line to be cleared through the gates.

Barely slowing, the motorcade raced inside the Kremlin. His car hadn't even come to a complete stop before Zatsyrko jumped from the back. Envelope in hand, he raced up the steps to the Grand Kremlin Palace. His shoes clicked urgently on the polished floor as he ran to the gilded door of the special conference room. He found the president of Russia waiting for him at a large table inside.

The president was a slight, balding man with clear eyes and a frowning face. He did not rise when the perspiring SVR head entered the room. At five feet four inches, Russia's leader was self-conscious about his height. To mask his diminutive stature, he stood only when absolutely necessary.

The men had been associates years ago. They had worked together back in the days of the KGB. Both men had been stationed in East Germany during those terrible days just before the Berlin Wall trembled and fell.

"What is so urgent that we could not speak on the phone?" the president asked his old comrade.

Russia's leader wore a grim expression. He had only just learned of the destruction of Mir.

So far there was no explanation among the world's scientific community for all that had been happening in space. Some were saying that a cloud of stellar dust particles had intersected with Earth, wreaking havoc on all orbiting devices. Others blamed increased solar activity. In spite of Anna Chutesov's opinion on the subject, the president of Russia still hoped that one of these theories was true.

Pavel Zatsyrko slapped the envelope down in front of the seated president.

"This was just received at my office," the SVR man said breathlessly. "I dared not show it to anyone else."

The envelope was light. When the president tore it open, he found just a single sheet of white paper. As soon as he pulled it out he saw that it was a printed copy of an e-mail.

When he read who had sent the note, the color

drained from the president's face. The line just below today's date read boris   feyodov@barkley.org.
His worried eyes darted across the lines of text.

Greetings, Little One:
By now you are aware that your space station
has been destroyed. The weapon used to accomplish this is yours, but it is currently deployed on the West Coast of the United States.
Since your precious Institute director is otherwise occupied at the moment and cannot do
your thinking for you, I volunteer my services
to help you sort through the predicament this
presents to you.
    Since it is no longer in your country, the
Americans can conceivably be blamed for what
has happened to Mir. Retaliation in this case
could be justified. Of course, since it is a rogue
group and not the American government itself
in possession of the weapon, such an attack
would be seen by Washington as unprovoked.
They in turn will retaliate. To further complicate your dilemma, I have already sent word to
the American president that it is a Russian
weapon on his soil that is responsible for the
random destruction of the past few days. I have
also mentioned that the secret test conducted
fifteen years ago from Sary Shagan was done
with this very weapon by order of the then-
general secretary. Given this information, he
might well attack you first. After all, the Americans prize their toys. And this event, while

many years old, could be construed as an act of war. Of course, passions have cooled on both sides, so the urge to retaliate might not be with the Americans as it would have been immediately following the event. Given this fact, time could work in your favor. That is, assuming you make your decision quickly.

That is my analysis of the situation. I am terribly sorry that I cannot help you reach a decision. Perhaps we can use this as a test, to see if you are big enough for the challenges of grown men.

I am curious to see if the embers still burn on either side as once they did.

Yours,
Boris Feyodov

When he was finished reading, the president crumpled the paper into a tight ball. Before the conference table, Pavel Zatsyrko studied the Russian leader's face. It was clear to Pavel that this had not been a wasted trip.

"I was not sure if it was as urgent as it sounds," the SVR head said. "Given his criminal ties, as well as his history, Feyodov's name was automatically flagged by our e-mail system. However, I do not know what this Institute is."

The SVR head was fishing for information.

The president didn't answer. He was staring blankly at the distant wall, his small hand still clutched tightly to the wadded scrap of paper.

"I do not know if it is connected," Zatsyrko ventured after a moment of awkward silence, "but one of my squads has gone missing. They were inactive now, but had been deployed on American soil at one time. According to my information, they left the country early yesterday with the highest security clearance. It superseded even my own."

The president finally looked up. His pale eyes held not a glint of emotion.

"Go," he ordered, his voice thick.

Pavel Zatsyrko hesitated. "What of Feyodov? These claims he has made are obviously outrageous, but surely you want me to send a team to retrieve him."

His subordinate's persistence raised a flash of the Russian leader's famous temper.

"Listen carefully, for this is an order that you will not disobey," the Russian president said coldly. "You will send no one after General Feyodov, is that clear?"

Coming to attention, Pavel Zatsyrko nodded sharply. No more words were necessary. Feeling the penetrating gaze of the president, the SVR head let the matter drop. The director turned and hurried from the conference room.

After Zatsyrko was gone, the president of Russia put the tight knot of computer paper on the table, smoothing it flat with the side of his hand. He scanned Feyodov's words again.

The former general was not a madman; that was certain. His analysis of the situation was essentially correct. No, Boris Feyodov was just a man. According to a months-old report from Anna Chutesov,

Feyodov was driven by the hatred of his own frailties. The Institute director had concluded that his self-loathing ran so deep there were no limits to what he would do to end his personal purgatory. And now it seemed she had been correct. As usual.

For almost two decades, in times of crisis Russia's leaders, both Communist and democratically elected alike, had relied on the intellect and resourcefulness of Anna Chutesov. He prayed that he would not be the last.

The president put his face in his hands. One way or another this situation would be resolved. With any luck it would not involve ICBMs dropping from the sky.

23

Mark Howard had no problem finding an office in Folcroft's administrative wing. Virtually every room on the second-floor hall other than Smith's was empty. Only a half dozen were connected with the sanitarium's routine business. For security's sake, Mark was put far away from those offices connected to the Folcroft Sanitarium cover.

The room Smith's secretary had found for him was so small he had to back tight against the lone window to allow the two struggling orderlies to carry in his new desk.

Of course in this case "new" was relative. While it was new to him, the desk was as old as the hills. Before being ordered up to this room, it had been collecting dust somewhere in a far corner of Folcroft's basement.

"Where do you want it?" one of the men asked.

Although it was clear to Mark the orderly wasn't joking, he might as well have been. There was really no choice. The room was so narrow the desk could only fit lengthwise. If he wanted it to face the other way, they would have had to take it back out into the hallway to turn it.

"Right here is fine," Mark said.

The two men placed the desk on the vinyl tile floor.

A quilted tarpaulin snugly enclosed the desk. Hand swipes were visible where the movers had brushed much of the dust away downstairs. Once they set their cargo down, the orderlies unsnapped the tarp and pulled it free.

A plastic sheet held to the desktop by packing string crinkled as the tarp was removed. Tape had specifically not been used to secure the plastic, lest upon removal it damage the oak veneer. After the string was cut, the plastic was rolled tightly, then folded inside the tarp. Holding the bundle of plastic and dust, the two orderlies left the room.

Mark quickly shut and locked the door.

In spite of the careful packaging, there was still grime on the worn oaken desk. He'd clean it later.

He picked up an old wooden chair from the corner, feeling a twinge of pain beneath his wrist cast as he did so. He was forced to jimmy the chair in between desk and wall.

From the footwell Mark hefted the desk on one shoulder, ever mindful of his aching wrist. With searching fingers he found the terminal wire that ran up the hollow interior of the right leg. It had been folded up on itself and fastened in place with gummy yellow tape.

Mark pulled the wire free, plugging it into the phone jack in the wall behind the desk. Settling into his chair, he found a concealed stud under the desk's lip. When he depressed it a computer screen that had been hidden beneath the surface of the desk rose into view, keyboard unfolding.

The old desk had once belonged to Dr. Smith. The CURE director had kept it for reasons known only to himself. Mark suspected that it was for emergency backup if his current desk computer ever failed him. He hadn't known Smith for a full day yet and already he knew the gray old man had not a sentimental bone in his body.

Before abandoning the desk to its lonely basement corner, Smith had removed all incriminating data from the system. Except for its most basic programming, the hard drive had been wiped clean immediately after Smith had switched over to his current desk six years ago. Not that it mattered. As soon as he'd plugged into the wall receptacle, the desktop computer seemed to take on a life of its own.

The screen lit up in user-friendly blue and the phrase "Download in progress. Please wait..." appeared in white letters in the upper left-hand corner.

Smith had instructed CURE's basement mainframes to automatically install everything Mark would need on his office computer. It took twenty minutes. Much shorter than should have been necessary, but an agonizingly long time for the young man seated behind the desk.

Once the download was complete, the screen blinked from blue to white. A window automatically popped up on the monitor. Contained within the box was a short paragraph.

At first Mark assumed he had been sent orders

from Dr. Smith. But when he started to read the words Mark Howard felt a chill grip his spine.

"We, the people of the United States, in order to form a more perfect Union, establish justice, insure domestic tranquility…"

The preamble to the Constitution. Just a few short lines, reprinted in its entirely. Mark carefully read the familiar words. And for the first time in his life they became more than just words on a page.

After reading the preamble, Howard quietly closed out the window. Jaw firmly set, he began sifting through the news digests automatically collected by the CURE mainframes.

He was stunned when he saw the top story. He had been so busy he hadn't heard the news until now.

By now the destruction of the Russian space station Mir was half an hour old. Mark quickly scanned the story.

Apparently, a Russian-manned Dutch rocket had lost control in space, slamming into Mir. Split in two, half the station was missing after the accident. The other section had spiraled into a higher planetary orbit.

A link at the bottom of the story connected to a related article. Mark's eye had not even scanned the entire story before his questing fingers accessed the link. He blinked in surprise as the computer switched to the next page.

This was just part of an ability he possessed that Mark had never fully understood. His fingers sometimes seemed to know more than his mind and helped steer him in the right direction. It was as if some unconscious part of his brain was always three steps ahead of his conscious self. He called this intuitive sense the Feeling, although he kept both ability and name to himself. An abnormal sixth sense wasn't an easy thing to explain to friends and family.

The second story was a wire report that had been updated eight times over the past twenty-four hours. In addition to Mir, there was another great ongoing catastrophe in space. Two dozen satellites had been rendered inoperable in the past day. The current speculation blamed a hail of meteors so small they were barely larger than dust fragments.

Mark had heard about the satellites. However, he had no idea that the number damaged had gotten so high.

At the bottom of the article, Zipp Codwin, the director of NASA, was quoted as saying, "We would already have the means to combat this terrible problem of killer stellar dust agents if only we had the funding to do so. According to NASA's own Director for the Eradication of Cosmic Dust and Interplanetary Space Soot, lack of proper funding has made us ripe for this kind of extra-earthly Mars dirt attack."

Howard frowned. Such talk was typical for NASA these days. Every problem existed due to lack of funding.

He closed out the story. When he leaned back in his chair his head bumped the wall. He automatically grabbed at his head, whacking his cast against the wall.

"Perfect," he groaned.

More carefully he pressed his head against the wall. He rested there for a moment, the elbow of his cast arm braced gingerly against his good wrist.

The Feeling was telling him there was more to what was going on in space than an errant cloud of dust. Something far bigger was at work.

After a moment's consideration he shut down his computer. As the monitor was slipping back into its hidden recess, he was squirming out from behind the desk.

Mark stepped into the hallway. When he entered Smith's office suite a few moments later, the Folcroft director's secretary looked up from her work.

"Oh, hello," she said uncertainly.

Mrs. Mikulka still seemed unsure what to make of this young man who in less than twenty-four hours had somehow gone from being a simple medical-supplies salesman to associate director of Folcroft Sanitarium.

"I need to see Dr. Smith," Howard said.

"Of course," Mrs. Mikulka nodded.

She started to buzz him inside, but then hesitated.

So many young men these days were so impolite. Keenan, her eldest son, had been like that. But here was a man unlike the rest of his generation. He had been so nice the previous day after waiting for hours. She had been thinking that this was part of some plan and that Dr. Smith had been testing him somehow. Whatever the case, right then and there Eileen Mikulka decided that she would do her level best to make this young man feel welcome at Folcroft. As

Mark passed her desk, she offered a knowing, motherly smile.

"He can be a bit intimidating," she confided in a whisper. "Very much a creature of habit. But don't let that bother you. Just as long as you don't vary from the routine he establishes for you, you'll do fine here."

Advice delivered, she pressed the intercom buzzer.

When Mark entered the inner office, Smith was just picking up the ringing White House phone. As the intercom buzzed and the door popped open, Smith froze. The old man's gaunt face was perturbed as he looked up at the intruder.

Seeing it was Howard, he frowned.

Smith's first impulse had always been to hide anything related to CURE from all prying eyes. It was axiomatic that this would include phone conversations with the President of the United States. It would take some time for him to get used to the fact that he was now going to have to include someone else in matters regarding the secret agency.

"Please take a seat," Smith instructed. With an arthritic hand he gestured to the chair in front of his desk.

As Mark sat, Smith answered the red phone.

"Yes, Mr. President," the CURE director said tersely.

"We just got another e-mail, Smith," the President's worried voice announced. "This one's from some Russian by the name of Feyodov. My people here say he was a general in Chechnya a while back.''

''That is correct, although he is no longer connected to the military,'' Smith said. ''He is currently involved in his country's black market. As far as we have been able to ascertain, it is he who is responsible for smuggling the particle-beam weapon to California.''

''Sounds like he's not content with using satellites for target practice,'' the President said grimly. ''Looks like now he's got his heart set on World War III.''

Smith's chair squeaked softly. ''Please explain,'' the CURE director said, his voice perfectly level.

Even as he was asking the President to elaborate, Smith's nimble fingers attacked his keyboard in order to access the White House e-mail system.

In programming the CURE mainframes to sort through any e-mail related to Barkley, California, or its council, Smith had neglected to list Boris Feyodov's name, assuming the Russian was merely a behind-the-scenes employee.

''It sounds like this Feyodov character has staged a coup from those secession kooks,'' the President said. ''He says that he's got control of the weapon now, and that he's going to keep using it no matter what we do. And that's not all. He also claims the Russians tested the thing once years ago.''

Smith's hands stopped dead over his glowing keyboard. As he read the note he'd just accessed, his own shocked face was reflected in the desk's gleaming black surface.

"My God," Smith croaked.

Sitting in his hard-backed chair, Mark Howard's face darkened at Smith's tone. The old man's skin abruptly went from sickly gray to deathly white.

"I take it you've just seen the letter," the President said dryly.

Smith was trying to absorb what he'd just read. Already the gears of his mind were turning at rapid speed.

"Feyodov is claiming that the Russians destroyed the space shuttle *Challenger,*" Smith stated.

Across the desk, Mark Howard's eyes grew wide. He shot to his feet and hurried around the desk. Looking over Smith's shoulder at the buried monitor, he scanned the note. Although the CURE director was uncomfortable with Howard's presence, he was too shocked to shoo the young man away.

"It sounds crazy, I know," the President admitted.

"No," Smith said, thinking rapidly. "No, it doesn't." The initial surprise was wearing off. "There were rumors of Russian involvement even at the time. Most thinking people dismissed the notion as ludicrous. But given what we now know, it is not so great a logical leap to take."

Howard had just finished reading Feyodov's letter. Knuckles leaning on the edge of Smith's desk, he glanced down at the seated CURE director. His youthful face was grim.

With a single troubled glance at Mark Howard, Smith leaned back in his chair.

"Given the current state of the Russian economy,

it would be impossible for them to develop such a device now," Smith continued. "Since we know one exists, we must conclude that it was built prior to the collapse of the Iron Curtain. As he mentioned in his letter, Feyodov was in command of the base where such a weapon would have logically been developed. This latter fact has been independently confirmed by my people. At the time in question the Soviet Union was on the verge of military, social and economic collapse. Having built such a device they might have—in a desperate hour—decided to test it on a high-profile enemy target. They would not have differentiated between civilian or military."

"But he's claiming the former president of Russia authorized this," America's chief executive insisted.

"There were still gulags in 1986, Mr. President," Smith said somberly. "If Feyodov acted without authority in this matter, he would have been punished. Instead he retained his commission in the army well into the following decade. If his claim is true, we can assume that he received approval for this at the highest level of their government."

The President's voice grew soft. "I wish he *had* acted on his own," he said. "The Russians would have dealt with him back then instead of dumping this problem on us." He sighed. "He's claiming he sent an e-mail about this to the Russian president, too. He's trying to stir the pot, Smith."

"That is likely the case," Smith agreed. "If there is such a letter, I will obtain a translation of it. Perhaps he never sent one, and this is all part of some elaborate bluff."

"He sounds pretty serious to me," the President said. "He says he just told the Russian president to nuke California to destroy all evidence of the weapon."

"Be warned that if this is the course of action they decide to take, it would almost certainly not just be limited to California, sir," Smith said, with a clinical detachment that made it sound as if he were discussing the following day's weather forecast. "If the Russians were to launch a first strike against us, I suspect it would be an all-out assault. Given those circumstances, we would have to respond in kind."

The President was quiet for a long moment. When he finally broke the silence, his voice was soft.

"Can this really be happening?" he said, more to himself than to Smith.

"It is," Smith said crisply. "For now we must do all we can to prevent the worst from coming to pass."

There was a deep sigh from the other end of the line.

"Guess the honeymoon is over," the President said. "I'd better send the Army in to Barkley."

"I would ask you once more to refrain from doing so," Smith said. "My men are in Barkley. Given the havoc being wrought on the global satellite network, I have not been in contact with them for several hours, but I am confident in their ability to handle this situation."

The President didn't seem convinced. "What about the Russian end? Maybe I should call their president."

"Unwise at the present time," Smith said. "As recently as last year they were threatening a nuclear strike. You no doubt recall the rather cryptic warning from their foreign minister when your predecessor declared a revived interest in creating a ballistic missile defense system for the United States. Rather than confess, the Russian president would certainly deny any involvement with the weapon. And cornered, guilty men have a tendency to lash out. For him to do so could have devastating global implications. At so delicate a time silence might be our greatest ally."

The President considered for a long time. "Still seems like we should do something," he said at last.

Smith's spine stiffened. "We are," he said in a certain tone. "Our best is on the ground. Now if you will excuse me, Mr. President, I have work to do."

The President's response was subdued. "Good luck, Smith," America's chief executive said. "To *all* of us."

The President's final words ringing in his ears, Smith gently replaced the red receiver.

"I guess I no longer need to tell you I think there's something bigger than a dust shower trashing all these satellites," Mark Howard said quietly as the CURE director closed his lower desk drawer.

Smith nodded. "That is the explanation that has garnered the most attention. With any luck the general public will never find out the truth."

"And sending the Army in might let *The New York Times* know something's up in Barkley," Howard said simply. Still standing beside Smith's chair, he was rereading the e-mail Boris Feyodov had sent to the White House.

Smith was surprised by the young man's deduction. It was one he had not mentioned to the President.

The greatest challenge for the CURE director had always been keeping a lid on various crises. Complete ignorance of events was always preferable, but sometimes problems were so big they could not be contained. And to have every dire predicament to face the nation suddenly and mysteriously solve itself would point to something unknown operating behind the scenes. Therefore, for those events that could not be concealed from the public, cover explanations like the one now being posited for the damage in space had always been acceptable to and, at times, encouraged by the CURE director.

Beside Smith, Howard was just finishing Feyodov's note.

"Sounds like this guy is the real deal, Dr. Smith," Howard concluded bleakly. "You said he and the particle weapon are in Barkley, California, right?"

Smith fidgeted uncomfortably. "Yes," he said. "At least there is no record of him leaving the country. Of course, he could have used an alias and had someone else send his messages from the Barkley address at a preordained time."

Howard straightened. "If he's sticking around town, he's running a big risk telling the Russians all this. He must know they'll be itching to erase their involvement. If he's still there I'd say the guy's got a death wish."

"I concur," Smith said. "Now, please excuse me. Given the circumstances I have much to do."

"I know it's my first day and all, but I *am* supposed to be your assistant," Mark pointed out. "Isn't there anything I can help with?"

Smith hesitated.

The CURE director was still reluctant to let Howard in on all the details of the organization. As it was, he had given his new assistant access to only a fraction of the CURE database. In spite of the events taking place in California, Smith had spent a chunk of the morning doing a hurried background check on the young man. So far, Howard seemed to be an acceptable candidate for CURE. Still, presidential appointment or not, it was far too soon to open the organization wide to an outsider. Harold Smith always erred on the side of caution.

"It isn't wise at the moment to involve you deeply," Smith said carefully. "I would prefer a calmer atmosphere to get you acclimated to your duties here. For now I will handle this situation as I have in the past."

"It's your call," Howard nodded. "Still, since you haven't given me any responsibilities yet, I'll keep an eye open from my office. Maybe I'll catch something you miss."

Mark was heading across the room when he suddenly paused. Taking a deep breath, he turned.

"You said to the President that you've got some field operatives on the scene," he exhaled. "I should tell you that I think I met them already."

Across the room, Smith had been leaning back

over his computer. Glancing up, he raised a dubious eyebrow. "That is unlikely," he assured the young man.

"It was a couple of weeks ago during that Raffair business," Howard pressed. "I was still with the CIA. I bumped into them in Miami. That's where I got this." He raised his arm. The cast jutted from his sleeve, wrapping around his hand between thumb and forefinger. "An old Asian and a young Caucasian, maybe a few years older than me."

Smith was stunned by Howard's words. The young man had indeed encountered Remo and Chiun.

The CURE director's uneasiness with the topic was evident. With everything else that was going on, he had not given much thought to how he would introduce this young man to Remo and Chiun. Like most things involving the two Sinanju Masters, he doubted it would go easily.

"You will meet them soon enough," the older man said, clearing his throat.

"I figured," Howard said knowingly. "All you've got are those two guys. You couldn't have squads of men roaming the country without someone finding out. Especially men like them. Oh, and for the sake of full disclosure, I should mention that we sort of met once, too, Dr. Smith. A while back you called Langley looking for an analyst to check some satellite data for you. You needed to find a missing boat in the Atlantic. I was the guy you spoke to."

It finally hit Smith. He thought he had recognized Howard's name when he read Mrs. Mikulka's Post-it note the previous day. He had dismissed it as a common-sounding name. Now he realized he had indeed heard it before. He was surprised it had not occurred to him during the background search he had conducted earlier in the day.

Smith's eyes were flat behind his clear glasses. "Did the President suggest it might be me, or did you surmise this on your own?" he asked evenly.

"I figured it out myself," Howard said.

"You did not share this information with anyone?"

Howard gave a lopsided smile. "No way," he promised, shaking his head. "I'm not like this Feyodov. I don't have a death wish, Dr. Smith. I just thought you should know."

Smith pursed his gray lips. "Your candor is appreciated," he said. "That will be all."

Nodding, Howard turned once more. His hand had closed around the doorknob when he glanced back one last time.

Smith was hunched over his computer. The glowing screen was reflected in his owlish glasses.

"One more thing," the new assistant CURE director said. For the first time there was hesitation in his youthful voice. "I think there's something else at play here. It's somehow connected to this whole satellite thing. It's not really big. Something small, behind the scenes. But it's the catalyst that set all the rest of this in motion."

Smith's gray face betrayed minor intrigue. "What makes you say that?" he asked, his tone curious.

Mark bit the inside of his cheek. "I don't know," he said, shrugging. "Just a feeling, I guess."

Before he could be pressed further on his hunch, the young man slipped quickly from the Spartan office. The door closed behind him with a soft click.

24

It was sleep without dreams. A great, oppressive blanket of black numbness the likes of which he had not experienced since before his earliest Sinanju training. When the darkness finally fled for Remo Williams, it was replaced by a blob of amorphous white and a nerve-numbing weariness that leached deep into bone. An eternity passed as the clot of shapeless white resolved into a more familiar environment.

He was in a room. By the looks of it, it was some sort of flophouse. A grimy lava lamp sat on a warped bureau. Behind it, a faded Jerry Garcia poster concealed tears in the fuzzy striped wallpaper.

Remo was in a bed.

No. As his senses returned, he realized it was lower than a bed. It couldn't have been more than just a mattress on the floor. A foul mustiness created by thirty years of human odors flooded up from the squeaky springs.

At first he had no idea how he had come to be there. It struck him all at once.

Something had happened back at the Barkley city hall. Something he had never encountered before. It was as if the air itself had drained the life from him. From him and—

His heart stopped.

He couldn't raise his head to look around the room.

"Chiun," Remo croaked. Though he tried to call out, his voice was barely a whisper.

When last he saw him the old Korean appeared to be dead. At least Remo had never seen him so drained of life.

Once the enervating sensation struck, Remo's own system had gone so haywire he couldn't sense any life signs from his teacher. He had drawn on reserves he did not have just to get them both to safety. After he had barred the door to prevent the Russians from following, he had collapsed.

There was no memory after that. No knowledge of how he had gotten from there to here. No way of knowing if his adopted father was...

"Chiun," he called again, his voice louder this time.

A concerned face appeared above him, blocking out the cracked, water-damaged plaster ceiling.

For an instant he thought he was dreaming. Then he remembered that Anna Chutesov had come back from the dead.

The Russian agent gazed down on him as she had in days long forgotten, a vision of beauty from another time.

"How's Chiun?" Remo croaked weakly. He braced himself for the worst.

When the reply he dreaded came, he felt the world drop out from beneath him.

"He's gone," Anna replied simply.

The words were like a dagger in his heart. Blood pounded through his veins, ringing in his ears.

Remo closed his eyes, too exhausted for tears.

His worst fear of the past few months had come to pass.

On the trip to Africa during which he had inadvertently taunted the gods into leveling a lifetime curse of Master's disease, Remo had been visited by the spirit of Chiun's son.

The little Korean boy with the sad eyes had prophesied a future of hardship for Remo. Ever since that time, Remo had harbored the secret fear that the Master of Sinanju himself would be part of the suffering he was destined to endure.

Lying in that squalid room, he had never felt so alone.

The loss of his home was nothing to him now. Everything else in life was dross. The one thing that mattered to him more than anything else in the world was gone.

"I have to see him," Remo said.

There was strength now in his hollow voice. Already he was wondering in which of his fourteen steamer trunks the Master of Sinanju kept his funeral robes.

Anna was sitting on a stool next to the mattress. She seemed unmoved by his loss.

"In a little while," she said as she squeezed out a damp facecloth into a cracked antique chamber pot on the floor. "You have been unconscious for hours. You need rest."

When she leaned over to wipe his brow, Remo grabbed her wrist, holding tight.

"I need to see him *now*," he insisted.

"You cannot," she said. "He and the FBI woman went out for food. They won't be back for a while yet."

A weight lifted from Remo's chest.

"He's alive?" he asked, scarcely daring to speak the words aloud. Her response sent his soul soaring.

"Of course," Anna said. When she realized what he had assumed, a spark of weary mirth came to her eyes. "I know he is like a father to you, Remo, but let us be realistic. If he ever did die, where would he go? Heaven does not want him and hell would not take him. May I have my arm back now?"

His heart singing with joy, Remo released her wrist. When he closed his tired eyes this time, they burned with invisible tears.

"Don't be too sure Chiun won't be the big man on campus of the afterlife," he muttered, trying to hide his great relief from Anna. "Most of the Masters of Sinanju I've met have been even bigger pains in the ass than he is."

There was a sudden trip in her voice. "There are other Masters of Sinanju?" she asked. "It was my understanding that the two of you were the only living practitioners of your martial art." The words sounded almost too casual.

Curious, Remo opened his red eyes.

Her face was etched in stone. Sitting on her stool,

holding her soggy facecloth, she seemed utterly indifferent to his interest. There was no visible reason to think she was making anything more than idle conversation.

"Long story," He sighed. "We're the only two alive. Well, the only two alive if you don't count the psycho-coma one who wants to kill us. Which I didn't for a long time until two days ago." His head sank back tiredly into the grimy mattress. "Ever wish you could take a vacation from living such an interesting life?"

"My life has not met your definition of interesting for many years," Anna replied. "My last active field mission was the one we shared. If not for the recklessness and avarice of the fool Feyodov, I would have happily lived out the rest of my life in anonymity."

"Yeah, renegade Russian generals with stolen doomsday devices do have a tendency to piss out the candles on the birthday cake." Remo struggled to his elbows. "How was Chiun when he left?"

"As usual he was concerned about you," Anna replied. "But physically he seemed fine."

"Really?" Remo said. His face clouded. He felt as if he'd been through the wringer. And Chiun was over one hundred years old. "I'm never gonna live this down," he sighed.

Anna understood his meaning.

"If you are worried that you should be more resilient, you need not be," she said. "You forced yourself to fight the neural disruption while Chiun did not. In fact, I doubt he *could* have at his age. He succumbed quickly and his body shut down, thus sparing him the effects of prolonged exposure.''

"Okay, I actually got the end of that," Remo said. "But what was that neural diddle-daddle you parked out front?"

"Your special training has rewritten your entire nervous system to a heightened degree," Anna explained. "You see, feel and hear better than the average human. For lack of a better explanation, your senses are tuned to the harmonics of your surroundings, absorbing the vibrations of your whole environment.''

"If this is going somewhere that's gonna make my head hurt more, I'm lying down," Remo exhaled. He pulled his elbows away, dropping flat on his back.

"It might," Anna said somberly. Her face was grave. "The weapon gathers protons from its surroundings during its charging phase. When it is fired, the protons are expelled in a particle beam, the energy from which disrupts the environment within a limited radius. Normal people within this field feel it as no more than a dissipating electrical charge. Apparently you and Chiun are affected more greatly. And since it is being used continuously now, the air around it would be polluted to someone with your skills.''

"Makes storming the Bastille kind of hairy for us."

"I would say next to impossible," Anna suggested. "After you collapsed it was all we could do to get the two of you to my car. Fortunately, Feyodov has limited forces in this town. We were able to get you to safety in this boardinghouse. However, they are doubtless looking for us. It is just a matter of time before we are found.''

"Not a problem," Remo said. He pushed up to a sitting position. His strength was flooding back. "We're outta here."

Anna seemed surprised. "You are not leaving?"

"You bet, baby," Remo said, swinging his legs over the edge of the mattress. "It's time to call in the marines. Or the Air Force. That portable-beam whatsit must be near the city hall somewhere. I'll get on the horn to Smitty and have him send a couple of bombers to boil their bong water."

"The phones do not work," Anna argued. "Your communications network is failing." She jabbed a thumb to the corner where an old black-and-white Magnavox TV sat on an overturned wicker basket. "I saw on the television that the remaining satellites have been overwhelmed by the demand. It could take you hours to get through, if ever. The damage they will cause between now and then is incalculable."

Remo sighed deeply. "Swell," he groused. "Wait a minute. The phone's out but the TV's working?"

"Just a few channels," Anna explained. "I was watching the network that was running the stupid comedian fund-raiser."

"Home Ticket Booth is still on?" Remo frowned.

Anna shook her head. "That does not matter," she dismissed. "What matters is that they have been covering the events taking place in space."

"What do you mean?" Remo interrupted. "Covering as in 'covering the news' covering?"

"Yes," Anna said impatiently. "Is that not what they do?"

"No, actually," Remo answered. "They pretty much just do movies. One good one on Saturday night, and then six days and twenty-two hours of *Earnest Licks a Lamppost* broken up by a half hour *Making of Earnest Licks a Lamppost* documentary midweek."

"Well, they are doing news now and it is not good," Anna said. "Feyodov has let his idiot employers destroy the Mir space station." Her expression was deadly serious.

Remo's brow furrowed. "So what?" he said. "Didn't you people abandon that floating Tinker Toy?"

"Only for a time," Anna said grimly. "It is back in service now. Or rather *was*. There were six cosmonauts on or near Mir at the time of the attack. Two that were on a capsule scheduled to dock with the station are presumed dead, as is one who was in the crew quarters. The other three are trapped in the command module. It is unlikely that a rescue effort can be mounted by my country in time to save them."

Remo tapped a thoughtful finger on the threadbare edge of the mattress. "Don't wanna seem like the coldhearted bastard that I am, but whoop-de-do. You're the clowns who gave General Feel-you-up a fistful of rubles and a pat on the fanny before setting him loose on the white elephant table at the Cold War carnival.''

Anna's eyes pleaded understanding. ''Don't you see, Remo?'' she asked. ''This attack has come from America. My government *knows* that. It does not matter who is in control of the weapon or whether Washington even knows of its existence. Up until now the random attacks have largely been against American technology, since America dominates space. If my nation begins to suffer losses as yours already has, it will not long tolerate them.''

''Hold the phone. Are you actually saying those borscht-slurpers in Moscow would nuke us because they let one of their own jerkwad generals swipe the only hunk of hardware they ever built that works?''

Still sitting on her stool, Anna placed her hands firmly on her knees.

''These are the same men in charge who for seventy years claimed the fruits of the Revolution were always around the next corner, this while people were starving in the streets and slave laborers were being forced to erect fences to keep the entire population from fleeing. You tell me, Remo, what they will do.''

Remo's face sagged and his shoulders slumped. ''This is all your fault, you know,'' he muttered. ''If you just had the decency to stay dead like a normal person, none of this would be happening.''

He had no way of knowing how true his words were. Eyes downcast, he studied the floor.

As he stared at the space between his loafers, Anna reached out absently, brushing a short lock of dark hair off his forehead. It was a casual movement, more an impulse stirred by memory than a conscious thing. The instant she realized what she was doing she pulled her hand away.

"I'm—" she started to say. Her jaw clenched. "You do not need this anymore." Flustered, she picked up the old porcelain bowl, taking it over to the bureau.

Remo watched her for an uncomfortable moment.

Although just shy of her fortieth birthday, she looked much the same as she had when he'd known her. Her hair was a little shorter, and there was a faint crinkling at the edges of her eyes. But her beauty was timeless.

"I'm not wearing a ring because I never got married," he announced all at once. His tone was soft.

Anna had wrung out the facecloth and was hanging it over the lava lamp to dry.

"Really?" she said, feigning bland disinterest. "I had assumed there was some Sinanju rule forbidding you from wearing jewelry."

"Actually, there is," Remo admitted. "Throws off the body's natural balance. Master Lom learned that the hard way when he accidentally strangled himself with his own necklace during an exhibition in front of Nebuchadrezzar." Still sitting at the edge of the mattress, he shrugged. "Anyway, I figured you should know about that whole marriage thing."

She had her back to him. When he finished speaking, he saw her shoulders sink. "There is something you should know, as well," she said quietly. She did not turn.

Her deeply serious tone instantly sent up a red flag.

He suddenly had a mental image of a little runny-nosed version of himself tearing around some Russian playground bending the monkey bars in his bare hands and pulling all the girls' pigtails.

"I didn't knock you up, did I?" he asked worriedly.

"No," Anna said somberly.

"Whew," Remo exhaled. "Dodged a bullet there."

At this stage in his life, Remo had already had more than his fill of those sorts of surprises.

"Remo, what I am about to tell you directly violates a standing order from the highest levels of the Kremlin. I am risking my life by divulging this information, but it is necessary for you to know so that you understand the urgency of the situation here. Before it was brought here, the weapon Feyodov stole was test fired. It was only one time and it was many years ago." She finally turned to face him. "My government is responsible for the destruction of the space shuttle *Challenger*."

It was like admitting a personal disgrace. Yet through her shame, Anna's eyes never left Remo's.

By this point Remo thought he was beyond shock. He was wrong. Her words brought him to his feet. Any residual lethargy he was feeling evaporated like morning mist.

"Who did it?" he asked coldly.

"Feyodov had charge of the weapon," Anna said. "The order to fire came to him directly from the

Kremlin. It was a stupid, stupid thing to do. Stupid men fearful of the future, lashing out in some insane attempt to prove their virility."

"Dammit, Anna, everything about guys isn't measured from the lap," Remo snapped. He was thinking rapidly. "Who was in charge over there back then? Was it the guy with the caterpillar eyebrows and the Edward G. Robinson bottom lip?" He shook his head unhappily. "Can't kill him, he's dead," he complained to himself.

"No," Anna said. "And that does not matter."

"Not to you, maybe," Remo said. He snapped his fingers. "I know who it was. It was that chrome dome with the Rorschach forehead."

"Remo, please," Anna pleaded. "I only told you this so you would understand how desperate this situation was before the attack on Mir. It has only gotten worse now. We must figure out a way to end this to the satisfaction of my government before the idiots in charge decide to resort to yet another insane face-saving measure."

"Right now, sweetheart, I'm not that all-fired worried about what satisfies your government," Remo snarled. "I've gotta find Chiun."

He flung open the door and marched into the hallway.

For a moment it was up to Anna Chutesov to worry about her government and the foolish decisions it made. Including the one, as yet unspoken, that she had hoped for ten years Remo would never learn of.

Cursing silently the testosterone-fueled madness that always seemed on the verge of destroying the human race, the head of Russia's top-secret Institute hurried out the door.

25

Theodore Schwartz of AIC News-Wallenberg marched briskly off the elevator and onto the thirtieth floor of the AIC News-Wallenberg Building in midtown Manhattan.

The towering glass building was home to what was inarguably the greatest telecommunications empire of the twenty-first century. And as CEO of ANW, Ted Schwartz was master of his domain. As he strode like a modern-day Midas down the gleaming executive hallway with its high-tech black surfaces and space-age silver accents, all eyes were glued to his powerful frame. Every face he encountered, he owned.

As usual, the staff cut him a wide swath. Grown men and women panicked and ran into offices to avoid him.

Their reactions usually brought him a silent thrill. The king who inspired fear in his subjects.

This day, however, was different.

Though as usual he was the eye of a gossipy hurricane, with tongues wagging and eyes flashing nervously in his direction, Ted paid no mind to the attention he attracted. He had more weighty issues to deal with than the endless nattering of his company's many proles.

In his corner office suite he passed through the outer room of secretaries without slowing.

Unlike most mornings, the many phones were silent. Bike messengers and FedEx men had apparently been delivering urgent letters since daybreak. The secretaries were tearing like mad through stacks of sealed shipping envelopes.

Notes from his rivals in the television and information business. Pleading for his assistance. They were turning on their TVs and finding dead air where their own networks should be. When they switched through the channels, the only thing they found were the News-Wallenberg networks.

His rivals wanted to know how he'd survived so long into the devastating storm that had crippled their industry. But without phones, they couldn't very well call. Hence the letters pleading to be let in on Ted Schwartz's secret.

Though it was exactly as he'd planned, at the moment he didn't have time for the sniveling pleas of his peers.

Ted's private secretary tried to stop him as he strode into her anteroom and swept over to his office door.

"Good morning, Mr. Schwartz," the shapely young woman announced nervously. "Scott Crouse already called twice today. He wants you to call him. He says it's urgent."

Ted Schwartz felt a blush of anger touch his cheeks.

That idiot Scott Crouse had been abusing special phone privileges like a madman, calling Schwartz's office a dozen times the day before.

Crouse had been chairman and CEO of America Internet Connection, the largest Internet service provider in the world. AIC had recently merged with the massive News-Wallenberg conglomerate. With the merger AIC gained access to the vast array of media outlets controlled by News-Wallenberg, which included hugely popular magazines, cable television networks, the Wallenberg Boys movie company and Wallenberg Music. But as a result of their recent business alliance, Crouse had been forced to take a back seat to Ted Schwartz. In spite of several months of abuse by the CEO, intended to either bring him in line or force him to quit, the young man had still not figured out the merger had reduced him to little more than a glorified mail clerk.

"I'm busy," Ted announced angrily. "And tell him if he uses anything other than the normal phone system once more, I'll tie a T-1 line so tight around his neck they'll be scraping eye juice off the screen of his Power Mac."

Flinging open his office door, the CEO slammed it shut in the face of his startled secretary.

He didn't need to talk to Crouse to know why the young man was calling. Ted Schwartz already knew.

Thanks to the disruptions in the satellite network, AIC customers all around the country were having an impossible time dialing online. It was a minor, anticipated glitch in an otherwise perfect plan. Besides, Ted thought to himself, AIC subscribers were used to getting busy signals.

Though the morning sun was crawling up between Manhattan's skyscrapers, the big office was bathed in gloom. The blinds were drawn tightly over mirrored windows.

Behind his broad desk, Schwartz scooped up the phone. The familiar buzz of a dial tone hummed in his ear. Unlike most of the phones in America this day, Ted Schwartz's worked. If it hadn't, Ted would have been pissed.

This was one of the most private lines in existence. At the moment only a handful of News-Wallenberg's top men had access to the top-secret satellite through which it passed. The satellite itself was installed with scrambling technology so sophisticated no intelligence service—either foreign or domestic—had any hope whatsoever of decrypting it.

Scott Crouse was wasting time on that selfsame satellite to whine about the phone-line disruptions that were preventing his teenaged AIC customers in flyover country from getting online to download their daily dose of Internet porn.

"You're not long for News-Wallenberg, Scotty boy," Ted muttered to himself as he stabbed out an eleven-digit number.

He had the number memorized. No way he was going to put this one on the speed dial.

It took seven rings for someone to answer. When a lazy voice finally said hello, Ted Schwartz was drumming his fingers furiously on the buffed glass top of his desk.

"Get him on the phone *now*," Ted ordered hotly.

It took less than a minute for a new voice to arrive on the line.

"Yes, sir," Zen Bower said, panting. He had obviously run all the way to the phone.

"What the hell is wrong with you?" Schwartz demanded.

"What do you mean?" Zen asked vaguely.

"Don't think you can pull that hippie-flashback-blackout bullshit with me," Ted snapped angrily. "You know goddamn well what the hell I mean. I gave you SPACECOM charts to follow. Dammit, there are only seven hundred satellites up there. You knock out some LEOs and a GPS to make it look good, then move on to the geostationaries. Bing, bang, boom, we're in business. Now tell me, moron, where in there did I tell you you could blow up the goddamn Russian space station?"

Zen took a deep breath. "See, there's a funny thing about that," he began timidly. "You know that Russian general I hired? Well, as you know, I fronted for you just like you asked. I took the money you gave me and turned it over to him. No problem with that. He got the weapon here and got it assembled and everything. It was all going along just like we planned. But—"

Zen paused, fearful to go on.

"First off," Ted Schwartz interrupted, "*we* did not plan. *I* planned. You were just some cockamamy Commie-loving retired ice cream pitchman when I found you. You were on the skids after your company had been bought out. You were blabbing like a baby to a reporter in one of my L.A. stations about how you wanted to break Barkley away from the United States and how you knew about some killer secret Russian weapon but that your black-market pal was asking way too much for it. I happened to be at the studio that day. You were delusional, but I decided your delusions were useful to me. *I* found you. *I* used you. Like everyone else in my life, you are nothing but a stupid, worthless employee. I own you. You pay the Russian with my money. I own *him.* Now, what's *my* Russian doing, and why'd he blow up his own goddamn space station?''

"Um, that's the thing," Zen said. "I really don't know. He just sort of went nuts and took over the particle gun. I think he might have issues, you know?"

In the artificial darkness of his high-rise office, the CEO of News-Wallenberg placed his hand flat on his desk. The glass surface was cold to the touch.

"Here is what's going to happen," Ted Schwartz said, his voice far colder than the tempered glass beneath his palm. "You are going to salvage this situation. You are going to pull the plug on that Russian, and you're going to go back to the original plan. I have *billions* invested in this. If you fail, so help me I will strap you to the front of that gun that I bought with *my* money, and I will personally pull the cord that'll blast your ass from here to Pluto.''

Zen's gulp of fear was audible over the crystal clear line. "I understand, sir," the ice cream man said.

"Good," Ted said. Pulling his free hand into a

fist, he shook his head. "Maybe the Russians won't give a damn," he grumbled to himself. "That station was in worse shape than their economy. Besides, no one's on to this yet. Thanks to some gentle massaging by me behind the scenes on CNC and HTB, the media's gobbling up the idea that this is some naturally occurring phenomenon. Course, if the shit hits the fan, we might have to go with the cover plan."

"Cover plan?" Zen queried.

Ted seemed annoyed to hear a voice coming from the other end of the line. This plan had been so top secret for so long he had gotten used to talking only to himself about it.

"Yes, moron," Ted snarled thinly. "The one where you announce to the world you've got a weapon of mass destruction that you've been using and will continue to use until the U.S. allows you to secede from the Union. You and the rest of that council of yours get a lot of press coverage, the likes of which you radical types just love. You take the fall for everything that's happened, become folk heroes, get Bob Dylan to write a song about you and Ed Asner and Danny Glover to protest for your release from prison. Then, when the dust settles in a couple of months, I use the best team of lawyers thirty billion dollars of annual corporate profit can buy to get you all set free." He clamped the mouthpiece to his chest. "Fat chance," he muttered.

When Ted brought the earpiece back to his ear, all he could hear was the sound of Zen Bower's nervous breathing.

"That was the *cover* plan?" the ice cream man

said anxiously. "You *sure* that wasn't the actual plan?"

Ted Schwartz's face grew as rigid as a death mask.

"What did you do?" the News-Wallenberg chief executive officer demanded in a voice like cracking ice.

Zen swallowed again. "I, um…well…that is, I might have already sent a teensy little note to the President demanding that Barkley be allowed to secede from the Union."

"You what!" Ted bellowed.

He could almost see Zen's wincing face.

"It's okay," the ice cream man said quickly. "He never got back to me. Probably too busy approving new killer strains of CIA-produced anthrax to release on inner-city slums or loosening the emission standards for SUVs. Who knows? Maybe they don't check their e-mail at the White House."

"Of course they check it," Ted Schwartz snapped.

His mind was reeling.

There wasn't any buzz at all about the Barkley threat. With the ongoing crisis he had practically cornered the market on news, and he hadn't heard squat. Either Zen was right and the electronic note had gotten lost somehow, or the government already had something planned.

Billions of dollars. His entire kingdom on the line.

Eyes wild, the ruler of the mighty AIC News-Wallenberg telecommunications empire gripped the phone.

"You fix this thing," he said to Zen, his voice a primal growl of low menace. "You fix it now or so help me…"

He let the threat hang in the air. Teeth grinding, Ted Schwartz slammed down the phone.

26

Anna's rental car was pulling up to the curb as Remo stepped off the porch of the seedy Barkley boarding-house. The Master of Sinanju and FBI Agent Brandy Brand were just getting out when another vehicle pulled up behind them.

The battered VW van looked as if it had spent the sixties carting Vietcong through a Hanoi minefield. When the side panel doors creaked open, Remo's hard expression grew darker.

A cloud of smoke rose into the gray morning air. In its wake a dozen people climbed out onto the sidewalk.

The men and women looked like tattered heroes from idyllic days, long gone, of the People's Park Barkley riots, when Tom Hayden and his Barkley Liberation Program had tried to enlist guerrilla soldiers as an army that could offer armed resistance against the local police.

They were tired, tie-dyed and bell-bottomed as they clustered together near their open van door. Brandy steered away from Remo and Anna, hurrying over to the new arrivals.

With a frown of deep annoyance, the Master of

Sinanju stepped away from them, moving to inter-
cept Remo.

"What the hell?" Remo asked as he watched
Brandy join the crowd of aging hippies.

Anna had hurried down the stairs behind Remo.
As she caught up to him, her pale face reflected deep
suspicion.

"Those are members of this city's ruling council," Anna Chutesov observed, her tone wary.

Remo studied the crowd on the sidewalk. The
only time he'd seen them, they were nothing but a
row of dirty feet sticking out from under a tablecloth.

"I'll take your word on that," he said dryly. "We
better see what they're doing here."

"Do not waste your breath," Chiun griped as he
padded up to them. "These rag wearers are here only
to prevent an old man from getting simple suste-
nance. When they approached us in the restaurant
parking lot the female-who-acts-like-a-man thought
important some nonsense they were babbling. While
I was left to starve, she led them back here."

A warning signal went up in Remo's head. Thinking his senses weren't yet properly attuned to sense
a trap, he quickly scanned the shadowy boarding-
house bushes in search of any skulking Russian
black marketers. He found none.

Having just been through the same draining experience as his pupil, the Master of Sinanju understood Remo's instinct to second-guess his own
senses.

"You are fine," Chiun waved. "If you must
know, in addition to forcing an elderly homeless

man to waste away to skin and bone, these dirty people said something about seeking an alliance with us. However, if you wish to hear the details you will have to ask them yourselves, for I could not hear their words over the grumbling of my poor empty belly.''

Remo looked over at the small group with greater interest. "Don't know about you," he said to Anna, "but it's got me curious."

Taking the lead, he preceded Anna and Chiun to the sidewalk. When he stopped beside Brandy, the FBI agent's youthful face was flushed with excitement.

"They say they want to help us," Brandy said to Remo.

Remo cast a skeptical eye at the crowd. "And we're now going to start trusting the senior-citizen contingent of the Black Panthers *because...*?" he asked leadingly.

Gary Jenfeld led the pack of city council members. He had been pleading with Brandy Brand, but with Remo's arrival he turned his hopeful gaze to him. A container of runny Rad Vlad Lenin Caramel Blast ice cream was clutched in his hands.

"You've got to help us stop our Soviet general," Gary begged. "He's costing us a *fortune*."

Never had Remo's skepticism been vanquished so easily.

That Gary was worried about his bank account was all it took for Remo to instantly believe the sincerity of the retired ice cream manufacturer. Much more than a romantic's love of jackbooted totalitarianism and a burning hatred of all things American, naked greed was the thing that most inspired all unrepentant sixties radicals.

Convinced now of the Barkley city council's sincerity, Remo folded his arms across his chest. With hooded eyes he stared down at Gary Jenfeld.

"Okay," Remo demanded. "Exactly what the hell is going on around here?"

IT WAS 7:30 a.m. on the East Coast, and Mark Howard was taking the long way down to the Folcroft cafeteria.

Over the past day he had been stealing spare moments here and there to wander the halls of the sprawling building. He wanted to acquaint himself with the sanitarium. Pushing open the fire doors, he entered the third floor of the public wing where Folcroft's regular patients were housed.

His new laminated lapel pass identified him as associate director of Folcroft. Apparently, word of old Dr. Smith's new assistant had filtered down to the regular duty staff. Although Mark drew a few furtive glances as he strolled the halls, no one approached him.

Mark was struck yet again by what a tight ship Dr. Smith ran here at Folcroft. Somehow the staff seemed to be unaffected by the disease of laziness that had been spreading for years through the managed-care industry. The floors were scrubbed, the patients seemed well cared for and the staff went about their duties quietly and efficiently.

Mark was heading for the distant stairwell, ready

for his usual breakfast of corn flakes and orange juice, when a muted sound caught his attention. It came from an open door to his right. Something made him stop and look.

An old woman in a paisley housecoat was propped up in a hospital bed. She was oblivious to Mark's presence. Her rheumy gaze was directed at a television set that was hooked to an angled shelf high in the corner of the room.

When Mark saw what she was watching, a deep notch formed above the bridge of his nose.

It was one of the regular network morning shows. A weatherman had just wrapped up his forecast, and the two hosts were talking about an upcoming celebrity interview.

As the cohosts jabbered, Mark Howard slowly shook his head. This was not right.

This particular network had been off the air in this part of the country since yesterday. The satellite system it used to broadcast its signal to the East Coast was down.

Since the previous evening, the only regular channels on at all were the Cable News Channel and Home Ticket Booth, both of which were owned by the massive telecommunications conglomerate AIC News-Wallenberg. So dire was the situation that HTB had suspended its regular programming of movies in favor of straight news. Somber-voiced anchors on loan from HTB's sister channel, CNC, had been warning the nation about the seriousness of the satellite outages.

But suddenly here was a normal morning show,

with the people on it behaving as if there were nothing wrong.

Something big and shadowy flitted unbeckoned across the back of Mark Howard's mind.

"Excuse me, sir."

He hadn't heard the nurse approach. She was pushing a wheeled serving cart filled with breakfast trays. She wanted to enter the room, but he blocked her way. Mark took a numb step back into the hallway, allowing her to pass.

Another TV played across the hall. The volume was turned down too low for him to hear, but it looked like some kind of nature show. A grizzled fisherman in a red slicker was hauling a bass into a boat.

And as he watched the flickering image of the white-bearded man, the shadow in his mind cleared.

In that moment something clicked for Mark Howard.

His breakfast forgotten, he turned and hurried back in the direction from which he'd come.

When he burst through the doors into the administrative wing a few moments later, he was already at a sprint. Racing into his office, he quickly locked the door behind him. Hands shaking with excitement, he booted up his computer.

His fingers flew across his clattering keyboard.

The Feeling was his guide as he instinctively searched through CURE's massive database.

Within minutes he had all the information he needed.

Mark looked around for a way to print out the data.

Of course, there was none. The desk had no hidden printer, and Mark hadn't hooked up a remote one.

Pasting and clipping like mad, he assembled the data into one big text file, sending it as an interoffice e-mail through CURE's closed system. He had no sooner depressed the Send key before he was shutting off his computer and scurrying out from behind his desk.

When he hurried into the office of Smith's secretary, Eileen Mikulka wasn't at her post. Not bothering to knock, he barged into the Folcroft director's office.

As usual Smith was sitting behind his desk. His morning plate of toast was empty and pushed to one side. Half a cup of coffee sat cooling at his elbow.

Even before Mark had pushed inside, the CURE director had been watching the door expectantly.

"It's Ted Schwartz," Mark blurted.

Smith pursed his lips unhappily. "Please close the door, Mr. Howard," he said tightly.

So excited was he, Mark had completely forgotten. "Oh," he said, nodding. He clicked the door shut, spinning back to the CURE director. "You got my e-mail?" he asked.

"Yes," Smith said, with a nod to his buried monitor.

"There's a lot there to get through, I know," Howard said. "I didn't have time to condense it. You can check it all out later." His wide face was flushed with triumph. "You know that thing I told you about before, the thing I said was the catalyst to everything that's been happening? It's Ted Schwartz, the CEO of AIC News-Wallenberg."

A flicker of something that might have been curiosity touched the gray depths of Smith's unblinking eyes.

"Why do you believe he is involved?" the old man asked.

"Something on TV tipped me," Mark said. "Actually, the fact that there was *anything* on TV other than the two News-Wallenberg networks. I knew CNC and HTB were still on, but I figured that was just luck of the draw. Their satellite just *happened* to not get hit. But then I saw some of the other networks were back on and, well, something just clicked. I did some checking, and I was right."

Smith leaned back in his chair. "Right about what?"

"About Schwartz," Mark said. "His company operates about one-seventh of the total number of satellites in orbit. Now guess how many of the entire News-Wallenberg conglomerate's satellites have gotten blown out of the sky?"

"I do not like to guess, Mr. Howard," the CURE director replied. "But I know that the answer is one."

"That's right," Mark said. "And that was just one of AIC's. I suspect that was just to make it all look good. And that's for Internet use, not broadcast. Besides, the rest of their network's already taking up the slack. Which brings me to the major point. The

huge number of satellites they have. There's no logical reason why they should have as many as they
do. The company's gone space-happy lately.
They've put up over a hundred satellites in the past
year. They were launching them like crazy from
everyone who would take them. China, Russia,
South America. And see, the thing is, with the GEOs
they've put on these suckers, they only need two or
three to blanket the whole country.''

A thought suddenly occurred to Howard. ''I'm
sorry,'' he said shaking his head apologetically.
''GEO stands for Geosynchronous Equatorial Orbit.
They're locked in place in a distant orbit above the
same spot. Since they're so far away from the planet,
they can cover a greater area.''

''I am familiar with the term,'' Smith said slowly.
His earlier curiosity was giving way to mild intrigue.

''Well, then you understand that there's no way
any outfit needs that many GEOs—even one as big
as News-Wallenberg,'' Mark insisted. ''So until two
days ago they basically had a hundred satellites
parked up there with nothing to do. Then they somehow get incredibly lucky when practically everyone
else's systems suddenly come crashing down at the
same time. Blammo, they're in business. Ted
Schwartz is already starting to cut deals with his
competitors to carry their signals for them. Probably
for a lot of dough, maybe in exchange for stock to
grow his own company. The exact details'll be
worked out later, I'm sure.''

Smith sat forward once more, folding his hands
on the edge of his desk. ''This sounds highly spec-

ulative," the CURE director said. "All of this could still be coincidental."

"Prepare for the biggest coincidence of all, then," Mark Howard said levelly. "The entire council of Barkley owns stock in News-Wallenberg."

"It is a large conglomerate," Smith said reasonably. "This could just be another coincidence."

Mark noted that there was little strength to the old man's arguing. It seemed more that he was playing devil's advocate than anything else. Howard frowned.

"In that case, here's the final coincidence," Mark said. "Ted Schwartz funneled money to Barkley so that they could get that Russian particle-stream weapon smuggled over here. It started a year ago, just when they began launching all those satellites. All kinds of transfers from a private offshore account of Schwartz's were directed to Zen Bower. The particular bank and corporate manipulations are incredibly convoluted, but I'm sure that given a little time I can unknot them. Schwartz is your guy, Dr. Smith. I'm *sure* of it."

Smith considered the young man's words for a long time. As he did so, he seemed to be nodding almost in satisfaction. At long last he took a deep breath.

"You are correct," the CURE director said simply.

Mark blinked. "You believe me?" he asked. He was surprised. He didn't think it would be so easy. His enthusiasm rapidly returned. "Great," he said. "He lives out on Long Island. When your two field operatives get back from California, you can send them there.''

''That will not be necessary,'' Smith said. ''Theodore Schwartz was arrested by federal marshals in his Manhattan office approximately ten minutes ago.''

Howard's face fell. Before he could ask his unspoken question, Smith broke in.

''I came to the same conclusion as you several hours ago,'' the older man explained. ''Once I had assembled the facts, I turned them over to the proper authorities. They will handle Mr. Schwartz from here.''

Mark's confusion was evident. ''But what about those two guys of yours? I figured you'd be using them.''

Smith's face grew serious.

''I am glad things have worked out as they have in this instance,'' the CURE director said somberly. ''For it has given you an early opportunity to see what your job here will truly entail. CURE has a single mission, Mr. Howard. We exist as a final measure to stop those who would attempt to subvert the law for their own ends. But there is one goal we always try hardest to attain, and that is to aid the law, not replace the criminal-justice system. For all the criminal activity that the mainframes sift through on a single day there are only a handful of occasions yearly that require special attention. Unless it constitutes a unique threat, we do not commit our agents to the field. And an attempt by a company—no matter how large—to corner a particular market does not warrant the risk of committing CURE's manpower.''

Howard absorbed the words, nodding slow understanding. ''But they're already working on this,'' he said.

Smith took on the posture of a fussy schoolmarm. ''Which is why this is a good learning experience,'' he said. ''Schwartz may have started this, but the events he was catalyst to have spiraled out of control. The situation in Barkley is dangerous and *does* threaten national security.''

Mark bit the inside of his cheek. ''It makes sense to limit their exposure,'' he said slowly.

''The more they are used, the greater the risk to exposure,'' Smith said. ''Therefore, they are used sparingly. As for the rest that goes on here, some would consider mundane the work that is done by CURE on a day-to-day basis.''

Mark offered a thin smile. ''You don't?''

Smith's back stiffened. ''I do not,'' he said. ''Our work is challenging, rewarding and vital.''

Even after all these years there was a flame of passion in the old man's words. Ignited by honor and duty, it burned with a patriotic sense to do what was necessary regardless of all the personal tolls it had taken.

''I understand,'' Mark said softly. He began edging for the door. ''Sorry I barged in here like that. I didn't know you'd already be on to all this. I figured you'd want the information as soon as possible.''

Smith nodded sharply. ''Your enthusiasm is commendable, Mark,'' he said. ''However, please be more attentive to security protocols in the future. Always be certain that my door is fully closed before discussing CURE matters.''

At the door Mark gave a little apologetic shrug before slipping out of the room.

Once the young man was gone, Smith leaned back in his chair once more. With a thoughtful expression he swiveled around. The morning light of winter glinted off the frothy surface of Long Island Sound. He watched the whitecapped black waves crash against the ice-rimmed shore.

He would never express the sentiment aloud, but Smith was impressed. He had severely limited Mark Howard's access to the basement mainframes, denying the young man entry into CURE's most sensitive computer data. Yet even without complete access, his new assistant had come to the same conclusion Smith had. As much as his abilities could be judged by this case, the man's instincts were sound.

Smith allowed his thoughts to drift from Howard.

Although the CURE director's work in the current matter was done, there was still a dire crisis on the West Coast.

It had been hours since he'd last heard from Remo. Fortunately, Boris Feyodov had gone quiet, as well. Through the previous night and into the new day there hadn't been a single e-mail note from the former general to either the Russian or American president. At first Smith thought this was the result of the malfunctioning phone system, but the satellite attacks had abruptly ceased. All had gone silent after the destruction of the Mir station.

He would have assumed success on the part of CURE's enforcement arm, but the silence had lingered for more than twelve hours and Remo had yet to contact Smith.

No, Feyodov was waiting. For what, Smith had no idea.

With tired eyes Smith watched the waves roll in across the Sound.

With any luck the resolution would come quickly and Smith could turn his thoughts to the future. Assuming, that is, the events played out in the world's favor and there was a future to be had.

27

By the time Gary Jenfeld finished explaining what was driving events in Barkley, Remo Williams was shaking his head in disbelief.

"You mean to tell me we're on a rocket ride to Armageddon because some billionaire bumwad wanted to corner the market on space trinkets?" he demanded.

They were all still standing out on the sidewalk in front of the boardinghouse. A weak smear of pink and orange stained the farthest edge of the bleary California sky. To the north, the great statue of Huitzilopochtli turned from midnight black to shadowy gray. Somewhere beneath, hidden by trees, was the city hall.

Gary cringed at Remo's accusatory tone. "You need money to save the ozone and protect the rain forest," he argued weakly. "And presidential legal-defense funds don't pay for themselves, you know. But none of that matters now. Our general's gone all Jack D. Ripper on us. He isn't following the rules anymore. You've got to *do* something."

"What I ought to do is get on the first stage out of Dodge and let you mopes figure out how to convince the incoming wave of Russian nukes not to blow you sky high,'' Remo said sourly. ''Here's a thought. Get a ladder and try doodling peace symbols on all the nose cones.''

''We cannot leave,'' Anna said firmly.

Remo shot her a withering look. ''Said the chick who left without a trace for ten years,'' he said sarcastically.

''I agree with the old woman,'' the Master of Sinanju said, nodding to Anna. ''Smith would not want us to leave.''

''If this is some fresh way of angling for a new house...'' Remo warned, raising an accusing finger. But the look on his teacher's face told him otherwise. Remo dropped his hand. ''Fine. We'll stay. But if we both wind up getting incinerated, don't come bitching to me.''

''I don't think the Russians will attack us,'' Gary said.

Remo's eyes were flat. ''Don't you people *ever* get tired of saying that?'' he asked, annoyed. ''Back in the sixties, when the Russians weren't invading someone they were waving their big Commie willies at everybody under the sun. They did it all on *your* watch, and all any of you did was slap on blinders and mulch your dorm-room pot plants while whistling 'Eve of Destruction.'''

''You don't understand,'' Gary said, shaking his head urgently. ''Feyodov stopped shooting the gun yesterday. Right after the two of you broke into city hall.'' He nodded from Remo to Chiun. ''I'm not sure, but I think if the Russians were gonna attack because of what happened to their space station, they would have done it by now.''

Remo allowed the words to sink in. He hated to admit it, but Gary was making sense. He glanced at Anna.

''He is right,'' she said simply. ''My president sees himself as a man of action. If his impulse was to attack, he would not wait twelve hours to do so.''

''Maybe the machine broke down,'' Brandy Brand suggested.

Gary shook his head firmly. ''No,'' he said. ''He charged it up one last time, but he's been sitting on it ever since. It's like he's waiting for something.''

Remo and Chiun exchanged tight glances. It was Remo who gave voice to their shared unspoken thought.

''Us?'' he asked.

The old Korean nodded. ''He knew of Sinanju,'' Chiun agreed with a puzzled frown.

''And he saw what happened to us when he fired that thing,'' Remo said with a scowl. ''Who the hell is this guy, and what's his beef with us? We can't get within a country mile of him, and he knows it.''

Gary Jenfeld looked anxiously at the rest of the Barkley city council. Fear filled their grubby faces.

''You have to figure out *something*,'' Gary said desperately to Remo. ''I mean, Feyodov's gone psycho. It's like he's got a death wish or something.''

''He has,'' Anna Chutesov said. ''But he is too cowardly to do the deed himself. He has seized this opportunity in order to get someone else to do it for him.''

"That's one problem I'll gladly help him with," Remo said. "But first Chiun and I have to figure out a way to snip the wires on that thing without frying our circuitry."

He turned to Gary. "Where exactly is it hidden?"

For an instant Gary's troubled eyes flicked over his shoulder.

An ominous black figure loomed far in the distance.

In the greasy gray sky of predawn, Remo saw the top of the far-off Huitzilopochtli statue in Barkley's town square peeking over the tops of the nearby trees and houses.

Remo wheeled back on the Barkley council.

"You hid it inside Mr. Slate?" he complained.

"It worked, didn't it?" Gary said anxiously.

Remo frowned. The truth was, it had. As a community Barkley had been so famously screwed up for so many years, he'd automatically dismissed a huge, four-story statue as just another part of the lunatic landscape.

Remo turned to Chiun. "How do we play this?" he asked.

"It is difficult," the old man said, thoughtfully stroking his thread of beard. He was studying the frozen face of Huitzilopochtli. The statue's black eyes stared coldly at the breaking dawn. "Does the power emanate from the stone god's eyes?" the old man asked Gary Jenfeld.

"You mean the particle stream?" the ice cream man asked. "The statue's hollow, and the top of the head is wide open. The mirrors that focus the stream are just below eye level.''

''We could use explosives to destroy it,'' Anna offered.

Chiun's face fouled at the suggestion.

Gary shook his head. ''It might look like a statue on the outside, but the thing's built like a missile silo. You couldn't drive a tank through the side of it. I don't think a bomb would make much of a difference.''

''What if we got a helicopter?'' Brandy suggested to Remo and Anna. ''If the head's open like he says, we could fly over and drop a bomb inside.''

Remo shot the FBI agent a skeptical look. ''They're shooting down satellites that are a million miles away and you want to try hovering over ground zero?''

''Oh,'' Brandy said, dejected. ''Hadn't thought of that.''

''But the hollow-head thing could work for us,'' Remo said thoughtfully. ''Chiun and I can't get close, but we can sure as hell lob something inside from a distance.''

Brandy cast a dubious eye at the statue. ''You must have one hell of a pitching arm,'' she said.

Remo ignored the FBI agent. ''Anyone here know how to make a bomb?'' he asked.

The entire Barkley city council with the exclusion of Gary Jenfeld raised their hands.

''Why did I even ask?'' Remo grumbled. ''Okay, put what's left of your brain cells together and come up with something that'll go boom. Preferably not in your hands."

"That'll be hard to do," Gary whined. "We banned explosives in town a few years back, along with all guns. And now the Russians are the only ones who have any weapons at all." He put on a pouty face. "They were supposed to protect us and now they've made us prisoners."

"And *that's* never happened before," Remo said dryly.

"We can come up with something," Brandy promised. "We'll have to swing by the hardware store. Let's go."

When the crowd turned to the curb, Remo took note of the ratty old van the city council had arrived in.

"Someone probably should go on the magic bus with the Doodletown Pipers," he said.

"Do not look at me," Chiun sniffed.

"*I* will go with them," Anna said.

Brandy took the wheel of Anna's rental car. Chiun and Remo slid into the seat beside her. Three members of the Barkley city council got into the back. Anna climbed into the van with the remaining council members. As the other car drew away from the curb, Gary Jenfeld was pulling his ample belly in behind the van's steering wheel.

The ice cream man was turning the key in the ignition when he felt something hard press against his neck. When he turned to see what it was, his face locked in paralyzed fear.

Anna Chutesov was sitting in the seat beside him.

To Gary's shock the Russian agent had drawn her automatic. The open mouth of the barrel tickled the graying whiskers that sprouted just below his ear.

Neither hand nor eyes wavered as she pressed the gun barrel harder into flesh.

"Now, idiot, take me to Boris Feyodov," she commanded.

And her steady voice was as cold as the Siberian Arctic.

28

All through the night, he waited. When day finally broke, he watched the light from the rising sun crawl down the hollow interior of the Huitzilopochtli statue.

When the fools from Barkley had first approached him a year ago, Boris Feyodov had given them the structural requirements that would be necessary for the device he had sold them. They had been as excited as all bomb-wielding anarchists on the day they presented him with the plans to the complex they intended to build.

A network of tunnels beneath the city hall and under the main town square would be built for the guts of the weapon. If anyone became curious, the construction would be explained away as structural maintenance on the old town hall building.

Looking at the blueprints, Feyodov saw no designs for the silo that would house the hardware and mirrors that focused the particle stream.

"These plans are incomplete," the general had said to Zen Bower, the de facto head of the Barkley city council.

"You didn't look at the page underneath," Zen replied with a wicked grin.

When Feyodov lifted the thick top paper, he found another blueprint. Schematics for the proposed Huitzilopochtli statue were drawn out in full. There was even a cross section of the statue in which tiny men had been sketched hard at work on the four levels of catwalks.

"You are joking," Feyodov said. But when he pulled his gaze away from the architect's rendition of the South American god, he found a look of sincere determination on the ice cream man's face.

And so the statue had been built. Four stories tall and smack-dab in the middle of town. And to Boris Feyodov's amazement, no one had batted an eye. The city of Barkley was truly an enigma, even by American standards. The former Russian general who had learned to play the capitalist system as well as he had ever played the Communist one had months ago given up any hope of understanding the collective mind of this hamlet of demented radicals.

Not that any of that mattered anymore. His thoughts this morning were less on the past than they were on the future. What was left of it.

Feyodov sat at the end of the main tunnel. The rough interior of Huitzilopochtli stretched high above, capped by a halo of perfect blue. All around was the constant, hair-tickling hum of energy stored in special capacitors.

If his life ended this day, it would end with the sweet perfection of exquisite irony.

It had become known through the night that there

were men still alive on Mir. The three surviving cosmonauts were huddled in the cramped Kvant science module.

In the old days they would have been abandoned. The station was the only thing important, and that was in ruins. Half of Mir had been propelled on the particle stream that had ripped it in two. Out of control, it was spiraling through empty space. The other half was still in Earth orbit but was completely unsalvageable.

The old Soviet Union would have taken the loss and moved on to the more important matter of retaliation against whoever was responsible for the destruction of state property. But so far Moscow was silent. Even though they knew full well who the culprit was, there had been no response to the e-mail Feyodov had sent to the president.

The former general was not a fool. He realized now the president was more patient than he'd thought. He was waiting Feyodov out. To see what he would do next.

But though the president had shown restraint thus far, it would not last forever. When the time came, it would be a simple enough matter to goad the little man in the Kremlin into a response. All would happen in its time. For the time being Boris Feyodov had opted for patience, as well. And his temperance had been rewarded in a way he had never imagined.

A plan to rescue the stranded cosmonauts was already under way. Of course the Russian government could never hope to launch such an operation without months of endless debate and planning. With their remaining systems failing, the men in space would be lucky to survive a few more days.

No, it was not the Russians, but the Americans who would be going into space to save Mir's crew. A space shuttle launch had already been planned for the next week. Given the circumstances, the time-table had been moved up.

When the image of the patiently waiting shuttle sitting on its launch pad in Florida was first shown on the news, Boris Feyodov could scarcely believe his eyes.

The old Communist general usually didn't believe in such things, but in this instance Boris Feyodov knew beyond a shadow of a doubt that this was the hand of Fate at work.

The particle gun would be fired one more time. And this sorry chapter in Boris Feyodov's life would come full circle.

Sitting in his chair inside Huitzilopochtli, Feyodov was wistfully studying the California sky when he heard the clatter of a lone pair of boots on the plank-ing that led from the city hall. The footfalls stopped beside him.

"Still no sign of them, General."

Feyodov rolled his head lazily to the speaker.

Oleg Shevtrinko's shoulder had been bandaged, and his arm was in a sling.

Feyodov had given his black market subordinates permission to leave hours ago. Loyal soldiers since the old Soviet days, they had to a man opted to stay.

Their courage gave him strength. From the start he was not certain if he would have the nerve to see this through to the end. Until the last he had planned for an alternative future. One in which he'd live the life of a fat, rich whore. The lure of comfortable retirement and his vast Swiss bank accounts had remained a temptation even as far as the previous day. But no more.

"They will come, Oleg," Feyodov promised. "It is the way the game is played."

"*Game?*" a mocking voice snorted from the silo floor.

Zen Bower had been despondent since Feyodov seized control of the weapon the previous afternoon. His depression had worsened after he had gotten off the phone a few moments before. Apparently, his benefactor in this scheme had been arrested.

"This was never a game," Zen lamented. "It was about power and money and making people do what's right because *I* told them it was right."

Feyodov had largely ignored such outbursts from the ice cream man. This time, he rolled an eye toward Zen.

The head of the Barkley council sat on the bottom metal stair that led up to the first catwalk. Hunching forward, his face was pressed firmly in his hands.

"It has never been that," the former general said with calm certainty. "Whether you knew it or not— from that very first meeting we had in Moscow— this has always been about revenge. And I have had my fill of you."

It was the coldness with which he said those last words that got to Zen. The council leader cautiously lifted his face from his palms.

Feyodov had borrowed Oleg's gun. He held it lightly in his outstretched hand. The barrel was aimed at Zen Bower.

The ice cream man's mouth dropped open in shock.

Defenseless at the hands of Barkley's supreme military commander, Zen suddenly had a deep and powerful appreciation of the true meaning of the constitutional right to keep and bear arms. For the first time in his life he was ready to march in lockstep with George Washington, Thomas Jefferson, John Adams and every other one of those powdered-wig-wearing, slave-owning, land-baron, dead white European males. Unfortunately, he had not the means to act on his newfound star-spangled patriotism. Before Zen could utter a single, flag-waving jingoistic word, Boris Feyodov pulled the trigger.

The ice cream man felt a sharp pain on the right side of his chest.

The bullet knocked him sprawling back on the metal stairs. Grabbing at the wound, Zen's fingers came back red. When he looked up, his face was horrified.

"Damn," Feyodov complained. "I am no good without my glasses. Finish him off."

He handed the gun back to Oleg. The Russian marched dutifully over to the staircase and finished the cringing ice cream man with a single shot to the forehead. His order executed, Oleg reholstered his gun.

The younger man's face was flat, as if he had done nothing more than squash an insect. It was the same face he'd worn that day back at Sary Shagan when he had helped execute Viktor Churlinski and the other scientists.

For an instant Boris Feyodov was transported back to that time. It had been the beginning of the end. And today, finally, the curtain would at long last come down.

"Will there be anything else, General?" Oleg asked.

Eyes vacant, Feyodov shook his head. With a crisp nod Oleg disappeared back inside the tunnel.

Alone, the former general stared at the distant wall. His thoughts were on Sary Shagan and the dark days since.

Anna Chutesov, the men from Sinanju. Russia, America. A great confluence of people and events and history. All had combined around a single human being. The result of that grand cosmic alignment was a hollow little man who had at one time been a god.

The words he had spoken to Zen were true. It *was* about revenge. The last years of his life had set the stage for this final act of vengeance. And the moment of reckoning was nearly at hand. When it finally did come, Boris Feyodov wanted to actually see it.

He got up from his seat. Hands clasped thoughtfully behind his back, he went off in search of his glasses.

29

They plundered all of the bomb-making materials they needed from the aisles of a local hardware store. When Brandy Brand and the three Barkley city council members exited into the parking lot, their arms were full. They hauled the materials to the open trunk of the rental car.

Remo and Chiun were waiting next to the car.

"No sign of them yet?" Brandy asked tensely as she and the others dumped armloads of sloshing bottles, propane tanks and mercury switches onto the spare tire.

Remo shook his head. "Even though this is their town, I wouldn't put it past those ninnies to get lost in their own driveway. But Anna's with them."

Chiun noted his pupil's worried tone. A troubled expression formed in the deep lines of his face. It was as if the past ten years had been erased. His pupil's words and stance made evident his concern for the Russian female.

Remo did not need this complication in his life. Not now, of all times.

As Remo watched the street, Chiun leaned close. "She survived for more than a decade away from your watchful eye,'' the wizened Korean said, his voice low.

Remo glanced down at his teacher. Chiun's weathered face held a troubled cast.

''Huh?'' Remo asked. It took a second for the old man's meaning to sink in. When it did, his expression fouled. ''It's not like that,'' he said.

''Would that I could believe you,'' Chiun said, shaking his head sadly. ''But I know you all too well.''

But Remo's tone grew certain. ''Not half as well as you think, Little Father,'' he said firmly. ''Yes, I had feelings for Anna at one time and, yes, it threw me for a loop to see her alive after all these years. But that was a long time ago. I'm different now. Plus there's the added fact that I'm more than just a little ticked off at her for that whole fake-death thing. So if you're worried that I'm harboring some hope of linking arms and running off into the sunset with her, don't bother. Whatever I had with her is over. But that doesn't mean I shouldn't be worried about the fact that she's tooling around this asylum in the Scooby van with a pack of Herman's Hermits rejects. They *should* have been right behind us.''

Chiun found great relief in his pupil's assuredness of tone. With a thoughtful frown he nodded agreement.

''Yes,'' he said, stuffing his hands deep inside his kimono sleeves. ''They should have. I for one, however, am not surprised. That woman has always been duplicitous.''

Remo looked down at his teacher. "You think it's Anna's fault they got lost?"

"They are only as lost as she wants them to be," the Master of Sinanju replied ominously.

Remo was about to question him more when the trunk of the car abruptly slammed. As the council members climbed into the back seat of the vehicle, Brandy hurried over to Remo.

"We're all set," the FBI agent said, fingering the car keys. "Shouldn't take more than an hour or so to get everything ready. We just need someplace quiet to work."

Remo nodded. "We'll go back to Anna's place," he said. "I'll drive, Bu—" He caught himself before finishing. For what seemed like the hundredth time he had started to call her Buffy. He stuck out his hand. "Gimme the keys."

As the three of them were getting back in the car, Remo's curiosity finally got the better of him.

"Why the hell'd you change your name anyway?"

By the look on her face, it was obviously a topic she didn't like to discuss.

"Some stupid TV show," Brandy groused. "They even stuck my old name in the title. I was Buffy all my life, then Hollywood's got to come along with some ridiculous fantasy show for arrested adolescents and make it impossible for me to do my job. When I got sick of the guys at the Bureau making fun of my name, I changed it. I *hate* that show."

"Really?" Remo said as he turned the key in the

ignition. He knew the show she meant. "I kind of like it."

She gave him a withering look.

"What did I tell you?" Brandy muttered unhappily to herself. She crossed her arms. "Arrested adolescents and dirty old men."

The rental car sped quickly out of the parking lot.

ONE CLEAN SHOT. That's all she needed and this madness would finally be over. This among other things consumed Anna Chutesov's thoughts as the Volkswagen van bearing her and the remaining city council members drove through the brightening streets of Barkley.

They had lagged behind Remo's car long enough to lose them. Once the lead car was out of sight, the Russian agent had instructed Gary to take a side street. After that, they steered a beeline for the city hall.

In the back five council members whimpered in fear. Behind the wheel Gary Jenfeld somehow managed through Herculean effort to keep his chocolate-and-ice-cream-packed bowels from releasing into his boxers.

"Is this some sort of Patty Hearst-in-reverse thing?" Gary whined. He pictured a brainwashed version of himself weeks from now being caught on blurry bank video, clean-shaven, dressed in a suit and withdrawing money to finance campaigns to get endangered spotted owl on the menu at the next RNC fund-raiser and build nuclear reactors in seal pods.

"Shut up and drive," Anna ordered.

Prodded at the point of her gun, Gary Jenfeld drove into the heart of Barkley. They passed beneath the great shadow of Huitzilopochtli. Anna sank back in her seat and watched the statue as they sped along. Her own face was stone by the time they circled the building and parked in a rear lot.

Anna forced the council members to surrender a few articles of clothing. When they climbed down from the van moments later, her blond hair was wrapped in a concealing bandanna. A bulky, gender-neutral jacket hid her natural curves. If one looked quickly, she could be mistaken for a council member. She kept her hand on the butt of her gun as she slipped it in her pocket.

"I don't like this," said Gary, who had decided that this was probably more an assertive-feminist thing than a brainwashing thing. "I understand your desire to express your gender superiority in this male-dominated environment, but what about that guy who knocked down all the doors and killed all those guys at Buffoon Aid? I know he's only a man, but he does have that whole upper-body-strength thing going for him. Let's go back and get him."

"Get me in to Feyodov," Anna said evenly.

Gary's rounded shoulders sank.

The ice cream man took the lead, steering the small group up the rear steps of the building.

An electronic lock was affixed to the wall. Gary's laminated security pass deactivated it. Once they'd gained entry to the city hall, they quickly headed down the first-floor hallway. Anna kept to the center of the small group, using their bodies as camouflage.

The back route led them up to the council chambers. Farther down the hall, Anna saw the backs of the second set of doors Remo and Chiun had knocked through. The thick steel was buckled around the locks, but they still stood. They were closed now, secured on the inside by a metal beam.

In spite of the fact that she had led them all here, Anna felt like a prisoner. All that kept her going was the gun in her pocket and the hope that she could end this before anyone learned the real truth.

As the group passed inside the council chamber they ran head-on into a trio of Feyodov's black market cronies.

"Oh!" Gary said, startled. "We didn't…that is, um…"

In the center of the crowd, Anna clenched her teeth.

The fool was panicking, spluttering like an imbecile in front of men who were already growing suspicious.

Anna shrank into herself. She was beginning to ease her gun out of her pocket when Gary struck on an idea.

"We caught one!" Gary cried. Wheeling, he aimed a pudgy finger directly at Anna Chutesov.

The other council members quickly picked up the thread. Before she could free her gun, they grabbed Anna roughly by the arms. One tore the bandanna from her head.

She tried to struggle, but it was no use. The men

swept in. A quick search turned up her gun. After that, the Russians themselves took hold of her.

"We've got another one in the van," Gary Jenfeld volunteered, backing quickly away. "Much worse than this one. A real secondhand-smoke-producing, hate-criming, Christian Coalitioner. Too dangerous for you guys. Tell you what, I'll go get him myself while you handle this one."

If the Russians heard him at all, they didn't seem to care. As Gary stumbled out the door, the black marketers were hauling Anna away from the remaining frightened Barkley officials. They headed for the back of the auditorium.

And with all hope of a simple resolution evaporating with every step, Anna Chutesov could do nothing but allow herself to be dragged helplessly along.

BOMB BUILDING was apparently to the Barkley city council what riding a bicycle was to the rest of the world. It took the two men and one woman scarcely an hour to tape, snip and wire together four makeshift bombs.

"These should pack enough of a wallop to knock it out of commission," Brandy Brand told Remo as she stuffed the last of the devices inside one of the big khaki duffel bags they had picked up at the hardware store. "But I still don't know how you think you're going to get them inside."

At the moment that wasn't worrying Remo.

He and Chiun had heard a vehicle arrive outside the flophouse a moment before. For the past few seconds Remo had been listening to a frantic, muted conversation downstairs.

After the speaker was done, he had hurried upstairs.

Brandy was in the process of closing up the bag around the last bomb when the sound of panting breath and pounding feet became audible to the others in the room. When the frantic, sweating man thundered inside the room an instant later, Brandy immediately whipped out her gun. With screams of ''narc'' and desperate denials of youthful ties to the Weather Underground, the three panicked Barkley bomb makers jumped for cover under the soiled mattress.

Gary Jenfeld recoiled at the sight of Brandy's gun.

"Don't shoot!" the ice cream man yelled. With cringing cupped hands and one upraised knee he formed a standing fetal position.

Remo and Chiun had both determined who the intruder was long before Gary raced into the room. Though Remo strained his senses, he detected no one trailing behind the lone council member.

"Where's Anna?" he asked.

Gary peeked anxiously out from behind his hands. "It's not my fault," he begged. "She made me do it."

He shrank more from the look Remo gave him than he had from Brandy's gun. Voice quavering in fear, Gary quickly told Remo of the events leading up to Anna's capture.

"She went all Helen Reddy macho on me," the ice cream man said in conclusion. "I blame the whole male-dominated hierarchical society that makes every woman feel they have to overcompensate for their innate superior femaleness.''

"I blame the fact that you wet your pants and turned her over to them," Remo said coldly.

"Well, there *is* that, if you want to get technical," Gary admitted. "Let's just split the difference and say the unfeeling patriarchy was at play here, too."

"You're two seconds away from getting your difference split," Remo snapped. As Gary cringed once more, Remo frowned. "We have to get her out of there."

"Why?" Chiun sniffed. "Not only has she always been a nuisance, but if we are to believe this one, her capture is a result of her own actions. I say good riddance."

"No," Remo said firmly. "We can't just leave her."

"You mean leave her as she left you?" Chiun suggested with an impatient scowl.

"That's not fair, and you know it," Remo said. "Anna did what she thought she had to do back then to survive."

The angry lines of the old man's face softened. "Think of our survival," the Master of Sinanju said. "And of the survival of our House." He pitched his voice low enough that the others couldn't hear. "It is too dangerous for you to risk your life at such a time as this, Remo. Or have you forgotten the reason for my dead son's visitation?"

The words and the urgency with which the old

man spoke them took Remo aback. "I haven't forgotten," he admitted.

"Then understand that this is one of the hardships you must endure," Chiun pleaded. "This woman you say you loved has come back to you, and now must die. Perhaps she is dead already. In either case you thought her so, lo these many years. If it makes it easier for you, pretend you never saw her again and leave her to her fate."

Remo considered his teacher's words. After a long moment he finally shook his head.

"Can't do it, Little Father," Remo said. "Sinanju has its traditions, but I have mine. And I can't just leave Anna hanging out to dry like that."

"Why not?" Chiun demanded.

Remo's eyes were level. "Because it's wrong."

A bony hand swatted the words angrily from the air. "Why do I waste my breath? Right, wrong. Even after all these years you cling to the childish concepts taught you by those carpenter-idolizing spinsters." He thrust his hands up his sleeves. "Very well. We will risk life and limb to retrieve your Russian harlot. But I am warning you, Remo Williams, if I die as a result of this fool's errand I will haunt you for the rest of your natural days."

"You shouldn't come, Chiun," Remo said seriously. "After what happened last time it's too dangerous."

But the old man's mind was made up. "If you die, then Sinanju lasts only until I draw my last breath, for it is far too late in life for me to train another," the Master of Sinanju said. "In that case, what good will a few more years of life do my village? We go together.''

Remo could see that there would be no arguing. With fresh concern for his teacher's safety, he turned to Gary.

''Okay, pinhead,'' he said to the ice cream man. ''Where exactly would they take her?''

30

Boris Feyodov's eyes sparkled with malicious glee.

He could scarcely believe it when his men brought the despised woman, Anna Chutesov, down to him.

Without his glasses he had not seen her very well during her earlier assault on the town hall. She had been far away then. All the way across the auditorium. A ghost of a figure from another time. Now she was close enough to reach out and touch. A beloved, hated vision from his past.

She was exactly as he remembered her. Beautiful, proud, antagonistic. The look of disdain she gave him as the black market soldiers forced her into a chair was priceless. It was a calculated contempt that made his bitter heart soar.

Although the men held her in place, Anna didn't try to fight. She just sat there in the rock-hewn tunnel beneath Barkley's city hall. Staring up at her traitorous countryman, her eyes were cold pools of ice-blue scorn.

Looming above the Russian agent, Boris Feyodov tipped his head knowingly. "You have not changed a bit since we last met," he said. Pausing, he held his hands out apologetically to either side. "I wish that I could make the same boast. However, the years have not been so kind to me.''

The look of disdain never left her face. ''We've met?'' Anna Chutesov asked blandly.

A smile spread across the flabby features of the former Red Army general. ''Do not make me think your reputation is undeserved,'' Feyodov said. ''You remember it well.'' The smile fled and his voice grew chilly. ''I certainly do.''

With great care he took a seat across from her. Dull eyes looked to his men.

''Release her,'' Feyodov commanded.

The black market men instantly did as they were told. Snapping to attention, they took a step back from her chair. Their hands never left their weapons.

Leaning back, Feyodov casually crossed his legs. ''It was April when we met,'' he said, his eyes growing distant. ''I had been director of the Institute for only a few months before I was relieved of duty. All because of you. You and some great secret you brought back with you from America. You barely acknowledged me that day you took command, just a glance and a nod as you carried your precious bag into your office. Into *my* office.'' He took a deep breath. ''That was the day we became enemies, you and I,'' he confided.

Anna finally had enough. Brow dropping low she shook her head firmly. ''Please keep your delusions to yourself,'' she said. ''I am not your enemy, *you* are. You hate your own cowardice and incompetence. You are a military man who had to live his entire career in the shadow of his own father. The

one time you were put to the test, you failed yourself, your country and the men under your command.
You are a tiny little failure and you have invented
pathetic phantoms to blame for your own weaknesses.''

Since his humiliation in Chechnya, the accusation
of cowardice was one that always brought swift anger from Feyodov. The reports were all clear on this.

Given the circumstances, Anna hoped to provoke
him into granting her a swift end. But instead of rage
a knowing smile cracked the sagging face of the old
general.

'''Phantoms.' An interesting choice of words.''
Feyodov nodded thoughtfully. ''Oh, and I am not
going to kill you. At least not yet. For all their faith
in you, you are really not as clever as they think you
are. For instance, the first thing you should have
done when you took over the Institute was change
the combination on my office safe.''

This drew a reaction. Nothing dramatic. A single
thin brow arched almost imperceptibly on her forehead.

The general leaned forward, dropping his voice to
a conspiratorial whisper. ''You left for a few hours
that first day. It was before you had changed any of
the security systems. I waited for you to leave, and
then I snuck back inside.'' His whispered voice became a rasp. ''I *saw* what you brought back with
you.'' Exhaling, Feyodov leaned back in his chair.
''Of course, I heard the rumors after that. When the
dark days came and Moscow fell to the capitalists,
I heard whispers of how the Institute alone was safe

from the mobs. I always assumed I knew why. Until yesterday.''

Feyodov would have said more, but at that moment a black market soldier came marching up the tunnel.

His arm bandaged tightly where Anna Chutesov had shot him, Oleg Shevtrinko glared hatred at the Institute head. After the events of the previous day, he now wore a bulky bulletproof vest, but it seemed to be doing little more than irritating his injuries.

''They have reached the five-minute mark, general,'' Oleg announced, shifting the weight of his vest.

Feyodov nodded silent understanding. With a wave of his hand he sent Oleg back up the tunnel.

''The Americans are about to launch a rescue attempt of the men on Mir,'' the former general explained to Anna. ''While they count down, so do we. Soon the world will know the truth of what happened at Sary Shagan.'' He tipped his head, considering. ''Fate is a powerful thing,'' he mused. ''The weapon that brought you here is the same thing that finally drew the men from Sinanju to me.'' A thought occurred to him. ''You were aware that when I was given my appointment at the Institute, they were supposed to come work for me?''

There was no point in lying. ''Of course,'' Anna spit.

Feyodov nodded. ''But then fate intervened, and they remained in America. As I said, given the reports I heard in later years, I assumed they had finally come to work for Russia. For *you*. It seems now that was never the case. Not that it matters. I possess the means to render them impotent. They share the blame with you for the life I now lead. Therefore, when they come to rescue you, they will die."

Anna Chutesov shook her head. "They will not come," she said firmly. "Those two are many things, but unlike you they are not fools."

Standing, the former Red Army general offered a tiny shrug of his shoulders.

"Then I will have to settle for your death and the annihilation of America and Russia," he said. "I suppose no plan can be perfect."

A thoughtful frown erasing his glimmer of a smile, the tired old soldier offered her his back. Leaving Anna Chutesov with the two guards, Boris Feyodov strolled down the tunnel. To watch history repeat itself.

A PAIR OF black market soldiers guarded the entrance to the city hall. They had been at their post for hours without incident. The streets of Barkley were empty. Its citizens had been ordered to stay in their homes.

The sun rose high and warm on the eerily calm scene.

It was just after 8:00 a.m. when one of the city hall guards felt a sudden light tapping on his shoulder. Startled, he wheeled for the source.

Someone was standing beside him on the high steps. A pair of deep-set eyes offered dark disapproval.

"No wonder you Commies lost the candy store," Remo Williams said. "You listen the same way you create systems of government. Shitty."

Another voice chimed in beside the second soldier, this one a high singsong.

"They stopped listening because no one in Russia has said anything worth listening to since the last tzar," Chiun squeaked. "I would turn a deaf ear, too, if I had to endure seven decades of bushy noses telling me why their hands were always in my kimono pockets."

Quickly gathering his wits about him, the guard near Remo grabbed for his gun. He found to his horror that he had nothing to grab with. His arms ended in bloody stumps.

"Sorry, but we need 'em for the next five-year plan," Remo said, tossing the man's hands into the bushes beside the steps. "But I'll see about requisitioning you a spare set of feet. Should be in the mailbox by May Day."

He finished the man with a punishing palm to the temple.

As the first man fell, the soldier next to Chiun tried to get a bead on the old man. Whipping his gun up, he squinted one eye. His eye was still squinting as his head bounced down the city hall steps and rolled under a shrub.

Remo and Chiun hopped over the pair of bodies and swept inside the big building.

The main door that they'd wrenched off in their previous assault on the town hall was still lying on the floor. It had been too heavy for the Barkley council to lift. Remo and Chiun bounded across it and raced up the hallway.

The second set of doors was warped around the handles. A pair of thrusting heels snapped a barricading bar and sent the battered doors screaming off their hinges. The two men raced along in their wake, slipping through the door to the auditorium. In the back of the hall they found a door precisely where Gary had said it would be. The room it fed into was small and windowless. Portraits of Marx, Mao, Lenin and other heroes of the Revolution hung on the walls.

A glass display case with a wide base sat in the middle of the floor. In it was a half-complete Barkley constitution that Zen Bower had started to write in a fit of delusional optimism. At a glance, Remo saw three misspellings and a dozen Wite-Out splotches in the preamble alone.

He didn't have time to read it in full. Grabbing one side of the case, he pushed. It rolled to one side, revealing a long set of stairs.

Remo shot a glance at the Master of Sinanju. "One of us really should stay out here," he said.

Chiun nodded crisply. "Agreed," the old man said. Hiking up his kimono skirts, he started for the stairs.

"Whoa, Nellie," Remo said. "I meant *you*."

"Who is Reigning Master?" Chiun sniffed.

They were both surprised by Remo's answer.

"Me," he said firmly. It was an instant before he realized he'd misspoken. "I mean *you*," he corrected. "But you can't always be pulling rank like that all the time."

Chiun remained frozen in place, a single sandal toe on the top step of the hidden staircase. He seemed to be waiting for his pupil to say something more.

"No," the old man agreed slowly, after Remo's silence had gone on more than a questioning heartbeat. "I cannot. Nor can I stop you if you choose to tag along on this misadventure of your creation. But I am going."

With that he floated like a wraith down the dark stairs.

Remo watched his bald head descend.

There was something in the moment that had just passed. Something small yet momentous. But for Remo it was like wrestling a shadow. He just couldn't grab on.

And then it was gone.

Shucking off a bout of momentary confusion, Remo's face steeled. With certain steps he hurried down the stairs after the Master of Sinanju.

ANNA WAS TICKING off the seconds in her head.

It had been two minutes since Feyodov's man announced the countdown. That meant there were only three left.

The world had not yet learned the truth of any of this. All the proof she needed was the fact that Barkley was not yet a radioactive crater. She would not have thought it possible but, remarkably, cooler heads were prevailing.

But the fact that no missiles had yet been launched would soon matter not. It would all be over once Feyodov shot down another American space shuttle. At that point the simmering pot would boil over.

If she could only find a way to stop him.

She glanced over her shoulder. The instant she did so, the men guarding her raised their rifles a hair.

She turned away. "Idiots," Anna muttered.

It was hopeless. Her weapon was gone. There was no way she could overpower the two black market men. All she could do was sit and wait for the end to come.

As she continued to count the seconds, her busy mind heard something down the far end of the tunnel.

It was hard to distinguish over the constant hum that filled the air. It was a sort of brittle crack-crack-crack. Like the snapping of dry kindling.

When she looked back she saw one of Feyodov's black market men running down the tunnel.

No. Not running. To run one needed functioning legs. Since his were knotted up to his pelvis in a flesh-and-bone imitation of a Christmas bow, it would have been impossible for the man to run. His feet dangled loose in the air.

Screaming as he flew down the tunnel, the man slammed with bone-pulverizing ferocity into one of the soldiers guarding Anna. The twisted bundle of arms and legs bounced off a workstation and collapsed in a deflating heap on the metal flooring.

"Strong routine, but weak on the dismount," a familiar voice called from down the corridor. "I'd give it a six-point-five. What does the North Korean judge think?''

"Hurry up, blockhead," came the squeaky reply.

The remaining guard was pulling his rifle high and twisting for the voices at the dark end of the tunnel. Anna didn't give him a chance to shoot.

As the man pivoted, she jumped on the first soldier's dropped gun. In a heartbeat she had the rifle up. With an explosive crack she sent a single bullet into the man's back.

The black marketer was sprawling facefirst on the decking when Remo and Chiun appeared.

Although Remo seemed unaffected by their surroundings, a hint of strain touched the Master of Sinanju's wrinkled face. He flounced beside his pupil like a fussy bird.

"What'd you do that for?" Remo groused at Anna as he glanced down at the body.

Anna hefted the gun. "Granted it is not as efficient as your plan of hurling crippled bodies around the room," she said blandly, "but the results are the same."

"Not really," Remo said. "Case in point."

He pointed down an adjacent tunnel. Even as his finger was unfurling, Oleg Shevtrinko came running into view brandishing an automatic pistol. His eyes went wide when he saw Remo and Chiun, wider still when he saw the bodies of his three compatriots on the floor. The Russian cursed hotly.

"See what I mean?" Remo said to Anna, unmindful of Oleg's gun. "Those boom noises always attract more boom noises."

Wincing at the pain in his bandaged shoulder, the black marketer whipped his gun up. Before Oleg could pull the trigger, Anna Chutesov fired.

The bullet struck Oleg hard in the center of his bulletproof vest. The wind punched from his lungs, the Russian fell back onto the floor. His gun clattered away.

"Stop *doing* that," Remo complained.

As he spoke to Anna, he felt a gentle touch on his bare forearm.

"Remo," the Master of Sinanju interrupted tensely.

When Remo looked down, he saw that the look of exertion on his teacher's face had grown worse.

"Right," Remo nodded, turning on his heel. "Let's get you out of here. We can sort out why you pulled this Anna-against-the-world crapola once this place is toast."

Anna shook her head. "Wait," she insisted.

"No time to fart around," Remo said tightly. His senses were focused on the far end of the corridor.

The tunnel arced around in the distance, making the end invisible. Somewhere far along was the Huitzilopochtli statue. Between there and here Remo sensed about two dozen more men. After Anna's two gunshots, some of the closest black market men had started to move in their direction.

"We cannot go," Anna insisted. "Feyodov plans to fire the weapon again."

"All the more reason for me and Chiun to get as far away as possible," Remo said. He grabbed her by the arm.

"You don't understand!" she pleaded. "He is going to destroy another space shuttle!"

This got Remo's attention.

"Dammit, what's with this guy?" Remo growled. "How much time we got?"

"Under two minutes," Anna urged. "And if we do not stop it, the global ramifications will be catastrophic."

"My worries go bigger than that," Remo said. He cast a concerned eye at the Master of Sinanju.

The old man was growing more haggard by the second. The very air seemed to be draining the life from him.

"You two get out of here," Remo said. "I'll take—"

He was shocked when he was interrupted.

Remo thought his senses had been working at peak. But apparently his body, like Chiun's, had begun to fall victim to the subtle disruptions in the air around them. He realized that the instant the pack of gun-wielding Russians charged into view at the far end of the tunnel.

He thought the tunnel had been longer, thought they had more time. Before Remo could reorient himself, before he could shout a warning to Chiun, before he could even utter a single word, the Russians fired.

And the tunnel flashed to explosive life with the deadly crackle of automatic-weapons fire.

31

To Boris Feyodov the distant gunshots were just so much background noise. He was standing over a computer console, his dark eyes glued to the screen. The tunnel ended directly beside him. The high walls of the Huitzilopochtli statue rose grandly into the blue sky.

"Is it done?" the former general demanded.

Seated at the control console, Professor Melvin Horowitz nodded. "It's synched with the NASA countdown and locked in to autofire forty seconds after the shuttle lifts off."

Feyodov glanced up the dark tunnel.

The shooting had intensified. Obviously, his men were encountering some resistance.

The two Sinanju masters. It *had* to be them. Up until now fate had finally been kind enough to supply him with all the tools and targets for his great act of vengeance.

"Can it be undone?" Feyodov demanded.

"It'd be tricky to do fast," the Barkley professor replied. "But I think I could do it."

Feyodov looked rapidly around the area. As Horowitz studied the monitor, the general quickly stooped. His fingers wrapped around a length of half-moon steel piping that encased the thick cables running along the edge of the tunnel. Picking up the five-foot-long section of pipe, he hauled back. With a triumphant grunt he bashed the hunk of steel viciously into the back of Melvin Horowitz's head.

Blood splattered across the monitor. Horowitz slumped forward, toppling sideways out of his chair.

Feyodov didn't even seem aware of what he had done. The pipe slipped from his fingers, clanging to the metal floor. His gaze was locked on the red-flecked computer screen.

Eyes ever alert, the former general watched as the digital timer flashed rapidly down to zero.

BEFORE THE BULLETS even started flying, Remo knew his body was out of whack. Not wanting to give opportunity to error, he grabbed the first protective shield he could find. Fortunately, it was a bulletproof Kevlar vest. Unfortunately for its owner, it was still wrapped around his body.

"Don't shoot, don't shoot!" screamed Oleg Shevtrinko as his black market compatriots trained their weapons at him.

The men down the tunnel didn't seem to hear him. They continued firing, trying to hit the target beyond their confederate. Bullets thudded into Oleg.

"Ow! Ow! Stop it! Stop shooting me!" Oleg yelled as round after round pounded into his chest.

Remo held the squirming Russian at arm's length like a knight's shield at the Crusades.

"Excelsior!" he yelled as he charged down the tunnel.

Chiun and Anna followed close behind.

Weaving and ducking, Remo harvested bullets from the air like autumn fruit. By the time they reached the group of Russians, Oleg's organs had been pounded to jelly.

Remo tossed the dead man unceremoniously to the floor. Like twin hurricanes of unbridled fury, he and the Master of Sinanju fell on the group of suddenly panicking Russians.

Beefy shoulders yielded arms. Thick necks surrendered heads. In seconds a grisly pile of twitching appendages was mounded on the cool steel floor.

Remo finished the last black market soldier with a heel to the jaw that sent the man's head spinning like a lead ball on the elongated end of his elasticized neck.

As the body fell, he twirled to the Master of Sinanju.

Chiun stood ankle deep in body parts.

The old man seemed no worse than he'd been a few moments before. But given his reaction the previous day, there was no telling how strongly he'd be affected if he was standing this close to the weapon when it discharged.

It would be easier if he just got out of there, but there was no sense wasting time arguing.

"We better do this fast," Remo said.

He hadn't taken a single step when a thought occurred to him. Glancing around, he saw only the

Master of Sinanju and the stack of Russian bodies.
There was no one else in sight.

When he looked back to Chiun, his deep-set eyes
held a glint of fresh concern.

"Where's Anna?" Remo asked warily.

WHEN ANNA ROUNDED the corner she saw the lone
figure standing anxiously over a distant computer
monitor.

So entranced was he with the action on the screen
that Boris Feyodov didn't even notice her. The body
of Professor Melvin Horowitz lay at his feet.

Anna had never been one to shrink from doing
that which was necessary. With Remo and Chiun
undoubtedly closing in behind, she would have to
act quickly.

Raising her rifle to shoulder level, she fired.

Down the tunnel the former Red Army general
didn't have time to react to the sound before the
bullet struck.

It bit straight through the arm, burying deep inside
his rib cage. The single shot sent him sprawling. He
fell into the arc of white sunlight that spilled into
the tunnel from the open top of the Huitzilopochtli
statue.

Feyodov instinctively began crawling across the
patch of light, out into the open-air safety of the
stone statue. With wild eyes he looked back over his
shoulder. When he saw Anna Chutesov approaching,
his face grew more panicked. He braced a hand
against his side to staunch the flow of blood.

"It is too late!" the general cried, still crawling.

Tables and consoles prevented Anna from getting another clear shot. She hurried after him, gun raised.

Far along, Feyodov pulled his hand away from the wound.

Blood. *His* blood.

A new look of deep fear flooding his sagging features, he flopped out into the hollow of the massive statue.

Anna would have continued after him if not for the strong hand that suddenly latched on to her elbow. Wheeling, she found Remo and Chiun standing behind her.

"Let's do this fast," Remo pressed.

"That was Feyodov," Anna insisted, struggling to break free of his grip. "I cannot let him escape."

"Dammit, Anna, stop making friends and help out here," Remo snapped. "He's not going anywhere. And you're the one who keeps saying the whole world's gonna go kerplooey."

The urgency of his words hit hard. The fight draining from her, she hurried over to the last console. Bracing her gun against it, she slipped into Melvin Horowitz's seat.

"The system is locked to fire," Anna announced after a cursory examination.

On the screen the counter flew below the sixty-second mark. Nearby television screens displayed images of the space shuttle on its Florida launch pad.

"Pull the plug," Remo commanded.

"It isn't a hair dryer with a cord plugged into the wall. To dismantle it would take time we do not have."

As Anna's mind raced desperately for a solution, Remo glanced at the Master of Sinanju.

Sweat had broken out across the old man's forehead.

Anna's earlier assessment had been right. Because of his advanced age, the Korean was feeling the effects worse than Remo. Not that the younger Master of Sinanju was immune. Remo doubted either of them could survive if they were this close to the weapon when it discharged.

"You better get out of here, Little Father," Remo insisted. "Anna and I will take it from here."

"If it cannot be stopped, there is no point in any of us staying," Chiun replied.

It was true. Remo nodded agreement, turning to Anna. "He's right," he said. "Let's amscray."

Anna had been looking desperately around the area. From where she sat she had a partial view of the statue's wide interior. A sliver of blue sky was visible at the top. Near it, something glimmered with reflected light.

She spun excitedly to Remo.

"The mirrors!" she announced. Breathlessly, she pointed up to the very top of the slender tower that stretched up from the floor at the center of the stone statue. "Shatter them and the beam will be unfocused."

Picking up the thread, Remo looked up the tower.

"Done," he said. He whirled to the Master of Sinanju. "Get Anna out of here, Little Father. I'll see you on the other side."

Anna was about to object when she felt a firm

hand grab her around the waist. In a trice she was up on the Master of Sinanju's shoulder and the old man was bounding back into the depths of the long tunnel.

Alone, Remo raced out into the belly of Huitzil-opochtli.

As he flew across the floor, his internal clock told him there were only forty-nine seconds remaining.

Boris Feyodov had made it as far as Zen Bower's body. His breathing ragged, the general lay next to the ice cream man's corpse. Blood gurgled from between his dying lips.

At Remo's appearance, Feyodov's eyes rolled open.

"You come to me at last," the old general coughed. Wincing in pain, he pressed his hand more firmly against his bleeding side. His pale fingers were already stained red.

"Love to chitchat with the suicidal general," Remo said as he flew past, "but I've got work to do."

A long access ladder ran up the side of the slender tower. Remo began scurrying rapidly up the metal rungs.

As Remo flew up the four-story tower, Feyodov's weak voice trailed after him.

"Work? You were supposed to work for *me*. You and the old one," the general called. "You never came. But *she* did. Thanks to you she took the last scraps of my life." His tone grew cryptic. "And she took even more from you."

Remo found that he was forced to concentrate

more than usual during his ascent. Staving off light-headedness, he was doing his best to ignore the ramblings of the dying man.

The ladder ended at a circular platform. By the time Remo reached it, only thirty seconds remained.

The cupped mirrors that focused the energy of the particle stream were aimed into the eastern sky.

"Ask her about the Institute," Feyodov called. "Ask her about Mactep. Ask her about what she—" he paused for a pained gasp "—what she...stole from you."

It was the intensity with which the words were spoken. From the top of the tower platform, Remo glanced down.

Far below, a thin smile touched the general's ashen lips. Pink froth bubbled from between them.

No time to ask.

Remo was about to shatter the thick mirrors when another thought occurred to him.

With two swift swats he cracked the mirrors from their swivel bases and repositioned them, each aimed in a different direction. His work done, he leaped from the platform over to the uppermost metal catwalk that rimmed the interior of the big statue. He scrambled up the inner wall of the statue, disappearing over the edge.

At the bottom of the hollow interior, Boris Feyodov watched Remo slip from sight.

Whatever the young one had done to forestall Feyodov's revenge, it was too late. It would come. Perhaps not this day and not as he had expected it to, but it was inevitable. The men from Sinanju didn't know it, but one way or another the former Red Army general would have some small vengeance.

A smile still on his lips, General Boris Feyodov closed his weary eyes. And when the death he had feared for so many years finally came to claim the old soldier, it was like welcoming an old friend.

32

Brandy Brand was standing anxiously on the sidewalk at the edge of the Barkley common when she saw Remo pop like a jack-in-the-box from out of Huitzilopochtli's stone head.

His descent was so rapid that at first she thought he was falling. He was halfway down the face when Chiun appeared from the door of the city hall. Anna Chutesov was flung over the old man's shoulder like a sack of potatoes.

Remo touched ground even as Chiun was darting down the steps. Racing full out, the two men met on the common. Side by side they tore across the grass toward Brandy.

The four bomb-filled duffel bags were at Brandy's feet. After Chiun had dropped Anna next to the FBI agent, the two men scooped up the bags, one in each hand.

"Bombs away, Little Father," Remo said tightly.

"But I didn't set the timers yet," Brandy insisted.

Remo and Chiun ignored her. Hauling back, they hurled their bundles high into the California sky. The four bags became specks of black in the vast blue backdrop.

Brandy barely had time to see them drop neatly, one after the other, inside the hollow head of Huitzilopochtli before she felt herself being swept off her feet.

With Brandy tucked up under one arm, Remo took off like a shot. Chiun kept pace with him, once more carting Anna.

With every racing step the old man seemed to grow more vigorous. Remo, too, quickly sloughed off the disharmonizing effects of the tunnel. They were two city blocks away from the town square when the ground began to shake.

It was a low, protracted rumble that started at the center of town and rolled toward the Barkley suburbs.

Once they had both determined they were at a safe distance, Remo and Chiun stopped running. They deposited the women on the sidewalk.

A mile from the center of town, all four of them looked back in the direction from which they had come.

The Barkley skyline had changed. Over the nearest buildings something was missing. For the first time since they had arrived in town, the evil eyes of Huitzilopochtli did not look out over the small California community.

The statue was gone. In its place was empty air. And then a column of dust rose up from the distant point where the ancient god had stood, obliterating the cheery pastel-blue sky.

IT TOOK half an hour for the dust to clear. When Remo, Chiun and the others returned to Barkley's center, they found the buildings around the grassy square in ruins.

At the last minute Remo had aimed one of the mirrors into the civic center where the Buffoon Aid concert had been held. The other he had aimed down into the statue itself.

The fractured beam had detonated the explosives and set off a chain reaction in the network of tunnels. When the underground complex collapsed, so too did everything above it. Including the city hall. Barkley's main civic building lay in cratered ruins. Before it the four-story Huitzilopochtli statue was little more than a pile of crumbled stone.

"Oh, my," Brandy said when she saw the rubble that had been the Barkley civic center.

"I figured that'd keep them from hosting any more of those ditzy benefit shows," Remo explained.

Brandy cast a worried eye at Remo. "But that's where the city council was hiding."

A flicker of genuine concern passed over Remo's face. "Any civilians with them?" he asked.

Brandy nodded. "They said Yippee Goldfarb and the other two Buffoon Aid hosts were in there. They were planning on starting that HTB fund-raiser again today." Her face troubled, the FBI agent wandered away from the rest, toward the bombed-out civic center.

Standing on the grass, Remo thought of the three famous actor-comedians. If Brandy was right, Yippee, Leslie Walters and Bobby Stone were probably buried somewhere under all that rubble. He thought of all the movies, TV specials and talk-show appearances they would never again make.

"I've done my good deed for the century," he said. With an expression of utter indifference, he turned his attention to Anna. "What's Mactep mean?" he asked sweetly.

Anna had been scanning the debris field. At his use of the Russian word, she glanced up. Buried in the depths of her ice-blue eyes was a hint of worried surprise.

"Where did you hear that?" she asked, her voice level.

"From the guy you were so eager to shoot holes through you took off on us *twice*," Remo said, his own tone flat. "And don't think we didn't notice."

"Yes, she was more of a single-minded nuisance than she used to be," Chiun agreed. "And given the mannish doggedness she has displayed in the past, that is saying much." With delicate fingertips he stroked his thready beard. "Perhaps it is due to her advanced age. It is a fact of nature that women past a certain time of life no longer produce feminizing chemicals. That goes double for Russian women, who at birth are already halfway to manhood."

"All the parts look like they're still in the right place to me," Remo said. His eyes never left Anna's. He was still waiting for an answer.

"You say that today," Chiun cautioned. "Tell me your opinion tomorrow when one of those parts is a mustache. And *Mactep* is Russian for 'Master'." His own gaze was curious.

The two men stared hard at the Russian agent.

Anna seemed poised on the edge of a lie. At last she relented. With a sigh, her shoulders sank.

"Mactep was the program intended to bring Sinanju to Russia," she admitted carefully. "It was begun many years ago under the auspices of a secret agency called the Institute. You recall the time when your Dr. Smith signed your contract over to our premier? Feyodov ran the agency that you were both supposed to come work for."

Remo had all but forgotten that time. It had been ages ago. It was during that particular crisis that he had met his bride-to-be, Mah-Li. After meeting her, the contract nonsense with the Russians had been just a pesky distraction.

For a moment he thought of the road not traveled. Of Mah-Li, of Anna. Of the future he would never have and the one he was destined to fulfill.

"Oh," Remo said, his voice small.

Chiun noted the pensive look on his pupil's face. Lest the boy lapse into another one of his maudlin funks or, worse, the woman read some romantic meaning into Remo's silence, he quickly chimed in.

"Sinanju contracts are nontransferable," the Master of Sinanju huffed, whirling on Anna. "Not that we would work for Russia under any circumstances. The entire nation smells like a distillery. Not to mention the fact that all the women are manlike and all the men are drunkards. Now, we could overlook the manful women because, let us be reasonable, you cannot help that. Besides, no one other than besotted Russian men are interested in coupling with them."

His voice dropped low. "Especially an Apprentice Master of Sinanju who can have his pick of comely Korean handmaidens," he added as warning. His voice grew loud once more. "But the rest cannot be easily dismissed. Tell your Kremlin masters that when you people stamp out alcoholism and do away with those silly little flirtations with communism and democracy you have engaged in these past few years, *and* are ready to install a new tzar like the beloved Ivan, *then* and only then will we talk. Until such time Russia is off-limits to our services. Consider yourselves under a Sinanju embargo." Face resolute, he crossed his arms rigidly. "Stand firm with me on this, Remo."

Remo seemed surprised to hear his name. He shook away the troubling memories. "Right," he nodded. He instantly shook his head. "No, wait. Wrong." His gaze grew hard, his jaw firmly set. "Before we put up Sinanju's version of the Berlin Wall, there's still one more Russian bill that needs paying."

And the seriousness with which he spoke the words caused both Anna Chutesov and the Master of Sinanju to share a rare, troubled frown.

33

The man whose actions had inadvertently destroyed an empire slept peacefully beneath his heavy woolen blankets.

The last premier to rule the Union of Soviet Socialist Republics was short and stocky, with a mild paunch and an affable face that, in slumber, made him resemble a human teddy bear. A white fringe of hair rimmed his otherwise bald pate. In the shadows of his bedroom, the famous wine-stain birthmark that was his trademark was a dark splotch.

He was a cuddly, grandfatherly figure with a pleasant smile and an open demeanor.

The blankets—which retained the aroma of mothballs from the upstairs cedar closet even this late in the Russian winter—rose and fell with each deep breath.

He had been a premier who called himself president. A powerful player on the world stage in days long gone.

These days he rarely dreamed of that old life. It had been years since his missteps had collapsed the Soviet Union. Years since he had been forced into private life. Years since anything he did mattered.

A final foray into politics a few years before had been humiliating. These days his life was occupied largely with global environmental causes.

As he slept this cold February night, winter wind rattling the windows of his cozy home, something seemed to creep into his consciousness. Snoring awake, the retired premier looked for the familiar glow of the digital clock. Through slivered eyes he saw that it was two in the morning.

He was closing his eyes when he thought he saw something dark move in front of the glowing red numbers.

For an instant his mind told him to be worried. But then a sudden intense feeling of drowsiness overtook him. With a big, growling yawn, he closed his heavy eyelids and fell into a deep, inviting sleep.

When he next awoke the clock read 4:00 a.m.

With another yawn, the old premier pulled himself out of bed and padded to the bathroom.

He was passing the medicine cabinet on his way to the toilet when he caught a glimpse of himself in the mirror.

At first he thought he was seeing things. The glow of the nightlight was too weak to be sure. He snapped on the wall switch. When he saw his reflection his jaw dropped.

During the night his forehead birthmark had mutated. The main blotch now seemed to form a number. When he rolled his head to one side he saw that a letter was beside it.

In a panic, he pulled from the closet a small handheld mirror that had belonged to his late wife.

He soon found that the letters formed a slogan. With a sinking feeling in his ample gut he tracked it all around his bald pate. It wrapped his head like the logo on a tire.

He could not believe his eyes. The former premier was already despised in his own country. Somehow someone had broken into his home and tattooed him with the one thing that would make him even more hated than he was already.

The slogan that spread like a rash from his birthmark all around his head read U.S.A. #1.

Shoulders slumping, Russia's retired premier dropped the small hand mirror into the marble sink.

Like the mighty empire he had once led, it cracked into a hundred jagged pieces.

34

Between flights, Remo called Smith from a pay phone at London's Heathrow International Airport.

"So that's that," he said as he finished explaining the details from Barkley and the side trip he and Chiun had taken to Russia. "If he wants to go hug any more trees, from now on he's gonna have to wear a hat or Crosby, Stills and Nash will stone him to death. Not that he wouldn't deserve it. After the *Challenger* he earned way worse than he got."

"I suppose I should be thankful that you did not eliminate him," the CURE director said thinly.

The Master of Sinanju stood next to Remo at the phone bank. The old man was staring glumly at the passengers as they hurried back and forth across the terminal.

"It is I who convinced Remo not to remove the fat Russian, Emperor," Chiun called.

"Please thank Master Chiun for his restraint."

"Now, there's a phrase you don't hear every day," Remo said dryly. "And don't be too free with the thanks until you hear whose ticket he wanted us to punch instead."

"Sinanju skills should not be wasted on some roly-poly retiree, Emperor Smith," Chiun said. "I wanted to remove the dangerous pretender who sits on Tzar Ivan's throne. He is a little man, and little men always have something to prove.''

Remo looked down at Chiun. At just five feet tall, the old man's bald scalp came up to his shoulder.

''Er, thank Master Chiun for the warning, but tell him I want no harm to come to their current president,'' Smith said.

''Don't thank him for that one, thank me,'' Remo said. ''I just wanted the old one. But I knew you'd go apeshit if I killed him. Besides, that thing on his head made a pretty good one. After that, the rest just wrote itself.''

''It is good you went no further,'' Smith said. ''Given the attempt by Feyodov to provoke a confrontation between our two nations, there is no telling how the Russians might react to the sudden, mysterious death of a former national leader.''

''Boo-hoo-hoo for the Russians,'' Remo said, scowling.

Smith forged ahead. ''As for the cosmonauts who were stranded on Mir, they have been rescued. The shuttle with them aboard landed an hour ago.''

''Send them a bill,'' Remo grumbled.

''But do not expect them to pay,'' Chiun offered.

''So that's it,'' Smith said. ''Theodore Schwartz, the man who financed this whole scheme, is in custody. You have taken care of Feyodov and the Barkley end.'' The older man hesitated, considering his next words. ''Now that this is over, there are things we need to discuss when you return.''

Remo noted the cryptic edge suddenly in Smith's voice.

"I don't like the sound of that. If you're thinking of throwing us out, don't," Remo warned. "Chiun didn't get the free house he was banking on and now with the three Buffoon Aid stars MIA, he's thinking he won't ever see one from that quarter. Though if we got one buck each from everyone who's ever had to put up with the multi-untalented Yippee Goldfarb on Oscar night, we'd be in clover."

"It has nothing to do with your living arrangements," Smith said. "It is more an organizational detail. If there are no other loose ends, we can discuss it when you return."

Remo thought of Anna Chutesov. A loose end that had apparently been dangling out there for more than a decade without any of them knowing about it.

The CURE director sensed something in the pause from Remo's end. "Is there something more, Remo?" Smith asked.

"No," Remo said. "That's it. See you stateside."

He hung up the phone.

As they walked back across the terminal, the old man gave his pupil a furtive look.

"You did not tell Smith about the woman," he said.

Remo shrugged. "Why bother stirring up that pot? And anyway, she bagged out on us as soon as we hit Moscow. Besides, we didn't see her for more than ten years. What are the odds we'll ever see her again?"

Neither man chose to wager. Both wearing thoughtful frowns, each man for a different reason, the two Masters of Sinanju walked silently toward the departure gate.

EPILOGUE

Her early-morning briefing with the president of Russia had not lasted long. The relief on his face had been great when he learned of Anna Chutesov's success.

In relating the details, Anna deliberately left out the involvement of Remo and Chiun. There had been too much stirring of old embers these past few days. At this point it would do no good to remind the Kremlin leadership of anything more to do with the men from Sinanju.

When she was through, she left the small man who led this weakened Russia to his celebratory glass of vodka.

Anna was bone tired as she drove her own car from the Kremlin back into Kitai Gorod. The Institute building rose up from the dirty streets like some great primitive temple of concrete and mortar.

She was passing the building and heading for the secret entrance when something caught her eye.

With a shocked gasp Anna slammed on the brakes. The car behind her screeched to a stop.

Anna threw open her door. Horns beeped as she

raced across oncoming traffic to the front of the building.

The gates to the unused driveway sat on the street. At her order, they were left closed in perpetuity, entwined with a rusty chain. Beyond them, up the short drive, was the sealed door to the underground garage. Neither gate nor garage door had been opened since Anna's arrival at that building more than a decade before.

This morning, the garage door was open wide. A great yawning black space stretched beyond.

The gate was still closed. With trembling hands Anna reached out to it.

The chain was broken. Within the chips of orange rust gleamed bright shards of twisted silver links. At her touch, the chain slipped to the ground, and the rusted gate creaked open into the driveway.

Behind her, horns blared and men shouted. Anna heard none of it. The shouting and honking were background noise.

As angry drivers began climbing out of their cars, she remained rooted in place. Her glazed eyes were distant. Her mouth hung open in shock. She said but one word, inaudible over all the yelling and traffic sounds.

"Мастер."

And for the first time in her life, standing alone on that Moscow sidewalk, Anna Chutesov felt the first thundering strains of true fear.

**Readers won't want to miss this exciting
new title of the SuperBolan® series!**

DON PENDLETON's

MACK BOLAN®
DESTINY'S
HOUR

THE
TYRANNY
FILES

BOOK I

War has arrived through America's backdoor, a strategic
offensive to turn the Nazi dream into worldwide domination.
The opening onslaught is a warm-up of chaos and blood, with
trigger incidents at crucial points. An evil force is boring
inexorably into the heart of the American nation. Bolan is
prepared to ensure that the republic sees another sunrise.
Even if it means his life...

Available in May 2001 at your favorite retail outlet.

James Axler

OUTLANDERS®

PURGATORY ROAD

The fate of humanity remains ever uncertain, dictated by the obscure forces that have commandeered mankind's destiny for thousands of years. The plenipotentiaries of these ancient oppressors—the nine barons who have controlled America in the two hundred years since the nukecaust—are now falling prey to their own rabid desire for power.

Book #3 of *The Imperator Wars* saga, a trilogy chronicling the introduction of a new child imperator—launching the baronies into war!

Follow Remo and Chiun and their extraordinary adventures... Don't miss these titles!

THE Destroyer™

GOLD EAGLE®

GDEBACK2